THE KEY TO FEAR

KRISTIN CAST is a worldwide bestselling author who was born in Japan and grew up in Oklahoma where she explored everything from tattoo modeling to broadcast journalism. After battling addiction, Kristin made her way to the Pacific Northwest and landed in Portland, Oregon. She rediscovered her passion for storytelling in the stacks at dusty bookstores and in rickety chairs in old coffeehouses. For as long as Kristin can remember, she's been telling stories. Thankfully, she's been writing them down since 2005.

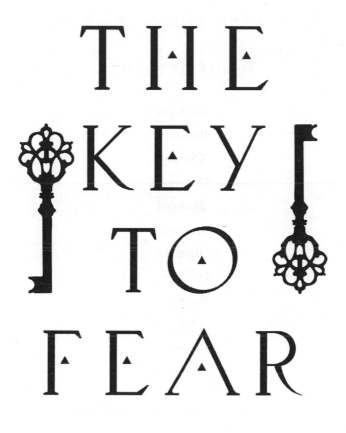

THE KEY TO FEAR

KRISTIN CAST

HEAD
of ZEUS

First published in the US by Blackstone Publishing in 2020.
First published in the UK by Head of Zeus in 2020

9 7 5 3 1 2 4 6 8

A catalogue record for this book is available
from the British Library.

ISBN (HB): 9781838933982
ISBN (TPB): 9781838933999
ISBN (E): 9781838933937

Printed and bound by CPI Group (UK) Ltd, Croydon, CR0 4YY

Head of Zeus Ltd
First Floor East
5–8 Hardwick Street
London EC1R 4RG

WWW.HEADOFZEUS.COM

To all of my therapists.
Thank you for helping me sort out my shit.

I

"Mommy?" The little girl closed her small, shaking hand around pale fingers stretched across the hospital bed. Fingers of the woman Elodie Benavidez had failed to save.

Elodie's chest tightened, her breath thick and hot.

"Mommy!" The little girl tugged, but her mother gave no response. Her hollow stare remained fixed on the ceiling.

Elodie's paper apron crunched as she forced her legs to carry her through the open door and into the cramped exam room. "Come with me, sweetheart," she said, her voice muffled by a thin mask. The warmth of the girl's fever seeped through Elodie's gloves as she grabbed the little girl's wrist and pulled her away from the bedside.

"No!" the girl screamed. Her tiny, shrill voice cracked the stillness of the room. "My mommy's sick!" She yanked her arm free and threw herself against the gurney, wrapping her petite body around her mother's dangling, motionless arm. "She's sick," she sobbed, burying her red cheeks against the corpse's naked shoulder. "Help her!"

"Sweetie, she's gone." Elodie tried to push back her own despair, but it clung to her voice like clay. She swallowed hard. "They all are."

"Mom—" The girl seemed to choke on the realization. "Dead?" Her breaths came in shallow, panicked gulps. "Like Daddy?"

Elodie had read the woman's chart. Her husband had been the first in their home to be infected. He'd died three days later. The virus had burned through him, used him up until nothing remained. Nothing but a flesh-covered sack of liquid jelly.

Elodie squatted, her eyes awash in unshed tears as she offered a delicate nod. "We have to go." The little girl winced when Elodie extended her hand. "Please, come with me."

The child shook her head, her blond hair matting against her sweat-stained cheeks and forehead. "She told me she wouldn't leave me." Sobs choked the girl's words, and they came out small and clipped. "She'll wake up." She rubbed the heels of her hands against her eyes. "Mommy doesn't lie. You'll see."

"Oh . . ." Elodie's voice came out a whisper as she wailed on the inside. She'd been assigned Long Term Care duty, and this was part of it. She stiffened, quieting her grief as she rose to her feet and smoothed out her crinkled apron.

The little girl clamped her eyes shut and bowed her head in one final plea. "Mommy, wake up." Her sweat-dampened hair slipped off her shoulders in tangled clumps. "Please, wake up."

Readying herself, Elodie let out a hot breath against her mask before clamping her hands onto the girl's shoulders and jerking, forcing her to release her mother's arm. The little girl bucked and kicked, but Elodie's grip only tightened. "You can't stay here," she grunted. "We have to get you into quarantine."

Elodie wanted to cry, *I'm sorry! I wish I could fix it! I wish I could do something!* but knew it would be useless. The girl was already infected. Elodie felt it in the heat of her skin and saw it in the broken capillaries inking thin red lines across the apples of her cheeks. In a few days, this girl would end up like her parents.

Elodie dragged her from the room, her little arms flailing for something to grab onto. *"Mommy, wake up! Mommy!"* She clawed at the metal doorframe, gripping it as if her strength could somehow bring back her mother.

Elodie yanked, and the little girl's grip broke free.

Arms outstretched, she screamed for her mother.

"Simulation complete." A smooth, calm voice interrupted the screaming of the girl, the heat of her flesh, her mother's vacant, endless stare, the hospital and its tang of death. The girl froze and became weightless in Elodie's grip, became colored air. "Simulation terminated," the disembodied voice announced as the scene in front of her blurred briefly before disappearing to reveal the real-life space around her.

Elodie had tucked her petal-pink bed cover meticulously under the mattress the same way as every morning per her mother's instruction. Her rock collection was lined up on her windowsill. The early morning sun's rays shone through the measured two-inch space between each stone, casting a gap-toothed shadow against the uncluttered surface of her desk. Everything in her room was perfect. Yet Elodie felt hollow, carved out, her insides replaced with a wriggling ball of nerves.

She pushed against the armrests of the desk chair she'd rolled to the center of her room before beginning the simulation, and tried to stand, but her legs melted under her and she collapsed to her knees, hands trembling as she tore free from her updated headset and visor.

A holographic image appeared near the foot of her bed,

carrying the same three-dimensional weight, three-dimensional *realness*, as the little girl in the simulation. Elodie stared down, half expecting the small heel of the hologram's pointed shoes to leave a divot in the plush carpeting. Elodie blinked up at the woman, whose short hair barely dusted her sharp chin as she glanced down at Elodie and claimed that cool voice. "Simulations such as these are necessary to illustrate the flaws in the medical systems of the past. The virus, Cerberus, originated in a hospital, and spread quickly to those in uninfected facilities because of inadequate to nonexistent containment protocols. Would you like to further review the points learned within the lesson fifteen simulation?" With her hands gently clasped in front of the white pencil skirt she always wore, the hologram blinked down expectantly.

A sob stuck in the back of Elodie's throat.

"Elodie, do you wish to review this lesson or proceed to the practice exam?" With a warm smile she tucked her hair behind her ear and cocked her head slightly. Although her hair was the same deep brown as Elodie's and her skin the same rich tan, the hologram (newly nicknamed Holly by the citizens of Westfall) looked empty. At least she did to Elodie. Everyone else had marveled at how life-like she appeared. This spokesperson for the Key Corp had always been smart, but she had also always been a voice—*only* a voice. Now, with her most recent update, she was a *person*. A person with a name. The face of the Key Corp and, in the same moment, absolutely no one, nothing but lights that were beamed from projectors the size of pinheads that had been planted throughout almost every home, building, street, and bridge throughout Westfall.

Elodie swallowed past the lump in her throat and brushed her damp hair back as she stood. She was glad she'd taken a shower before beginning her lesson, as the line of nervous sweat dampening her brow was indistinguishable from her wet hair. "I'm done for today. I don't want to be late."

Holly nodded. "I've bookmarked your place, so we can pick back up whenever you're ready. Don't forget, your final exam for this quarter is in four weeks."

"I know. Thanks, Holly."

Holly's Key Corp–red blouse shimmered as she waved politely. "See you at the MediCenter, Elodie," she said. Her image blurred and then vanished as quickly and soundlessly as she'd appeared.

Elodie checked the time on her Key Corp–issued cuff. She was still ahead of schedule. She was *always* ahead of schedule. Tardiness was the one thing she had complete control over.

Elodie glanced over her room to ensure everything was in its proper place. A few of the smooth river rocks she'd collected on the banks of the Columbia were askew. She hurried over to the window to straighten them before taking another final look around. Satisfied, she stuffed her damp hair into a beanie, hefted her clear backpack onto her shoulders, and jogged down the stairs into the kitchen.

Gwen perched on the edge of a barstool at the expansive center island, her finger poised over the illuminated surface of her holopad. "Did my daughter just come downstairs, or was that a herd of wild beasts?"

Elodie's lips stretched into an automatic smile. "Morning, Mother," she chirped, diverting her attention to the smoothie waiting for her on the counter. She lifted the straw. Beige clumps slid off the metal and into the lumpy mixture in the glass.

"Don't play with your food, dear," Gwen said without looking up.

"This isn't my usual. This is . . ." Elodie wrinkled her nose, " . . . something else."

With a sigh, Gwen tented her hands and cast Elodie a concerned glance. "I noticed you were getting a little bigger around, you know, *this* region." Gwen extended a finger and drew a circle in front of her daughter, encompassing every inch of her not hidden by the kitchen island. "Seems I've been indulging you." Her laughter was like glass breaking. "So I decided straight protein, no fruit sugars or nut butters, was the way to go."

Elodie's fingers flew to her collar. "Thanks." She squeaked as she rubbed the stiff fabric of her scrub top between her thumb and forefinger.

"You have that horrid hat on again." Gwen brushed back her own bangs from her unlined forehead and fluffed the curled lengths of her artificially blonde hair. "Is something the matter?"

Elodie stiffened. She'd hidden her damp hair for a reason. This morning's interaction with her mother was already off to a bad start—typical, but bad nonetheless. But without the *horrid hat*, it would be so much worse.

Elodie stuffed her feelings into the pit of her stomach and covered them with a large gulp of the pasty drink. "Just not that hungry, I guess."

"Good. See? It's working already." Gwen's blue eyes twinkled, in stark contrast to the acid spilling from the lips below, plump with fresh filler.

"I'm going to be late," Elodie offered with the same false urgency she'd used with Holly. It wasn't a lie. Just an unrealized truth. Before Gwen could land another blow, Elodie hooked her thumbs around the straps of her backpack and cut through the open kitchen and living room to the foyer. She'd almost made it out the door when her mother's shrill call struck her back.

"Oh! Elodie! Your father said he'd be home for dinner this evening, so think about what you're going to wear."

Elodie's surge of excitement was quickly squelched by common sense. Her father was full of promises. If they held any weight, he'd have already sunk to the center of the earth.

"*I* was thinking the green dress with the flowers," Gwen continued. "It makes you look so thin. I'll pull it out and have it pressed. Think of jewelry to go with. *I* was thinking—"

Elodie closed the front door and sagged against it. "Four more months," she muttered. "You only have to live with her for four more months." She adjusted the straps of her backpack and softened as the spring breeze caressed her cheeks.

The best part of her day was about to begin.

||

Aiden's boots were dirty. He didn't know how it happened, or where, but he knew if anyone at the Key Corp MediCenter saw, they'd tack the noncompliance to the end of the *Shit You've Done Wrong So Far Today* list. And, although the sun had barely taken its position in the sky, he knew that list was already a mile long.

"Let me get this straight." Dr. Cath Scott paused to remove a nearly invisible speck of lint from the crisp sleeve of her tailored blouse. The soft wrinkles on the back of her ivory hands told the story of her more than fifty years better than any other part of her. Though if Aiden tilted his head and squinted just right, he could catch a glimpse of the lines feathering around the corners of her kind eyes. "You decided that simply not showing up to your designated workplace was the right thing to do because you . . ." Dr. Scott paused, flicking her fingers across her holopad as she scrolled through Aiden's most recent disciplinary action sheet. "And I quote, 'don't like the job.'"

Aiden closed one eye, then the other, back and forth, back

and forth, making her form shift ever so slightly. He'd sat in Dr. Scott's office in the same stiff plastic chair, an arm's length from the rounded edges of her sparkling white desk, and had a version of this conversation more times than he could count. Mornings were his favorite time to get called in, when the sun crested the tall buildings of downtown Westfall and its brilliant beams reflected off the iconic pale pink tower across the street from the MediCenter. Dr. Scott's wall of windows provided the best view in the entire building. Maybe that was why she remained pleasant even though they continued to meet like this. Aiden would remain pleasant, too, if each morning he was bathed in gentle magnolia light.

The rays seeped through the towering windows, staining Dr. Scott's mane of blond curls. "What were you thinking?" She squinted, and those thin lines around her eyes flashed to life.

The zippers lining Aiden's black synthetic-wool coat scraped against the chair as he shrugged and slouched a bit lower. "Like you said, it was simple. And yeah, I don't like it. Babysitting surgical bots is boring. They're bots. Get better engineers if their bots are so shitty that they need looking after."

"*Ai-den.*" Dr. Scott accentuated each syllable before pursing her lips.

He slouched a little lower.

With a labored sigh, she continued to scroll though his seemingly unending file. "Aiden, you're in my office at least once a month."

He brushed his fingers across his full lips, hiding a mischievous upturn of his mouth.

She set down the holopad and tented her fingers. "I'm running out of ways to punish you that aren't . . . *harsh*." A silent threat lingered behind the word.

His gaze washed over the pink building and the MediCenter's reflection trapped in its windows like the two were locked in a staring contest. Aiden didn't bother wondering which would win. The MediCenter would. The Key always won. His toes clenched in his boots. "Be harsh. I can handle it."

Again, Dr. Scott's thin lips tightened. "This is serious. If certain people were to get wind of the fact that you've been bouncing around from career to career, you would end up in Rehabilitation."

Each muscle in Aiden's back stiffened. "I haven't really been bouncing around." He straightened and slid to the edge of his seat. "I'm trying to figure some stuff out, but I've stayed within the same career, more or less—"

Dr. Scott pushed the holopad across her desk. The transparent screen lit up, blue-tinged white and black text came into focus. "You've trained as an anesthesiologist, a surgical core technician, a long-term patient care tech, a *short*-term patient care tech, in the pharmacology department, the behavioral health department, as well as medi-bot maintenance, cancer research . . . the list goes on and on." And it did. So much so that the last line was partially blurred by the bottom of the screen.

Instead, Aiden sat back in his chair and propped his ankle on his knee. "Yeah, but is it *really* hopping if I'm staying in the same field?"

"Yes!" With a jolt of exasperation, Dr. Scott tossed her finely manicured hands in the air. "And of course you're staying in the same field. Your tests revealed an aptitude for the medical sciences. We know this is where you'll thrive."

He sagged again, plopping his elbows against the plastic armrests. "Maybe I don't want to have a career yet. Is that something your tests took into consideration?"

Dr. Scott swept the holopad back to its place in front of her.

"You are almost eighteen. People your age have been in their assigned career for years and are racing to the top of their field, not dillydallying, trying to *figure some stuff out.*" Dr. Scott adjusted the row of styluses on her desk until they were all parallel with the edge. "Aiden, there's nothing to figure out. It's better to follow the path chosen for you, and the Key has made it simple. *I* have made it simple. And Rehab—"

Aiden lurched forward. "You know I don't need Rehabilitation." He scrubbed a hand along the smooth undercut lining his mohawk's tight curls. "I can't go. I won't. Put me in whatever career field you want. I'll stay with it."

Dr. Scott's thick brows lifted, deepening the creases just below her hairline.

"I swear." And he meant it.

Her nails clicked against the polished white desktop. "You've run through too many other careers. I'll do my best, but chances are you won't like where you end up."

"Anything is better than Rehab. I've heard stories." His gaze fell to the dirty toes of his heavy boots. "I won't survive there."

The pink light had drained from the office as the sun cleared the buildings, pinning itself high above the city.

Dr. Scott folded her hands across her desk. "This is the last time I can reassign you. I'll get it sorted and have your new career assignment within the hour. You know where to find the details. It'll start today. Go home and change, but don't be late. You want to make a good impression on your new supervisor, so no stopping somewhere that will get you into more trouble."

Aiden stood and nodded stiffly, the delicate tinkling of his zippers at war with the heavy clomp of his boots as he shuffled toward the door.

"And, Aiden, tread lightly. You don't want all that dirt you're tracking in to give someone a heart attack."

He gingerly lifted each foot, admiring the powder of dirt left behind. "Guess it's a good thing we're in the MediCenter." With a grin, Aiden strolled through the open door, dirt crunching in muted applause with each step.

III

Elodie had never been so relieved to leave for work. As long as she could keep from thinking about her mother and about that disturbing lesson fifteen during her ride on the commuter train, she'd be fine. Once she got to work, she'd be swallowed by her job, and the little girl's screams would be scrubbed from her memory to make way for more pertinent information.

Focused on the day ahead, Elodie jogged down the wide front stairs of the renovated Craftsman she shared with her parents. She paused at street level and pressed the small, purple button on her Key Corp–issued cuff. A comforting sound hissed, like a match being lit, as a translucent violet bubble expanded from the cuff and encased Elodie. The Violet Shield Personal Protection Pods weren't mandatory while walking around in Zone Two, but judging from the number of hazy purple spheres bobbing along the pedestrian walkways like grapes, they made everyone, Elodie included, feel a little bit safer.

Clutching her nursing textbook inside the bubble, Elodie

turned to the right and walked briskly along the wide sidewalk to the MAX transit center hub that would take her downtown to Zone One, and Westfall's central MediCenter.

It was late April and the prettiest season in Westfall, the only city in the West Coast sector of New America. The heavy gray clouds that had loomed over the city, promising rain every day from late fall to spring, had finally lost their battle against the sun. Now the glorious yellow orb dried the streets and added color back to the streets. Elodie breathed deeply as she passed a bush heavy with purple flowers, thankful that the latest updates to Personal Pods allowed scents to pass through the Violet Shield.

As always, she'd timed it perfectly. The train's arrival bell chimed exactly as she rounded the corner to the MAX's platform. Keeping her distance from those around her, Elodie hung back and allowed the other Zone Two residents to enter before she slipped between the slowly closing doors and into the slick, pristine interior of the MAX car, spotless from its daily sterilization.

The scent of bleach tickled her nose. It was the way life would always smell, a fact Elodie found reassuring. Actually, she found it *more* than reassuring. Bleach was sterile. Bleach was safe. And, therefore, *life* was safe.

Elodie bathed in the sharp scent as she settled into one of the few aluminum seats. She'd read somewhere once that prepandemic, the seats on the MAX were all squished up right next to each other. With a grimace, she glanced at the empty space on either side of her.

It's no wonder Cerberus claimed ninety percent of the population. They were entirely too close to each other—all the time.

She sat back and relaxed. Her attention automatically flicked to the digital clock in the wall of the train. It was exactly 0900. It would take twenty minutes to get to the MediCenter, which meant she would arrive at work ten minutes before her morning shift began.

More importantly, she had a whole twenty minutes all to herself.

She eyed the other passengers before cracking open her textbook just enough so only she could see the pages. An icy wave of adrenaline tickled her spine as she took another glance around the car. None of the other passengers were even looking at a book, much less one as special as hers.

Elodie was breaking rules. *In public.*

She ran her fingers over the forbidden sheets she'd so carefully pasted to the pages of her textbook, and she could hardly keep still as she began to read.

"And that, my friend, is why life is worth living. Or, in your case, worth dying . . ." With a grimace, Vi shook her head. The blunt ends of her blond wig barely moved with the gesture. "Forgive me, Johnny."

Johnny Diamoto jerked away as Vi leaned in from behind and rested her pointed chin on his shoulder. He was slick with sweat and stank of fear, ripe for the plucking.

Vi sighed. "That was a shitty line. I'm trying to come up with a catchphrase, but can I be honest?" Vi didn't wait for a response. Instead, she stood and tightened the garrote around his fat, hairy log of a neck. Slowly. Not wanting to shed light on the shadow of hope hanging dark in the stuffy room.

She'd turned the heat up before he'd arrived at the swanky downtown hotel. *The Honeymoon Suite, tonight 7p.* That's all his text had said. Honeymoon suite. Typical. Men like him loved dressing up their double life, making it seem like there would be a fairytale ending if the woman could just hold on long enough.

Admittedly, Vi had hung on too long to this one. She'd lavished in the gifts, the trips, but now he wanted more. He'd "bought" and "paid for" enough. It was time to "see some returns."

The timing had actually been perfect. Home Office was crawling up her ass about finishing the job. And finish, Vi would.

Diamoto's sausage-roll arms strained against the silk ties she'd used to secure him to the chair. What was it with men and wanting to be tied up?

"Well, this whole catchphrase thing is not really working out for me," Vi said. "I definitely thought it'd be a lot easier. I'll have to get back to you."

Wet, strangled grunts burbled through Diamoto's swollen lips as she pulled on the ends of the wire.

"Did you have a thought, Johnny?" she purred. "Something to add?"

The chair creaked in response.

"What do you think my catchphrase should be?" Vi liked to leave them with a question. A small thread of connection she could twirl between her fingers after the job was done and she was back to being alone.

A final fighting burst surged through Diamoto, and his right arm freed itself from its binding.

That was the last time she would use silk.

Keeping her gloved hands securely wrapped around the wire, Vi dodged his arm as it flailed back, reaching for her. His waist was still tied in place, but Diamoto's stumpy fingers found her wrist. His thick paws wildly clawed at her, pulling at and crashing against her leather-clad forearms.

"Bad . . . boy . . . Johnny," Vi grunted as she tore away from him and crossed the wire behind his neck.

She leaned into him and pulled.

Johnny Diamoto shuddered and his hand slapped against hers like a wet, dying fish.

Vi breathed in a lungful of air as his ran out, and the world, no doubt, darkened around him.

Vi knew what that was like. Once upon a time, gloved hands had kept her from breathing. Left her for dead.

But Vi was better than that man. Vi always finished what she started.

The train clunked to a stop and the doors slid open with a hiss. Elodie glanced up as one person boarded. One person *without* his Violet Shield up. It wasn't technically illegal to use public transport without a pod—as long as you followed the Hands-Off Protocol and kept distance between you and other passengers.

The man scanned for an empty seat, his gaze pausing, lingering on her. He ran his hand through his swirl of blond hair, his lips quirking up in a charming half smile. Elodie's cheeks heated and she flicked her eyes down to her clean white sneakers. She felt his eyes still on her, heavy yet inviting, as he found an empty seat at the back of the train car.

Astrid would've chided her, saying something like, "You can still talk to people even though you have a fiancé. If he's telling you that you can't, you have a real problem." But this was something Elodie's cheery, talk-to-anyone best friend would never understand. It wasn't that Elodie wasn't *allowed* to talk to other guys. She was her own person and could do what she wanted (within reason, of course). Plus, Rhett would never even know. No, it wasn't an issue of allowance, it was an issue of her actual human capabilities. She just . . . *couldn't*. Most real-life interactions were so rushed and uncomfortable. Words wouldn't even come out of her mouth and she ended up *stuck*.

The sterile white lights of the MAX flashed purple, and Holly materialized in the center of the small commuter train, her hands gently cupping The Key's flowering red logo hovering just in front of her chest. "Please do not be alarmed." Her smile was broad and white and calm and perfect. "The Violet Shield has been activated for your protection. You may continue with your activities. And remember, no touching today for a healthy tomorrow." She paused for a few moments, blinking rapidly as she tested the MAX's system, before repeating the message in the same steady, almost lullaby tone. Elodie recognized it from earlier. It was the same timbre Holly had used when Elodie had come out of lesson fifteen, when the weight of an awkward glance would have broken her into a million pieces.

The train fell eerily quiet. The young man who'd gotten on without his pod activated was now encased in his own purple haze. Apparently, all it took was one routine test to make sure everyone was doing what, in Elodie's opinion, they should have done the moment they had left the house. Elodie shifted in her seat as thick ribbons of tension snaked around her. Why was everyone being so quiet? This happened every Tuesday. Transit Test Tuesday. That's how she remembered to anticipate Holly's appearance, so she wouldn't freak out and think something bad—

Incoming call from Astrid Fujimoto.

A line of block-lettered text scrolled along the bottom of Elodie's field of vision, announcing the call from her best friend. With a thought, Elodie answered. A translucent gray rectangle filled the left section of Elodie's vision, partially pasting over the scene in the train. Like the sunrise, Astrid's image faded into view, dim at first and then bright and vibrant, the other MAX passengers only visible behind her when they moved.

Astrid's melanite black hair hung from her slick high ponytail in a giant frazzled knot against her chest as she stared wide-eyed at Elodie. "The shield is on in the MAX, isn't it?" She didn't waste any time. "They're on throughout Zone One. And they're on here, too."

Elodie shifted nervously, all too aware that her voice was one of only a handful of other passengers who whispered to each other. "That's weird. They normally only test the MAX's shield on Tuesdays." She hiked her shoulders. "But I guess it does make sense to do the train and all the zones in the same day."

Astrid's round face scrunched. "Yeah, that's great. What does it have to do with today? *Thursday.*"

Thursday? A strangled breath squeaked past Elodie's lips. It was Thursday. "Wait, the shield is on where you are? In Zone Two? There shouldn't be any reason for it to be on that far from city center. There's nothing but houses out there."

Astrid twisted the length of her ponytail, only adding more tangles to the nest. "It was a germ stack. The shield is on in case it's airborne."

The same hard lump Elodie had felt earlier that morning returned to the back of her throat. "Where—" She cleared her throat in an attempt to break through the fear tightening her airway. "Where is it?"

Astrid's lips firmed into a thin line. "Tilikum Crossing."

Elodie pressed her back against the cold seat. "That's a major MAX stop. Everyone traveling across the river switches trains there."

Astrid's eyes were wide and frantic. "It went off right before the train doors closed. Whatever was in the stack . . . it's trapped in there with all of those people."

Elodie stiffened. These kinds of things didn't happen in West-fall. These kinds of things happened in other cities. Far away cities. Cities that weren't filled with kind, rule-abiding citizens.

She chewed her bottom lip. She didn't need to ask who'd set it off. She already knew the answer.

Astrid's dark gaze fell and she let out a shaky breath. "It was Eos." Again, she mussed her hair. "Two seconds and I'll have the feed to you."

Silence stuffed Elodie's ears as she stared through Astrid at Holly standing in the middle of the train with her perfect smile, blinking through a test that was not routine after all.

Do something! she wanted to scream at the holographic woman who was everywhere and nowhere—the face and voice of the company that had saved their species from extinction. The Key Corp had set up rules to keep its citizens safe, but Elodie began to feel that protective shell crack. She shuddered at the thought of what could come in.

The MAX slowed to a stop. When Holly instructed all passengers to disembark, Elodie leapt out of her seat and darted through the open doors, the image of Astrid projected ahead, as though she raced backward through the crowd. With their Violet Shields engaged, the other riders purposefully hurried to their destinations. Were they really supposed to just *go on*? Everyone acting like nothing was happening when just a few miles away, living, breathing human beings were already marked as dead? Those citizens would never see their families again. They'd never see anyone again. The Key would take them into quarantine where they'd be put into a medically induced coma while bots monitored them until they inevitably died of whatever disease was packed into the germ stack. If they were lucky, the Key would put them out of their misery. Either way, no one ever survived Eos.

"Just sent it your way. Pull it up. It's wild." Astrid leaned back, cradling her head, her fear quickly sliding away, lacing itself with the glassy-eyed amusement of a spectator.

Elodie paused, hesitated. She didn't want to watch the feed. It wasn't going to be *wild*. It was going to be heartbreaking, nauseating, sad. She exited the MAX stop and walked with purpose down Third Avenue.

Astrid waved her hands in front of her face, her image drifting through other pedestrians also learning about Tilikum Crossing on their own private screens and text messages. "El? Hellllloooo? Where arrrrrre youuuuu?"

"What? I'm right here. Obviously. You can see me." Elodie forced one foot in front of the other, forced herself to match everyone else's pace.

"Physically, sure, but mentally." Astrid tapped her temple. "Light years away."

"Can't I take a few seconds to think about things?" An escaped clump of damp hair slapped against Elodie's cheek, and she tucked it back under her beanie. "Serious stuff is happening right now, and I need a minute."

"You can take as long as you want, as long as you aren't thinking about Vee again."

"Vi," Elodie corrected automatically.

"I knew it!" Astrid clapped. "I knew you were still reading those books. Getting lost and daydreaming about those ridiculous stories. All books like that do is cause problems. And they're banned, Elodie. They'll get you into so much trouble. You have to stop." Her ponytail swished from side to side to punctuate her point. "I mean, next you're going to tell me you believe in New Dawn."

Elodie quickened her pace. Her gaze darted suspiciously at the passersby, monitoring every little reaction for fear they'd somehow heard Astrid's side of their private conversation, though she knew it was only in her field of vision, pumped into her eardrum via implant. "I was not daydreaming. Plus, I don't do that anymore. I turned all of those"—she checked her surroundings before whispering— "*illegal books* over to the Key's librarian myself." It wasn't exactly a lie since she planned on doing just that as soon as she finished the entire series. "So there's no reason to talk about it again." Her brow furrowed. "And I would never say that I believe in New Dawn."

Astrid smoothed a finger over her perfectly plucked eyebrow. "Well, they're both made-up stories."

"But one is a *book*," Elodie whispered. "It's art, Astrid. And the other is a lie Eos created to drum up recruits. Not the same at all." She shook her head and Astrid's image moved in unison with the motion. "Play the feed," Elodie commanded her vidlink before Astrid had a chance to comment.

A gray rectangle appeared above Astrid's image. The shape bisected the translucent panel covering the left side of Elodie's vision and created two separate panels—the lower was Astrid, and the upper was the live feed of Tilikum Crossing.

The first thing Elodie noticed was all the people lined up, each on their backs with their arms in an X across their chests. Hazmat-clad soldiers pointed guns at each person while trash can–sized bots sped around the bridge spraying every surface with liquid.

Her breath hitched in her chest and her legs ceased moving. This time, she couldn't force herself forward. She couldn't make her body blend in with the others who moved around her, swerving so as not to bump into her, not to *touch* her, everyone a little more cautious, a little more anxious, as the morning news spread. Maybe they could do all these things at once, their bodies continuing through the world on autopilot while their minds attended to more important matters, but Elodie couldn't do it all. She felt too much.

The drone transmitting the live feed didn't supply audio and was too high above the scene for Elodie to tell whether or not the eyes of the men and women lying on the bridge were closed out of fear, obedience, or death.

Elodie's fingers tingled. "Are they dead?" she finally heard herself ask.

Astrid's ponytail slid from her shoulder as she shrugged dismissively. "If they aren't now, they will be soon."

Elodie wanted to run until Westfall was nothing but a distant haze, but she would only be able to go so far. The Key had locked down the city at the threshold of Zone Seven. And for good reason.

Astrid cocked her head. "You think one of those soldiers is Rhett?"

Elodie squinted at the image, but it was no use. With their shiny Key Corp–red Hazmat suits and black weapons, the soldiers resembled a swarm of ladybugs. "I hope not. I don't want him anywhere near that kind of stuff."

"Even if he is, they have such intense sanitation procedures that there's no way Rhett could get infected." Astrid's gaze slipped to something out of Elodie's line of sight before she continued. "Key soldiers are always safe. No one fights against them and no germs can get to them. It's pretty much a no-risk job."

The scene on the bridge froze and dissolved into the gray hold screen before blinking white. Elodie opened her mouth to speak, but the Key's red logo unfurled across the small box in her vision.

Astrid resumed twirling the ends of her glossy ponytail. "You getting this?"

Elodie nodded as a woman strode into view, but it wasn't

Holly. The woman's hourglass hips swished hypnotically as she took her place. She clasped her slender, earth-brown hands in front of her hips and locked her hazel eyes on the camera.

"Good morning, citizens. By now, I am sure you have heard about the attack on *our* city."

Elodie's brow furrowed. "She sounds so familiar . . ."

"Like Holly?" Astrid let out a slight grunt of admiration. "That's Blair Scott. The hottest thing since VR. Like, Icarus-too-close-to-the-sun hot. Blair developed Holly's new coding, and as a signature, used her own vocal pathways in the new-and-improved Holly."

Elodie adjusted her beanie, hiding her grimace behind her hand. She barely noticed the other pedestrians racing by in either direction. The thought of creating a weird voice-twin made her skin crawl.

Blair continued. "Eos is trying to shake us, but they will fail. Westfall and its citizen are stronger than their hate. While we do not yet know how the attack on Tilikum Crossing happened or why, this is what we know for certain—

"You. Are. Safe." Her tender smile lifted her round cheeks but stopped short of her eyes. Those remained unchanged—smooth and fierce.

"Mere moments after the attack, the Key Corporation activated Westfall's intense containment protocols, and we are pleased and *thankful* to be able to say that our city is one hundred percent free of any infective agents, and no one outside of the immediate attack zone was exposed to any pathogens."

Elodie released a stored breath and scooted out of the way as a group of button-down-clad men approached.

"Another win for the Key!" one of the men cheered as they passed by.

Had Elodie really been standing in the middle of the sidewalk like a dolt? Mentally, she shook herself and continued her walk to her office building as she resumed listening to Blair Scott.

"We are safe, and we owe that safety to the Key, and the more than five decades of work they have put into protecting us. That is why we know for certain that the corporation is truly the key to health, the key to life, and the *key* to our future."

Recognizing the end of a Key Corp message, Elodie focused on ending the feed. "Doesn't it bother you how they're always saying that? *The key to our future.* It's creepy, right?" she said as Astrid's image expanded to full size.

Astrid shrugged. "It might seem a little intense if it wasn't true, but isn't it just a fact? I mean, if it wasn't for the Key, we wouldn't even be here. Our species would have died out forever ago."

"Fifty years ago," Elodie corrected.

"Since you and I have only been here for seventeen, it might as well have been forever ago." Astrid punctuated with a flick of her ponytail. "Either way, we're alive because of the Key."

"You're totally right," Elodie said, more to remind herself than in response to her best friend.

The gray stretch of pavement beneath Elodie's feet abruptly changed to rust-red brick when she reached the front of the MediCenter. "I'm at work. I'll call you after," she said, suddenly remembering she could finally remove her hat. She yanked it off her head and stuffed it into her backpack before shaking out her dark curls. Instead of cascading around her shoulders in beautiful waves as she'd imagined, her wet hair splatted against her shoulders in two damp clumps.

Astrid's eyes widened for the zillionth time that morning. "Is your hair *wet?*"

Elodie scooped her hair off her shoulders, leaving behind two wet shadows across her top. "I took a shower. It's no big deal." If she'd had more time, she would have taken another one after her nursing lesson. She needed a real shower after that nightmare; needed to feel the steaming torrent of water against her skin. She needed to feel clean.

"Hmm." Astrid pursed her pale pink lips. "I don't want to say it's weird, but, you know," another shrug. "It's weird."

"*You're* weird." Elodie batted down her insecurities with a forced chuckle.

"Thank you much." Astrid grinned, straight and shiny. "Hey, even though everything is good now, don't take the MAX home. Take a Pearl."

Elodie snorted. "Yeah, maybe I'll think about it in twenty years when I'm head of the nursing department. I get that you work with your genius dad, but us normal people don't make thousands of bits each year to go spending on fancy Pearl rides."

The rosy red of Astrid's cheeks deepened. *Bits.* That was the one thing that would embarrass Astrid every time. Each coin her family made seemed to add to her shame. Elodie didn't understand. If she had that much money, she'd be long gone. Across the ocean and deeply rooted in foreign lands. Westfall would become nothing more than the place she'd come from. The place that made her unique, different from everyone else. Her stomach clenched with the lie. As much as she wanted to believe she'd be anywhere else, her place was in Westfall, with Rhett, in the MediCenter, with her plain, safe life.

Astrid pulled a thick curtain of hair across her face like a mask. "Shut up," she teased, releasing the dark strands. "We're working on a new Pearl prototype and need people to test it out. I'll send one to pick you up. *For free.*"

"A prototype? I'll have to figure out if I would rather die in a fiery ball or test my luck in some horrible germ attack." The men and women laying on the bridge, X's on their chests, flashed behind Elodie's eyes. "You know what," she cleared her throat. "That was stupid. Don't listen to me. I'll take your free ride."

Astrid plucked the air with a delicate wave. "Later, later."

The image filling the side of Elodie's vision went gray and disappeared as she ended the call and stared up at Westfall's downtown MediCenter building. Bronze sconces framed the smooth concrete facade, their tines stretching toward the sky like points on a crown.

Elodie's clear plastic cuff flashed green as she approached the spotless glass doors. They opened noiselessly, their shiny gold handles glinting in the dappled sunlight. How long had it been since anyone had actually touched them? The handles on all of the entrances in the remaining buildings in Zone One were now nothing more than metal jewelry for doors.

The scent of fresh pine, of the forest after a rainstorm, swirled through the air.

"Is this one of those experiments where someone stands in the middle of the walkway to see whether or not people are gullible enough to start a line behind them?"

Heat flooded Elodie's cheeks and she flicked her gaze to the pavement behind her and the owner of the deep, silky voice and source of the piney scent. How had she missed those giant boots clomping up behind her? The boots moved, leaving a dusting of dirt across the red brick. Elodie grimaced. Who even knew where to find that much dirt?

"You *are* going in, right?" The owner of the boots spoke again.

Elodie jerked forward and absentmindedly shook her head at the dingy, mud-splattered yellow laces. "No. I mean yes." She forced her attention to the ground beneath the nearly silent shuffling of her brilliantly white sneakers. Maybe she did get lost in her thoughts way too often. "Yes, I—" The glass door clanged surprisingly loud when Elodie smacked into it.

The heavy boots clomped up behind her, bringing with them more of the crisp evergreen scent. "Oh, shit. Are you okay?"

Elodie's vision danced as she waited for the doors to reopen before attempting to walk through them again. "Yeah." She rubbed the side of her head and stayed facing forward, refusing to look at whoever had just witnessed what had to be the most embarrassing moment of her life. The doors opened and Elodie concentrated on proceeding as calmly and incident-free as possible to the bay of elevators. "Eleven," she squeaked after scanning her cuff beneath the elevator's control panel.

The heavy, crunchy footsteps continued to shadow her. Elodie pressed her eyelids shut and held her cool palm against her flaming cheek as she waited to see which elevator would descend first.

Another beep of the control panel. "Twelve," the boots' owner said with a muffled groan.

Or maybe Elodie was the one groaning.

Her eyelids fluttered open and she cast a sideways glance at the dirty brown boots waiting by her side. There was no way she could board an elevator and ride all the way to the eleventh floor with that forest scent, with someone who had just watched her walk into a door. Not with the morning she'd been having. She smoothed her wet hair over the tender knot forming on the side of her head.

An elevator chimed its arrival, and Elodie darted away from the opening doors and the heavy boots.

Today seemed like a really good day to take the stairs.

IV

"*And* the key to our future. The key to *our* future. The *key* to our *future*." Blair bit down on her nail, silently scolded herself, and then clasped her hands in front of her as she hurried down the MediCenter's glass-lined corridor. "Damn. I could've done better. That's the worst part about going live. There's no opportunity to make adjustments or edits."

"Nonsense. You did great." Blair's new assistant's words were rushed and breathy as her short legs worked to keep up. "Really, Ms. Scott, you are an asset. A real asset. Everybody thinks so." Her assistant's constant need to please made Blair's teeth hurt.

"Your name," Blair snapped her fingers. "I've forgotten it already."

"Wyndham, Ms. Scott. Maxine Wyndham."

Sure, Blair might seem a bit tough, and may have gone through more assistants than years she'd been alive, but that was only because none of them were a right fit. She needed someone dedicated. As dedicated as she was. And that wasn't easy to find.

Blair would have a cot brought to her office at Westfall's

downtown MediCenter, which served as the Key Corp headquarters of the New American West Coast, if it meant a greater career edge. She'd once considered curling up on her plush throw rug, but felt it would create the wrong optics. Each one of the assistants Career Placement had assigned her had pretended to feel the way she did, but it was obvious they didn't possess the same strain of dedication Blair had coursing through her veins. She'd even weighed letting her brother give it a shot, but she knew how that would end.

The Leightons, Blair's parents, had both worked hard for the long, prestigious titles they'd tacked in front of their surnames. After their deaths, Cath Scott had adopted Blair, and the Key had pressured her to take Cath's last name. Unity, that's what the corporation had been striving after. That's how battles were won and power reigned, and Blair understood those facts completely. It was a fair trade-off. The silver lining to her unbelievably stormy life. A new last name that practically oozed power in exchange for her fate as an orphan. Even if she'd had a choice, she would have taken that name. Cath had not only completed a doctorate but had also risen to director of Career Placement at the MediCenter. That made Blair as close to an example of *born and raised in* as anyone was going to get.

But, for some reason, every assistant placed with Blair assumed that her desire to be on top meant that she needed some kind of yes person. That, however, was not how the saying went. *Behind every strong woman was a sea of strong women,* not *behind every strong woman was a sea of yes-minded drones.* Why didn't anyone understand that?

Blair turned down the corridor that led to her office and stopped short of the door. "Ms. Wyndham." She swiveled to face her pretty new assistant. "I appreciate all you've done . . ."

Black.

She categorized the lie immediately. Although, black was far from the worst kind. Blair was always lying to someone. Like luggage on a trip, lies followed her to each destination. She had to pack them up every night just to unload them in the morning. To keep track, she'd developed a sort of guide. It also served as a guilt meter—Blair felt it was the least she could do to make note of how guilty she should feel if she ever decided to turn that part of herself back on.

Red lies were lies that, if they were corporeal, would draw blood. And then there were black lies. Blair would never feel anything about black lies. They were empty holes of nothingness. Words slid so gracefully into conversation that their absence would have been felt more seriously than their addition.

Blair hooked a soft smile to the corners of her lips and continued. "But I really don't think you're right for this position."

Maxine's cheeks flushed and the tip of her thin nose turned pink. "I don't understand. I thought everything was going well."

"It is . . ." *Black.* "But our styles are too different."

Maxine's nose twitched, and she rubbed her red, puffy eyes.

Blair forced her palms flat against each other to keep them from balling into fists. People where always hemorrhaging their feelings all over the place. If Blair could keep hers buttoned up, there was no reason why others couldn't also. "Now, Maxine, please don't cry."

"I'm not." She pulled a handkerchief from her pants pocket and dabbed her eyes.

Blair dug her pinky nail into her palm, relaxing slightly as a jolt of pain sparked up her arm. "Really, tears are nothing to be embarrassed about."

Black.

Blair unclasped her hands, unfolding herself in an attempt to look more open and approachable. "So far, what I need and what those assigned to me have been able to supply have been two vastly different things. It's nothing personal."

"This," with the square of fabric Maxine gestured to her sliminess before slipping the handkerchief back into her pocket. "Is because of my allergies. They always flare up this time of year and turn me into a leaking mess."

"Oh." The revelation stung. Blair possessed an uncanny sense for sniffing out others' lies, and this had the air of truth. She didn't necessarily want to make people cry. But she did want people to want to work for her so badly that the thought of getting fired would at least have them on the verge of tears.

"If I'm honest, Ms. Scott, and, may I be honest? Actually . . ." Maxine waved her hands as if erasing the question. "I'm going to be honest whether or not you want to hear it. This *style* doesn't work for me either. When I received word that I was assigned this position, I was ecstatic. We're both twenty-three and I am in awe of what you've been able to accomplish. I thought working for you would be an amazing learning experience. Then I heard about the ways your past assistants had treated you. So, in order to work with you, I became that. And I have to say that I really don't like it. You're great, but you already know that. I hate being the person who follows you around with the sole purpose of managing your ego. It's insulting." Her pointed chin lifted. If not for the fact that Blair was a head taller, Maxine would have been looking down the end of her nose at her new boss. "Insulting to both of us."

Blair inhaled, slowly and deeply.

"Ms. Scott," Maxine continued, "I do want to stay, but only

if I'm able to be honest with you. I also have a lot of connections and can—" Blair held up a finger and Maxine's jaw clamped shut.

There might be a nice balance with Maxine. A fiery subservience Blair could enjoy.

Blair scraped her gaze down the petite young woman, her straight blond hair, snowy complexion, and pointed heels. "Call me Blair." Her office doors opened with a hiss as she passed her cuff under the scanner. "And, Maxine, when the bots come by with my coffee, tell them I want it black."

From the second Aiden stepped off the elevator and into the twelfth floor Career Center Receiving Area, he regretted everything. Okay, maybe not *everything*, but a lot. What he regretted most of all was that he had used up all of his free passes. The next step was getting shipped off to Rehab. How had he reached the end so quickly?

"Next citizen, please." The Holly that haunted the MediCenter pointed to a line of low-tech lighted arrows built into the floor. They flashed green, leading him to a wall of private booths. The accordion doors opened automatically, and Aiden stepped through the Violet Shield's stream of purple light, before plopping down on the metal stool protruding from the floor like a tooth.

The computer screen in front of him flashed white and gray and then white again before the Key Corp's red logo faded into view and uncoiled before him, staining the small booth with its tendrils of red light. "Welcome," the computer's robotic voice croaked. It was different from Holly's, not as alive or real, though hearing Holly always brought goosebumps to his arms and a heaviness against his back as if he was being haunted. "Please scan your citizen identification cuff and state the reason for your visit. I understand complete sentences."

Aiden tapped the toes of his boots against the floor. "You don't, actually. But it's good to see you again. I've been reassigned to janitorial duty. At least, that's what the message said this time." He scanned his cuff and left the computer to sift through the extra words he'd provided. Each time he'd visited the career center, he'd said something a little different to test the computer's abilities. It said it understood complete sentences, when what it meant was that it understood certain words spoken in a certain order. But that was probably too much explanation and actualization for such a low-tech device to comprehend.

"Citizen 1782445, your reassignment has been updated." The computer whirred and an arrow appeared on screen, pointing to a narrow strip of paper poking out from under the monitor. "Please take your printed reassignment update. Have a pleasant day."

Aiden pulled the paper free and read aloud. "Reassigned. Report to basement level room forty-four at 0930." He glanced up at the screen. "Reassigned to what? There's nothing even halfway decent down in the basement."

The arrow flashed in response.

"Great. Thanks a lot." Aiden nearly ripped the flimsy door off its ancient sliders as he shouldered his way through the tight opening. He clomped toward the elevator, his boots still leaving a trail of dirt behind him.

This morning was turning to shit.

But at least he hadn't walked into a door.

VI

Elodie arrived at the Long-Term Care Unit breathless, at exactly 0930. Precisely on time. Although, to Elodie, who was habitually ten minutes early, being *on time* felt unnervingly close to being late.

And like every day he was scheduled to work before her, Gus sat ready and waiting, his back to the door. "Almost, Elodie. Al-most." Gus waggled his finger at the clock glowing down at them from the corner of the holoscreen that monitored their patients. From the back, Gus looked sharp in his maroon Key Corp LTCU scrubs with his shaggy hair and lanky, unassuming figure, but when he turned around—

"You're wet." Confusion creased Gus's bushy, dandruff-flecked brow.

Elodie pulled her towel-dried waves into a tight bun and smiled politely. "Yeah, I showered." Sure, Westfall citizens opted for light baths instead of the water showers of the past, but that didn't mean she *shouldn't* take a *real* shower. There wouldn't have been one in her house if it was against the rules. "Are you planning on giving me an update before you head out?"

"Don't I always?" Gus pursed his thin lips, instantly transforming back into the impatient employee who treated every workday like it was the worst day of his life. But how could it be? This is what the Key chose for him, for both of them. And it wasn't an idea the corporation plucked out of thin air. No, the Key had taken their time. And Gus and Elodie and everyone else in Westfall and cities around the globe had done their part and taken the series of tests to determine not only what would make them happiest, but also what they would excel at. The Key had done an impeccable job placing them (not that Elodie would ever think that the Key would do anything less). Elodie was happy. Her parents were happy. Her friends were happy. Gus . . .

"I already did a Violet Shield once-over on the Control Center." Gus brushed his hand through his dishwater brown hair. Specks of dandruff leapt from his scalp, adding to the light dusting on his shoulders. "Oh, and there was a transfer last night." He motioned to the final patient care chart in the line of five that glowed paper-white on the holoscreen. "Don't know what her deal is, so you might want to run the shield again soon, just to be on the safe side."

Elodie's gaze scanned the row of patient care chart thumbnails. "A new patient? I thought we were full."

"We were." The bruise-purple rings around Gus's eyes seemed to swallow them as he squinted. Too many hours spent in VR. "Then they sent one out to the MediCenter in Zone Two, the *lesser* MediCenter, and brought this one from . . ." He hiked his shoulders. "I don't know. Somewhere else."

Elodie's hands tightened into fists. *This one, that one.* You're a step away from referring to them as *things* instead of people."

He further rounded his slumped shoulders with a shrug. "They're in medically induced comas until they either get put down or get better. Bots take care of them—"

"*We* take care of them!" she said. Gus's slack-jawed expression mirrored the shock tingling through Elodie's limbs. It wasn't technically an outburst, but it was definitely more bursty than anything Elodie normally said.

He held up his hands in surrender. "Yeah, fine. You're right. We take care of 'em."

Elodie let out a puff of air. She needed to get herself under control. "*Who* brought the patient from *where*?"

"Hell, Elodie, I don't know. I just run the Violet Shield and make sure none of the pumps malfunction and no dumb bots get stuck in doorways. I'm not in charge of intake. That's your job."

It was times like these when Elodie wished she had Vi's covert assassin abilities. "Well, since it *is* part of your job, did you make sure all of the treatment pumps are full enough to get me through the day?"

"Yeah, yeah. I did everything I'm supposed to do. It was a busy night, but I'm not stupid." He rubbed the small diagonal scar behind his right ear and stared blankly at the empty space above Elodie's head.

Automatically, she rubbed the matching scar behind her own ear. The bump from the implant had faded long ago. A small strip of smooth skin was the only outward evidence of the tech that had been injected under her scalp shortly after birth, same as every other citizen. The implant had grown up with her, grown *into* her, *learned* with her. It made her, and everyone else's, life so much easier. Although Gus's habit of touching the implant point every time he checked his schedule, mail, or a plethora of other things Elodie was thankful she couldn't see, was a constant and obnoxious reminder that he wasn't paying her any attention.

He let out an exasperated breath "I have VR surf lessons scheduled in exactly thirty minutes, so I'm out of here." He jogged to the elevator and waved his cuff under the reader. It beeped, beeped, and beeped again as Gus flapped his arm under the beam of light.

"You only need to scan it one time," Elodie muttered.

Gus tapped his foot against the tile. "Unlike *some people*, I have a life outside of work that I'm ready to get to."

"Oh, yeah? Well, *I* happen to like my job." Elodie spun around as the elevator doors swallowed her coworker. "Damn." She dropped into the hard plastic chair in front of the control panel and quickly scanned the steadily blinking peaks and valleys of the new Patient Ninety-Two's heartrate monitor before she hefted her backpack onto her lap and unzipped the center pouch.

"I do too have a life outside of work." The neon lights of the holoscreen glimmered off the slick cover of her nursing textbook. "Actually, I have *lots* of lives outside of work."

VII

Blair felt eyes on her as she stood outside of Cath's office. She pulled her fingers away from her mouth and clenched her teeth. Her adoptive mother had an open-door policy, but it was controlled by the slowest woman Blair had ever had the displeasure of dealing with. And the ninth floor was not a place where Blair wanted to be stuck. The entire space was filled with clear partitions, giving the regular working masses the illusion of having their own office. But a true office wasn't a glass box, it was a room made of solid walls that deflected unwanted glances. It was a space like the one Blair stood outside of, but, if this septuagenarian had her way, would never be able to enter.

Open this door, you insufferable reject! Blair's thoughts burned as she offered a polite nod to Cath's elderly assistant.

The old woman smiled. "She's on a call, dear. It'll be just a moment. But it looks like you have a visitor yourself." She tilted her chin in the direction of the sharp, clicking footsteps closing in on Blair.

Before Blair could make up an excuse to come back later or break down the door herself, the footsteps halted, and a booming voice struck Blair's back like a battering ram.

"Well, well, well, if it isn't Blair Scott. A meeting with your mommy bring you down to the ninth floor? Is baby brother in there too? A little Scott family get together on Key Corp hours?"

Blair's teeth scraped together as she turned and lowered her gaze to meet the man. "Preston, it is *so* nice to see you."

It doesn't get blacker than that.

Preston's strong jaw twitched. "That's Council Leader Darby, Blair. *Council. Leader. Darby.*" He thrust his coffee mug for emphasis. Brown droplets sloshed onto the pristine floor. "I worked hard for the title."

Blair tightened the corners of her snarl into a broad smile. If Preston Darby had ever worked for anything, Blair wasn't quite sure what it had been. All he had to do to attain his title was draw breath and walk around Westfall as a more handsome, clone-like version of his father, who had been Council Leader until his untimely death.

Preston clicked the heels of his shiny black boots and nodded over his shoulder at the glass-encased audience staring wide eyed at the scene unfolding outside Dr. Cath Scott's door. The list of people who could admonish Blair was a short one, and Preston Darby was near the top. "Wouldn't want the masses to think the Council has gone soft."

"Soft, you? *Never.* I'm sure you're hard in every way that matters, Council Leader Darby."

"Well, I, uh . . ." He cleared his throat and took a quick drink.

Getting a reaction from Preston Darby had always been easy. So easy that it hadn't been fun since he'd dissolved into a mushy bag of snot and tears during their final year of schooling. That last semester had shone a spotlight on Blair. The corporation had been correct when they'd chosen her for leadership training. Blair had been named the Key's student body liaison and, in all of her correspondence with the corporation, he'd been listed as Preston Derpy. It hadn't even been Blair's mistake. It had been their virtual assistant's. Blair just didn't correct it.

The door slid open behind her and Cath's crone assistant made a small coughing noise. "You can go in now, Ms. Scott."

Blair nodded. The assistant's timing had been perfect. Perhaps Blair should learn her name . . . "If you'll excuse me, Council Leader, I have a meeting to—"

"I saw your broadcast," he boomed with another surge of his mug. "It was—" He paused, tilting his head from side to side as if weighing his words. "Let's just say you can tell it was your first time. But don't worry, Blair. Practice makes perfect." He took another drink, the corners of his lips curving into a grin around the mug's black rim.

Heat painted Blair's stomach. Derpy was upping his game.

Blair scanned the sets of eyes patiently peering from their glass boxes. She could practically feel gossip churning inside them. *Did you hear what the Council Leader said to Ms. Scott? No one talks to her like that. And then she ran away to her mom's office!*

That couldn't be the office chatter. It *wouldn't* be. Blair slid her tongue across her lips.

"You'll have to forgive me, Council Leader. I was taken aback by your gorgeous shoes." She pressed her hand against her chest and peered inquisitively down at Preston's petite feet. "It's about time a designer came out with a line of heels for men."

Now *that* would make for some excellent office goss.

Coffee sloshed to the tiled floor as Preston whipped around toward the bubbles of laughter erupting from the glass boxes behind him.

Blair's prey was wounded, but she needed Council Leader Preston Darby dead. Figuratively, of course. "They're beautiful, Council Leader, just beautiful." Blair squatted as much as her slim skirt allowed. "Is that a two-inch lift? I'll have to see if they have them in my size."

Preston's face lit up stoplight red. "This is the last time you make a fool of me." More coffee leapt from his mug as he clicked off toward the elevators.

Blair smoothed out her skirt, nodded at Cath's assistant, and strode into her adoptive mother's office. A chorus of laughter erupted as the door slid closed behind her.

"You shouldn't have done that, Blair." Cath tapped her pursed lips with her index finger, her perfectly manicured Key Corp–red nails in stark contrast against her pale lips and white desk.

Blair waved away the comment. "Preston deserved it." She fluffed her wild curls over her shoulder. "I don't know who that short little gnome thought he was talking to."

Cath hid her smile behind her fingertips. "He can make your life more difficult. And Denny's."

Blair snorted. If Preston Darby dared to mess with her brother, she'd have his tiny feet stuffed and mounted.

Cath chuckled lightly. "*Short little gnome . . .*"

Blair ran her fingers over the cracked spines of the reference books lining Cath's bookshelves. "Did *you* happen to see my broadcast?" Blair pressed each word against the back of her teeth, forcing them out slowly, subtly, as if that one question hadn't been the reason for her visit. "I feel like it went okay," she continued, strangling her footsteps the same way she choked her words, with practiced ease. "I didn't have a prompter or anything. There wasn't time. But I guess that *is* the nature of an emergency. I ended up having to wing it." She came to the end of the bookshelf and flicked an invisible speck of link from her fingertips before making her way to Cath's desk. "Any thoughts?"

Blair clamped her mouth shut as anxiety clacked her teeth together. If she could reach inside herself and punish her nerves, she would. She hated the way they popped beneath her skin, the pressure building until she felt like she might explode if she didn't vent. And her current go-to was Cath. Who was she kidding? Her go-to was always Cath. It had been since Blair had turned thirteen. Since her parents—

Blair shook her head. There was no point in thinking about the past. She wasn't there. She was here. She was now. "The whole time I was up there I was thinking about what you would have said and what I as a citizen would have wanted to hear from you, a Key representative. No one helped me. My assistant pulled me out of my meeting, gave me bullet points, and next thing I knew there was a camera in my face."

Cath patted her desk. "Sit. Relax." She smoothed out the crisp sleeves of her blouse. "You did fine."

Blair slid into one of the uncomfortable chairs facing Cath's desk. "Just *fine*? I suppose my inflection was a little off . . . Like I said, I didn't have time to prepare."

A soft grin creased the corners of Cath's warm brown eyes. "You delivered the message well. It was clear and concise."

A compliment, but not exactly what Blair was looking for. She forced her spine straight even though every ounce of her deflated. "The whole point was to try and make the citizens feel like we're on the same team. Like they can trust the Key and, by extension, they can trust me."

Cath gently folded her slender arms across her desk. "I thought the point was to let citizens know that the city is safe, and that they don't have to worry about infection or about Eos."

"Well, yeah. I mean, yes, of course. That was definitely the main point. That goes without saying."

Black.

Cath cocked her head. "You *were* told that the city is safe now, *weren't you?*"

Did Cath not know for sure? Or was this a test? What if Cath was fishing? What if the powers that be had given Cath information they hadn't given Blair? Or what if they had told Blair something they hadn't told Cath? Maybe the corporation was trying to pit them against one another since a new position was opening up soon. Maybe they wanted to see if Blair was able to keep from spilling Key secrets to a person as close to her as Cath.

Well, Blair had never failed a test before, and she wasn't about to start now.

With deliberate absentmindedness, Blair brushed back a few curls that had freed themselves in front of her eyes. "I hear Holbrook is being put down. That'll mean his MediCenter Director title will be up for grabs."

Cath's gaze fell to her hands. "I can't imagine what he's going through. Having the date of your death set, each second ticking by, bringing you closer to the end." She shook her head. "His heart has been bad for a while, but the whole thing is . . . sad." Her eyes glistened when she finally looked up.

Cath cared so much. Blair needed to try to care more too. It might make people warm up to her, and it would be easier to do her job if her employees' loyalty rested on the fact that they truly liked her.

Blair slumped her shoulders slightly, a mirror image of Cath's sadness. "Mrs. Holbrook is probably broken up about it."

"I've spoken with her. She understands that it's time, but that doesn't make it any easier. To survive the virus just to be put down fifty years later . . ." Cath plucked at the air with her fingers as her thoughts swallowed her.

Blair studied the ragged edges of her nails. She should contact the old bag's wife; she was on the MediCenter board, and if Blair had any hope of being nominated for Director Holbrook's job after they finally put him down, she needed to make nice with whomever she could.

Message to Maxine. Blair thought, blinking long and slow. When her lids lifted, the transparent gray messaging box appeared, only slightly blurring the vision in her left eye. *Find Holbrook's address and send his wife whatever I'm expected to send to a person whose husband is on the bullet train toward death.* The bold text appeared as quickly as she thought it, and sent just as fast.

"Blair, you should come too."

"Sorry, I can't." She'd missed what Cath had been saying, but she knew without hearing it that she didn't want to attend. She loved Cath, but she didn't particularly like spending time with her. Cath was always doing things that bordered on *strange*. Okay, to be honest, they were frickin' weird. Canoeing and running and hiking all out in the real world like some kind of Zone Six dip who couldn't afford a new VR kit. It was gross.

Cath frowned. "He's the director of the MediCenter. You really should make time to come to his funeral. Everyone will be there sharing stories, memories. If it makes you feel better, we can go together. I know it would be easier for me if I had you by my side."

Blair sucked in a breath and nodded. "Oh, the funeral. Yes, I'm definitely attending. And we *should* go together." If what Cath said was true, and *everyone* really was going to be there, it would only make Blair look better to arrive with the ever-popular Dr. Cath Scott.

Ever-popular. Blair kept herself from rolling her eyes like a petulant child. She could be loved and admired too, if she really wanted.

Blair cleared her throat and shook away the sudden spike of jealousy heating her stomach. "I have the perfect outfit for a funeral. However, it's deep navy, not black. Do you think that's appropriate?"

Sunlight streamed in through the wall of windows behind Cath, framing her in an ethereal glow. "Perhaps you should focus on the meaning of the proceedings and less on your attire. Don't you think that's more important?"

Blair bit the inside of her cheeks. "Yes, of course."

Black.

And I'll be dressed in navy.

It wasn't her fault Cath didn't understand that the funeral was going to serve as the first in-person interview for Holbrook's position. And *that* was really the most important thing.

Holbrook would be dead. He wouldn't need their regurgitated memories or their tears. But Blair, who was very much alive, did need his title. It was what she'd been working toward since she'd begun her career. A career that was taking off unlike any other. She was the MediCenter's rising star, and she wouldn't burn out because of the death of some old man. No, she would be a phoenix and rise from that old bastard's ashes.

VIII

Aiden was only slightly late for the first morning of his new career assignment when the elevator doors slipped open and he shuffled, heavy footed, into the light-soaked hallway. The small rectangle of paper listing his room forty-four reassignment stared up at him, its bold text washed out under the glare of the bulbs.

He shielded his eyes and squinted as he reread the room number. "Remember never to come in hungover."

Aiden didn't bother to look through the hazy, Violet Shield–covered doorways that lined the hall. There'd be plenty of time to investigate his surroundings when he made the exact same walk every morning of every day for every year of his life until he retired. And by that time, he might as well be dead.

Yep, having a career chosen for you was absolutely fantastic.

A big "44" glowed at the end of the hall, black digits backlit by white light. The orchid-like biohazard symbol bloomed around the block numbers with bewitching beauty, even though Aiden knew each petal symbolized death and destruction.

Haunting Holly appeared as Aiden closed in on number forty-four, the only entrance in the long, brightly lit hall with its doors closed. "Hello and welcome to the End-of-Life Unit. Only authorized citizens and MediCenter employees are allowed entry. The Key Corp thanks you for your understanding and for your help in keeping our city and its citizens safe."

Aiden tugged at the too tight collar of his scrub top. "The End-of-Life Unit?"

The hologram's sterile smile was right at home in the bleached-out corridor. "That's correct. Please place your cuff beneath the scanner." She motioned to the panel at the side of the door. "All authorized citizens and employees will be granted entry."

"Hang on. There must be some mistake. *This is the morgue.*" As he said it, he knew this was no mistake. Cath had put him here on purpose.

Haunting Holly clasped her hands in front of her hips and nodded. "Yes, you've reached the morgue. Or, as we like to call it, the End-of-Life Unit, or ELU."

Aiden stared at the overly chipper face and hollow eyes of the MediCenter's seemingly omnipotent mega computer. "This can't be happening." He stumbled backward, reaching out for something to hold onto as his world slipped out from under his heavy boots.

The morgue? *The fucking morgue?* That's where Cath sent him? This is the place he was going to have to spend the majority of his life? No, not even just the majority of his life. He'd end up here after he died too. He was going to spend his entire earthly existence *in this morgue.*

Haunting Holly tilted her head to the side. Her hair fell away from her cheek, revealing a small, Key Corp–red gem dangling from her ear. The corporation really had thought of everything.

Her delicate eyebrows lifted. "Please place your cuff beneath the scanner. All authorized citizens and employees will be granted entry," she repeated.

Aiden held out his arm and didn't stifle his groan when his cuff flashed green and the double doors slid apart with a quiet hiss.

"Welcome, Aiden." Haunting Holly walked backward into the reception hall, arms open as if these first steps of the rest of his life were something to be revered instead of reviled. She pointed to the glass reception desk gleaming like a crystal in the corner of the giant room. "Octavia will get you checked in for your first day. I look forward to assisting you during your career in the End-of-Life Unit."

Aiden paused in front of Haunting Holly and her clasped hands and brilliant smile, forgetting for a moment that she was what her name implied—a hologram. "You say it like it's a good thing." He stepped through her. As though he were in a rainstorm of color, light misted around him. He stared at his palms, painted Key Corp–red by Holly's blouse. If he ever felt empty, he'd remember this. He'd remember Holly, all seeing, all knowing, all nothing.

Haunting Holly blinked out of existence—well, *this* existence—and Aiden was left gazing at the deep umber of his own skin. He cleared his throat, stuffed his fingers into his shallow pockets, and proceeded toward the giant crystal of a desk and the young short-haired woman seated behind it.

Octavia didn't look up from the holopad balanced on one hand. Aiden stood there a moment, shifting uncomfortably in the silence. "Hey, I'm—"

The petite young woman held up her hand, stripping Aiden of his introduction.

"Okay," he said, "I'll just stand over here and wait until you're finished doing whatever it is you're doing."

She let out an annoyed puff of air. "Do you not know what it means when someone holds up their hand like that?" With a flick of her wrist, she reenacted the move. "It means you need to stop talking, not switch subjects."

Aiden pulled at the short sleeves of his uncomfortably small shirt. "Sorry."

"It's too late." She tapped purposefully on the glass desktop. "I had the perfect conclusion to my paper, but it's gone now."

"We'll have time to do classwork down here?" Maybe it wouldn't be as horrible if he had time to work on his studies. After all, he would be starting over . . . again.

Her glitter-lined eyes narrowed into sparkling slits. "No. I only had time to do my work because the guy I'm waiting on is late."

"That's me." Aiden poked himself in the chest. "I'm the late guy."

Octavia pursed her lips, the pink slivers almost disappearing completely. "Yeah, I realize that." Aiden waited in another awkward silence as she scanned her holoscreen. "You're wearing the wrong scrubs," she finally said, her vibrant blue eyes boring into Aiden. "Ours are blue. You're wearing chartreuse. Surgical wears chartreuse."

Aiden glanced down at his slightly too small scrubs. "They're the only clean ones I had."

"But we wear blue." She gestured to her top as if doing so would magically change the color of his outfit.

Aiden tapped the toe of his boot against the floor. "I, uh, I'm not sure what you want from me. I didn't choose to come here. This is where I was assigned."

"Great." She tucked her holopad into the front pocket of her top, shoved herself away from the desk, and took off toward the other end of the expansive reception room. "They're always sending down idiots who have messed up their lives and are now here to mess up mine."

Aiden stepped forward, paused, and then took another tentative step. "Am I supposed to follow you?"

Octavia's neon pink–tipped hair didn't move as she whipped her head around and cast an exasperated glance over her shoulder. "Obvi."

Aiden hurried to catch up to her, then raced to keep up. For having such short legs, she was a surprisingly fast walker.

Octavia pointed her piercing blue gaze up at him. "Do you even have an aptitude for the medical spectrum, or is this some kind of punishment?"

The tight, unforgiving fabric strained against Aiden's shoulders as he shrugged. "Both, I guess."

She halted abruptly, her pointer finger trained on his chest. "No. It can't be. You're either supposed to be doing this *or* the corporation has sent you here to learn a lesson. To scare you so badly that you won't ever do whatever idiotic thing you did ever again."

Aiden chose his next words carefully. "What if I don't know what I'm *supposed* to be doing? What if I do have an *aptitude* for this, but it's buried under the desire to do something else entirely?"

She scrunched her small face. "That's stupid. How can you not know what you're supposed to be doing? The corporation literally tells you." Another scrunch. "I can tell by your age that this is a punishment, not a serious aptitude-based life decision."

Octavia turned and pointed down the end of the hall to the vending machine packed with individual vacuum-sealed blue scrub sets, a row of thicker orange packages, and plain white orthopedic sneakers. "Holly will get you what you need. And don't listen to her when she says to call me Octavia. It's Tavi. Holly's just being a birth record—quoting bitch. Also, you should for sure size up your scrubs." Scrunch. "You look like you squeezed yourself into your little brother's uniform."

Aiden's brow furrowed. "What do you mean you can tell by my age that this is a punishment? I'm not that much older than you."

With a groan she tilted her head back. "So tedious." She leveled her glitter-rimmed eyes at him and crossed her arms over her chest. "You're what? Eighteenish?" She was correct . . . ish, but didn't wait for a response. "Well, I'm sixteen and have been working in the ELU for three years. In two more years, I'll probably be in charge of my own examiner bot. Not starting fresh."

Aiden hooked his thumbs into his pockets. "I don't think 'fresh' is an appropriate description for anything down here."

"Yeah, well, I don't think I like you." With a final scrunch of her face, Tavi spun on her heels, her pink and blond hair firmly helmeted to her head as she stomped back toward the reception hall.

"Then it's a good thing we'll be working together. Every day. For the foreseeable future." He called after her as she turned the corner, her sneakers squeaking on the tile as she disappeared from sight.

Aiden dragged his calloused hands down his face. "Unfucking-believable."

Haunting Holly chose that moment to return. "Hello again, Aiden. I see that you're in need of my assistance."

Aiden grimaced. "Unfortunately."

"Great! What can I help you with?"

"I guess I need a new pair of scrubs." He looked down at his boots. "And shoes."

She followed his gaze down to his feet. "Ah, yes."

For an instant, Holly's warm and knowing smile was a balm on the chapped and irritated surface of his heart. It was easy to understand why the citizens of Westfall and beyond would want to trust that face . . . that voice. What he couldn't comprehend was how they could believe her words.

"Scan your cuff, and I'll get you taken care of."

Aiden's plastic cuff flashed, and Haunting Holly's eyelids fluttered as she sorted through the data. "Looks like you've been approved for five pairs of scrubs, two biohazard suits, and one pair of shoes. Would you like to collect all of these items now?"

Aiden stared at the orange biohazard suits all neatly folded and tucked innocently away in their plastic sheets. "This assignment keeps getting better and better."

"If you would like, I can give you a detailed explanation as to the uses and features of the ELU's biohazard suits."

Aiden held up his hands. "Nope. I would not like. If you tell me, I'll probably run out of here."

"Unless an emergency arises, running in the End-of-Life Unit is prohibited."

"I didn't mean—" He pinched the bridge of his nose. "Never mind. Go ahead and give me a pair of scrubs, a suit, and the shoes."

Haunting Holly noiselessly clapped her hands together. "Excellent. Anything else?"

Aiden slouched against the wall. "You wanna tell me the secret to working with dead people?"

"Tea tree oil right here." The hologram brushed her finger across her upper lip and winked.

Aiden rolled the back of his head from side to side against the wall. "You can make a joke, but you can't understand an exaggeration?"

Haunting Holly flashed another perfect smile and vanished.

The vending machine spit out a tray holding the scrubs,

biohazard suit, and sneakers. Reluctantly, Aiden scooped them up and followed the signs to the unit's locker room. The door slid open automatically, and Aiden's palms went clammy before stepping through the haze of purple light. In the locker rooms, there was always at least one person in a stage of undress. To the Key, bodies were just that—bodies.

No touching today for a healthy tomorrow. One of the corporation's favorite phrases. One of their favorite laws.

There were punishments for touching, swift and just. After all, according to the Key, a touch could spread disease, create another pandemic. Without touching, there should be no desire, no lust, no aching need. Cerberus should have sent those feelings to the grave along with the billions of people the virulent strain had claimed.

The fear of touch and the laws against it for the past fifty years meant that it wasn't only the Key that regarded bodies as sexless. It was everyone, *most* everyone. And, according to most everyone, all bodies had the same basic needs and, therefore, shared the same locker room. Each MediCenter unit's locker room was identical. Each had a wall of Key Corp–red lockers with cuff-activated locks and automatic doors, squeaky clean black-and-white tile floors with benches sprouting like metal hedgerows, two light-bath stalls bisecting the room, two toilet stalls, and one old-timey water-shower stall, although Aiden had never seen one in use.

He shuffled to the closest locker, unlaced and kicked off his boots, and stripped out of his too-tight chartreuse uniform. He wadded up the pants and top and did a little hop as he tossed them into the nearest refuse receptacle before waving his cuff under the locker's sensor. It popped open and Aiden stuffed his dirty boots, one on top of the other, into the narrow metal box.

Behind him, the bulbs from the light bath hummed to life. He turned, the hairs on his arms rising as the empty stall illuminated and exhaled cleansing light. A petite, red-haired woman had slipped into the stall without a sound. She tilted her chin toward the ceiling. Her waterfall of hair brushed against her naked back, coming alive in the changing light that flowed through each color of the spectrum.

Aiden couldn't pull his gaze away from the shadows that scooped out homes against her curves as she swayed, or from the light that pooled in the gentle dip in her lower back.

She gathered her hair, fastened it on top of her head, and turned.

Aiden's breath knocked against his ribs as he became all too aware of his own bare chest and bare legs, and the thin, white underwear stitching it all together.

She grinned and swiped at the living rainbow spilling down her bare shoulders. "I haven't seen you before. Are you new to the End-of-Life Unit?"

Aiden swallowed. Another fifty years could go by and he'd never get used to the self-consciousness that quaked in his stomach. "Um, yeah." He nodded and tried his best to pretend like this was normal, like *he* was normal. "It's my first day."

Light sank into the hollows of her pale collarbones. "I work upstairs in MediCenter marketing, but there's a problem with our showers." Another grin. "Which ELU department are you starting in?"

Aiden cleared his throat. "They haven't assigned me yet."

Air conditioning threw a cool gust across his bare thighs and he shivered slightly.

She brushed her hands down the slopes of her waist as if each touch would assist the light in cleansing her further. "Oh, you're *super* new." Her hands crossed over her bare stomach. "Pray you don't get incineration. That one's rough," she said as she slid her hands across the stretch marks running in powerful arcs along her naked hips. "Everything else in the MediCenter is either safe and boring or dangerous and interesting."

Aiden took a moment before asking, "Which are you?"

She released her hair and it rained against her bare breasts. "Dangerous and interesting."

The lights clicked off and she stepped through to the other side of the open stall.

A sudden shock of cold bit at the backs of Aiden's legs as he dropped onto the bench in front of the lockers and busied himself with stripping the vacuum-sealed plastic from his new uniform. He shook out the folded pants and a small, rectangular card floated to the floor. Aiden picked it up. *End-of-Life Unit—blue scrub set* was printed on one side. He flipped it over: *No touching today for a healthy tomorrow*. Aiden balled up the words, the warning, in his palm and threw the crumpled card into the open locker.

No rule, regardless of the punishment, could eliminate desire. And Aiden's desire was a river dammed just beneath his ribs. There were others out there like him, hiding in plain sight, faking emptiness to blend in. If there was only some way he could tell who felt the same . . .

His lips ticked with a grin as his thoughts wandered to the girl who'd run into the front door and then fled up the stairs.

But there was no use in thinking about her, about the woman in the shower, about desire, about any of it. Those thoughts were difficult to mask and, right now, Aiden needed his disguise firmly in place.

By the time he finished dressing, the red-haired woman was gone. It was for the best. Aiden didn't need anything else dangerous and interesting in his life.

Elodie swiped her cuff under the scanner next to the glass-top control panel. The Key's red logo swirled to life on both the panel and the holographic screen.

To health. To life. To the future. We are the Key.

"Welcome back, Elodie."

For the first time since she'd arrived at the MediCenter, Elodie felt at ease. Monitoring patients, making sure their needs were met, discharging patients and preparing for new patients to arrive, this is what she was good at—even when Gus left her with vague and incomplete new patient information. It also didn't hurt that this version of Holly was the one Elodie was most comfortable with. Helper Holly, or at least that's how she thought of the disembodied Holly voice, who stayed at the MediCenter and served as Elodie's nursing assistant.

Careful not to press unnecessarily on the expansive control panel, Elodie rested her forearms on the desk and studied the holoscreen as it scrolled through each patient's information. Bots beeped and hummed mechanically as they passed through the shield of violet light staining each patient's doorway, which protected those outside from any deadly microbes that might try to escape.

Everything looked normal. The Long-Term Care Unit physician had come through earlier and hadn't marked any patients as contagious, including the new one. No doses needed to be changed. No one else was being transferred out or in. Since Gus had left her with zero specifics about the new patient, Elodie double tapped on her chart to review it more closely. Patient Ninety-Two's health information was as normal as Elodie's other patients, steady rhythms, no present contagions, nothing out of the ordinary.

Elodie dropped her chin into her palms. It shouldn't be disappointing. Everyone was healthy. And she really had had enough excitement for one day.

Lights reflecting off the cover of her textbook drew her attention. She should probably hurry and finish reading the second book in the series so she could move on to the third book, then the fourth, and the fifth. After she finished, she'd be able to turn them over to the Library or incinerate them herself.

She warmed as she thought about how many more adventures she and Vi had left. But Astrid was right. Elodie's stomach squeezed. She could end up getting in trouble for something as stupid as reading unsanctioned fiction.

If the Key did find out, how bad would the punishment actually be? It was only reading, and reading never hurt anybody. Now, what would be painful was not knowing how Vi's story ended. It would make Elodie distracted and angsty, and all of that negative energy would spill into her work and her social life. Not finishing the series would be more harmful than keeping the books for a little while longer.

Excitement flapped in her chest as she turned to the dog-eared page.

Vi's heartbeat ticked up a notch as the wire dug into her custom leather gloves. The pressure made her jaw slacken and fire spark to life deep within her belly.

Vi enjoyed killing. Not in the way someone enjoyed a vacation or a free day off work. That enjoyment was a pacification—a scab protecting the world from what would happen if freedom really meant a person was free.

And Violet Jasmine Royale had let herself loose.

But what Vi liked more than the kill, what she craved more than a tall glass of double malt and a thick cigar, was the moment after. The brief second of swollen silence stretched thick and hard between her and her victim.

Vi's lip twitched with a sneer.

Victim. Yeah, right.

The word implied that Johnny Diamoto had been worth saving. It implied that he was innocent, and Johnny Diamoto was far from innocent. He was a liar. They all were.

Johnny's lies had attached to his soul and fed from any goodness in him like a leach, getting fat and bloated, infecting him with darkness. They had poisoned him and now, Johnny Diamoto was as healthy as the lies he told.

The cavern the garrote had carved into Johnny's neck squelched as Vi pulled the wire free. It hung from her fingertips as she, breathless and satisfied, strode into the Honeymoon Suite's luxurious bathroom. She ignored her reflection as she made her way to the marble double sinks. There was no reason to look at herself when she really wasn't herself at all. Johnny had liked them blond haired, blue eyed, and beach-bum tan. Violet wasn't any of those things.

She stole a glance in the mirror as she rinsed the garotte and peeled off her gloves. She'd been made over so many times, costumed as so many different people, that she had trouble remembering exactly what she'd looked like before. Again, she averted her eyes and busied herself with drying her things. There was no use in thinking about what she looked like. Tomorrow, she'd report into the office as this tan blond and leave as someone else. It was a fair price for getting to do what she loved, and for getting revenge.

Vi tucked her most prized possessions into her overnight bag before she checked the time. The cleanup crew wouldn't arrive for another hour. The corners of her lips curled into a grin as she eyed the jetted jacuzzi tub. After the night she'd had, she deserved a soak.

Water surged from the faucet as Vi turned the knob to hot. She squirted in a glob of complimentary bubble bath and watched the water foam as she kicked off her stilettos and wiggled out of Johnny's favorite lacy negligee. She turned on the jets and sank into the steaming water, closing her eyes as the bubbles puffed up around her. There really was peace in death. Hopefully, this time, it would last until she got home.

Block letters formed at the edge of Elodie's vision and snapped her from Vi's fantasy to her mundane reality.

Incoming call from Rhett Owens.

Elodie groaned.

With how often she was interrupted, she might end up keeping *Death by Violet* forever.

Elodie pressed her back into the chair's hard frame as if to distance herself from the message scrolling past her vision. It wasn't that she didn't want to talk to her fiancé. After all, they were in a stage that Astrid kept referring to as romancia-landia. Or maybe it was a place? Elodie wasn't quite sure. What she *was* sure of was that she and Rhett had definitely never even passed through romancia-landia.

Choosing at the last moment to forego the video portion of the call, Elodie activated her comlink. "Rhett, hi. I'm at wo—"

"I want to assure you that there's nothing to be afraid of." Rhett's tenor voice was smooth and clear in her ears. "I'm sure you saw Ms. Scott's situation update, but I know how sensitive you are and that you would still be shaken up."

Elodie's brow furrowed. "I'm not overly sensitive, I—"

"I didn't say *overly*, El. But you are a woman."

Elodie's mouth went dry, her tongue a hard lump of sand behind her teeth. Rhett wasn't wrong. She was a woman. But the way he'd said it was a slap, not a statement.

Rhett cleared his throat and continued. "Everything is being taken care of. My team and I were the first called out to Tilikum Crossing. It's fine now." His voice was curt. His words clipped, like he was presenting a briefing, not talking to the woman he would marry in a few months.

Elodie stared at Patient Ninety-Two's steadily blinking heart-rate monitor. "That adds to my relief, but I am still really worried about all of those—"

"Grant Holbrook, the Director of the MediCenter, which means he's pretty much Director of the Key itself, called me up to request that I gather my team and head to the site post haste."

Post haste? Was Elodie really going to spend the rest of her life with a guy who said *post haste*? She opened her mouth to comment but Rhett continued as if she wasn't on the other end of the call.

"At least, that's what he would have said if I had spoken to him directly. It was one of his assistants or someone, but I'm sure I'm the only person you know who gets calls like that."

Elodie squirmed in her chair. Her back itched in a place she couldn't quite reach.

Rhett grunted. "No one *ever* gets a call like that." He reiterated with a bit more gusto. "I mean, you haven't heard of anyone who has, have you?"

"Yeah. Yep." Elodie rubbed the heels of her hands against her eyes, glad he couldn't see her. "Wait. No, sorry. I haven't heard of that before." She picked at the dog-eared corner of her textbook. "Rhett, I'm actually really busy, so—"

"I'll get those Eos lunatics, El. I promise you I will."

"Oh," she bit her bottom lip. "You don't have to do it for me."

"Of course I do," he said, his voice softening a bit. "I want you to be safe. I want our family to be safe. In order for that to happen, Eos must be dealt with. There are things I know about Eos, Elodie."

She dropped her forehead into her hand. What was wrong with her? Rhett was great. He'd do anything to protect her. The Key had matched them, had chosen her for him, for a reason. And she had fallen in love with him. Or at least something very close to love. They might not currently be in romancia-landia, but Elodie would help them find their way there. "Hey, Rhett, want to move our date night up? Or maybe even add another night to the schedule?"

Or blow the schedule up completely and be utterly spontaneous?

On second thought, it was probably best to ease him in slowly.

Rhett paused for so long that Elodie would have thought

he'd ended the call if not for the *Connected* signal blinking at the bottom of her vision.

Finally, he sucked in a sharp breath. "Is something wrong?"

She shook her head automatically. "No. I just want to see you."

There was a rustling on his end of the call before he spoke again. "Activate your camera and we can see each other right now."

Elodie took a deep breath, plastered on a smile, and activated the videolink. The transparent gray box appeared, and Rhett came into view.

"See, that's nice, isn't it?" The shadows cast by Rhett's black helmet made his prominent brow even more menacing.

Elodie sat up a little straighter and made sure to keep her smile in place. "I meant I want to see you in a fun date setting. Not while we're both working."

His amber eyes deepened with a squint. "You said you didn't like it when I called you with my squad around, so I found a booth. I'm alone. My attention is on you. How is this different than date night?"

Elodie's smile slipped.

Rhett's brow creased. "I'm trying to do everything you want, El."

"Yeah, no, you're right." She remade her smile. "I did say that I wanted you to call me when you could focus on our conversation and not be pulled in all different directions. So, thank you for that."

The corner of his smooth lips tipped with a crooked grin and he nodded. "Anything for you."

Elodie's eyes dropped to the control panel. Why couldn't she feel the way she was supposed to?

"Is your shirt wet?"

Elodie snapped her attention back to him as she ran her hand across her chest. "I don't think—"

"Your shoulders." He stabbed the air with his index finger. "How did your shoulders get wet? It didn't rain this morning."

"Oh." She smoothed her fingers over her still damp waves. "I washed my hair. It was before this horrible nursing lesson and—"

Rhett's wide nose wrinkled in disgust. "Why?"

She hiked her shoulders. "Hygiene? But I should have waited until after my lesson. It was terrible. I'm studying—"

From the monitor for the patient rooms, a wet cough scraped over the hum and clank of the bots and the repetitive beeping of the control panel, and crashed into Elodie.

Rhett's eyes widened, his golden irises completely visible. "What was that?"

Elodie stilled, straining to hear past the beeps and the whirs and Rhett's thick tenor.

Another cough struck out. Elodie flinched. Her breath released in tiny hiccups as she flicked her gaze to the patient rooms.

Rhett leaned forward. "Is someone cou—"

It was Elodie's turn to interrupt. "I have to go." The vidlink box emptied to gray before clearing from her vision.

She could barely breathe as she slid to the edge of her seat and waited. Nothing. She blew out a puff of air and collapsed against the unforgiving plastic. Of course it was nothing. Some bot probably got tripped up on something and—

Cough.

Elodie's skin frosted, goosebumps springing to life across her arms. That was a cough. Undeniably so. Was a patient moving? Was a patient *awake?* She pulled up the live feed in each of the patient rooms.

Still.

Still.

Still.

Still.

Moving.

Elodie's heart beat against her chest. "Holly, show me information for the new patient."

"Sure thing." The detailed chart appeared on screen the moment Holly responded.

Elodie read it aloud. "Patient Ninety-Two, Aubrey Masters, age eight." She gripped the edge of her seat as she quickly looked over the first page of the chart. "It says that she's been in the MediCenter since she was four. What was the original reason for admission?"

"I'm sorry, Elodie, but you do not have clearance to access this information."

"That doesn't make any sense." Elodie chewed the inside of her cheek and drummed her fingers against the smooth edge of the control panel. "Holly, I'm Lead Nurse for this shift. I have clearance to access any information about any of my patients. Why was patient Ninety-Two admitted to the MediCenter four years ago?"

"You do not have clearance to access this information."

Cough.

Elodie read through the patient info, swiping each useless page off screen until there was nothing left except the live feed. "This has nothing in it. It's all useless, generic."

Cough.

"Holly, if you won't tell me why she was admitted, give me a detailed health report. Nothing I have means anything. The physician was in earlier today. She must have uploaded something."

"I have it right here." Again Holly brought up Patient Ninety-Two's records. This time, she'd highlighted the physician's note. "Quote: *Patient Ninety-Two is currently in healthy, stable condition. End quote.*"

Cough.

"Yes, I can see that." Elodie pointed to the holographic image and the column of green checkmarks lining the patient's health assessment. She boosted the levels for Patient Ninety-Two's monitor. "You're literally showing me that information right now. But healthy, stable patients don't end up in the Long-Term Care Unit."

Haggard coughs echoed from Aubrey's room, and Elodie winced at the labored breathing that followed. "They also don't cough like that, and I know you can hear her. You hear everything. That's not in line with healthy New American standards."

Cough.

"Patients like that belong in the Quarantine Unit, not my LTCU. There is something wrong with her, and I need access to more than these surface files so I know what to administer. Show me *something* I don't already have."

"Error." Holly honked.

"You can't simply say *error*. What kind of error?"

"Error." Holly repeated.

Another bout of wet coughs erupted from Aubrey's monitor. "Momma?" She wheezed weakly, the steady beeping of her heart-rate monitor spiking.

Elodie's stomach churned and her heart slammed within her chest. Her patients didn't speak or cough or wheeze. Except for the monotonous robotic beeping, her unit was silent. *Always* silent. That's what she expected. That's what she liked.

"Holly," Elodie whispered. "Increase sedation to Patient Ninety-Two by two units."

"Unable to comply. Sedation pumps are empty."

"Dammit, Gus," she hissed. "You said you'd refilled all of the patient pumps! Holly, flag Aubrey for immediate transfer. How long until a maintenance bot is able to refill her sedation meds?"

There was a pause while Holly calculated. "I've submitted the patient transfer request, and a maintenance bot will be available to refill the sedation pumps in forty-seven minutes."

"It hurts," Aubrey choked through tiny sobs.

Cold sweat sprang up on Elodie's brow. She was back in lesson fifteen. Back with the little girl screaming for her mother. Back with the virus as it painted bloody prints across the girl's small cheeks and turned her pores into gateways for its escape.

Elodie could barely swallow past the knot in her throat. "We don't have forty-seven minutes. This is an emergency. Override whatever else the bots are working on and send one to the basement to refill the tubes. *Now.*"

"I'm sorry, Elodie. There are eight work orders before yours, and it's not within my abilities to override them. The maintenance bot will arrive at the medi-pump lab in forty-six minutes."

"Mommy?" Aubrey's pained plea squeezed Elodie's heart.

"Dammit!" Elodie's knuckles whitened as she pressed her fists against the desk. "Holly, find the MediCenter's schematics and upload the map to my vidlink."

Aubrey's coughing continued, wet and painful.

Elodie's hands trembled as she hurried from the command station toward the elevator.

"Schematic uploaded to your vidlink. Do you need my assistance in locating an area?"

"The medi-pump lab." Elodie held her wrist up to the scanner, and gulped in air, trying to calm her frayed nerves and speeding pulse while the little girl's coughs echoed behind her. Her cuff flashed green and the elevator yawned open. The metal box threw distorted images of her through the open space. In some reflections she was tall, others short, wide, or thin, but in each one fear stretched her round eyes wide.

And Violet Jasmine Royale had let herself loose.

Elodie turned and charged toward Aubrey's room.

The eight-year-old's cries grew louder as Elodie reached the windowless door to Patient Ninety-Two's room. Elodie stopped just short of the Violet Shield. Her breath came in short, panicked puffs. Each exhale passed through the haze, scrubbed and sanitized by the purple light, and clean and new by the time it fogged the surface of the door.

A wet series of coughs erupted from inside the room.

Elodie took a step back. What was she doing? She was about to risk her life to . . . do what? She wasn't Vi. She wasn't a rebellious assassin. She was studying to be the Long-Term Care Unit's Chief Lead. She was going to get married. She was going to be normal and healthy and safe.

Elodie nearly collapsed back into the silence of the LTCU. "Holly, we, uh, we—" She paused and took a shaky step away from the door. She had to get a handle on her panting breath and speeding heart. She had to get control of herself. Calm determination, that's what would be expected from the Chief Lead.

That's what Elodie should expect from herself. "Help me find the medi-pump lab. I'll change out the sedation pumps myself."

"I've submitted a work order to have a bot fill them," Holly countered.

"It's going to take way too long. That little girl is awake." Elodie stabbed the air in front of the door. "She is crying and in pain and calling for her mom!" She wrung out her trembling hands and shoved them into her pockets.

Be calm. Be calm. Be calm.

"My patients are all sedated. I don't know what to do when they're awake. I'm not trained to know what to do." Elodie balled her still quaking hands. "Now ping the location of the pumps. I'll take over from there."

Holly remained silent, but a map of the MediCenter formed transparent over Elodie's vision, along with two blinking lights signaling her current location and the location of the pump room.

Elodie itched to leave the LTCU and retreat into the elevator. But she couldn't. Not yet. The part of her that had almost carried her into Patient Ninety-Two's room without a second thought was begging for resolve. "Can I see her?"

The door slid open and Elodie shuffled toward it, but not through. The Violet Shield danced in front of her as she peered into the room. Bands of white plastic held Aubrey's thin limbs against the gurney she'd called home for the past four years. Her hands and feet twitched with each weak attempt to pull free. A thin sheen of tears coated the girl's round, pale cheeks. Elodie flinched against the frightened whimpers and labored cries that tore at her ears—but she did not enter.

Heat pricked her eyes. "Close it." The door hissed shut as Elodie marched, calm and determined, to the elevator.

Tavi drummed her fingers on the desk, her pointed nails clicking against the glass. "Took you long enough."

Arms out wide, Aiden glanced down at his uniform. "Why, yes, Tavi, I do look rather charming in this bright orange trash bag. Thank you."

Tavi rolled her eyes so dramatically, she might have caught a glimpse of her brain. "Anyway, there are several things you need to learn, and, lucky for you, you have the best teacher in the entire unit."

The tight elastic ankle cuffs dug into Aiden's calves with each step toward Tavi. "Great." He wiggled a bit as he walked. The constrictive orange fabric kept riding up. Leave it to Aiden to get another uniform that felt entirely too small. "Where do I go to meet this master teacher?"

Tavi cleared her throat, the corners of her mouth twitching with a smile. "At the end of next week you'll have a test on what you've learned." She steepled her fingers, pressed them against her thin lips, and continued. "If you pass, it'll determine which

section within the End-of-Life Unit you're best suited for. If
you fail, well, you're kicked from the program and will have to
head back to career placement. For what, I assume, is the three
hundredth time. Now," her hands slapped against the desk as she
stood, "some newb instructors go easy on people who are sent
down here, but others—" She sucked in her lips to keep from
smiling. "Others have been here longer and know what's expected
and how to weed out *losers*." Her gaze narrowed at him as she
enunciated the word. "And the like. Others—" Another twitch
of her lips. "Like me." *Twitch.* "And, like I said, I am the best."
The smile broke free, curling up mischievously as she grabbed her
holopad and shoved it into her pocket.

Aiden felt his expression abandon his carefree facade and
twist into a grimace. Tavi hated him, thought he was a loser, and
now she was the person in charge of teaching him everything he
needed to know to be successful in the ELU. Aiden tugged at the
orange fabric zipped up to his throat. "This should be fun."

Tavi blew past him, her pink hair still unmoving despite her
speed. "What part of death, exactly, is supposed to be fun?" she
tossed over her shoulder as her short legs carried her down another
long corridor they had yet to explore.

Aiden slumped forward and dragged his hands down his cheeks.
Why? Why? Why? Why? Why?

But he knew *why.* He even knew *how.* Cath Scott was trying
to save him and prove a point at the same time—better this than
Rehab.

"It doesn't look good to constantly lag behind!" Tavi's shout
hammered his internal mutterings.

With the enthusiasm of a person who'd spend the rest of his
life surrounded by death, Aiden shuffled after his instructor.

-:-:-

Aiden followed Tavi around the bowels of the MediCenter for what seemed like a million hours. She pointed to a thousand different rooms, explained to him exactly why he didn't qualify for access to see what was behind each shiny, windowless metal door, before pursing her lips, shaking her head, and doing the same at the next door they came to.

Aiden checked the illuminated number on his cuff. 10:52.

He fought the urge to tilt his head back and groan. *No way have I only been down here for a little over an hour.* He dragged his fingertips along the wall as he trailed Tavi and her fluorescent pink and blond hair helmet. "What a time suck," he muttered.

"Hm?" Tavi's sneakers squeaked against the floor as she stopped abruptly in front of another metal door.

Aiden snapped his hands to his side and stared ahead attentively. "Nothing." He couldn't bare another lecture about his "lack of interest and what that said about his character."

Tavi shrugged and typed a few notes onto her holopad before looking up. "Now, *this door,* you're actually allowed to go through."

"I'm honored." Aiden attempted a bow but thought better of it as soon as Tavi's glare sliced through him.

She passed her cuff under the control panel and motioned for him to enter as the door slid open.

It was exciting, and, if Aiden was being honest, a little intimidating to finally gain entry into one of the mysterious rooms. He'd assumed they would walk around the entire basement and end up back at the intake desk before he was actually allowed to touch anything.

Inside, white light beamed from overhead even brighter than

the scorching light of the hallway. Aiden's eyes watered, and he squinted, barely getting a peek at Tavi's pink-tipped bob before it disappeared around the corner. Aiden rubbed his eyes and rushed to keep up with her.

"Cold Storage is through that Violet Shield barrier," Tavi said as, with a sweeping gesture, she motioned across the bright room to the floor-to-ceiling pane of violet. "Although you'll never have to mess with anything in there. Humans are *not* allowed past the barrier. Well, not *living* ones anyway." She let out a tinkling chuckle. "Now, we can start in here with the cadaver examiner bots, or go over to the lab and begin with sample testing and storage. Either way, we'll *begin* begin with containment protocols." Her fingers flicked across her holopad like the legs of a bug. "We have to cover all of it, so it's really up to you, which is something you won't hear me say very often."

Aiden's eyes finally adjusted, and his hand fell by his side. The hairs on the back of his neck rose as he fought to keep his gaze from locking onto the Cold Storage shield and the rows of death beyond.

"They're clear." He relinquished control, tossing his attention to the room past the violet wall. "All of it is clear. You can see . . . *everything.*"

Tavi's thin shoulders hiked. "They're just bodies."

Aiden's heart knocked against his ribs. "They're people."

She snorted. "They *were.*"

He didn't know what to say to that. In a way, she was right.

"Look, Aiden, you seem like a . . ." She paused, scrunching her face in that disapproving way of hers. "*Guy*—I don't know. My point is that we have amazing protocols down here. Part of the reason that Cold Storage is filled with clear cases is so that we can more easily monitor the bodies, and we aren't only relying on bots to relay all of the necessary information. Cerberus pretty much liquified people, and with clear cases that's super easy to spot." She crossed her arms over her chest and tapped her fingers against her thin lips. "Not that it would actually get that far. I mean, the bots take samples, spray down the bodies and the cases and the walls and the floors, plus the Violet Shield and the—"

Aiden shook his head. "I don't need an explanation." Tavi opened her mouth to object, and Aiden added, "At least, not yet. I just—" His shoes were the same sharp white as the floor and the ceiling and the walls and the lights. "I need a minute."

Tavi balled her hands into fists. Her scrubs hung loose on her petite frame. If he'd looked like he was wearing his little brother's uniform earlier, she looked like she was wearing her mother's. "Another break? Yeah, sure, fine, whatever." Exasperated, she threw her hands into the air. "Take another one. Take all of the breaks you want. I'm not the one who has to pass the Level One Orientation Test next week. You are." Scrunch. "And don't get all queasy and barf on my floor."

Aiden wasn't in danger of throwing up. He wasn't in danger at all. With everything the Key had done to keep Westfall safe, any danger he could end up in he'd have to search out himself.

His stomach hollowed as he sped toward the door that would free him into the hall and lead him back to the expansive intake room. He couldn't help but take another look back at the storage boxes and the pairs of feet pressed against the end of the clear rectangle. All different sizes. All different colors. All waiting for dissection. All waiting to burn.

"And we'll meet back in the lab." Tavi's voice was tinny as his heartbeat slammed against his eardrums. "You're *so* not ready for cadavers."

XII

Elodie winced against the harsh white light that flooded the elevator as it yawned open and revealed her first glimpse of the MediCenter's eerily quiet basement. Trepidation quaked within her limbs as she shuffled down the brightly illuminated hallway, following the path Holly had highlighted.

Vi had almost gotten Elodie in trouble. Possibly horrible, life-ending trouble. Maybe that's why the Key Corp had disposed of so many works of fiction, directing current authors to write tales that actually mattered and inspired today's citizens, instead of books that planted false and dangerous ideas within their readers. And the corporation was right to do so. Elodie hadn't even finished Vi's series of books, and she had already come entirely too close to making a choice she would regret. The rules were there for a reason.

The rules are there for a reason.

The blinking light on Elodie's vidlink ate up more of the highlighted path as she turned down another barren, light-soaked hallway.

But Violet Royale hadn't given her the idea to put her life in danger. Elodie was quite capable of coming up with her own original thoughts and making her own decisions. What had reading about Vi made Elodie do, anyway? Nothing! It had simply given her a little more . . . *confidence?* No, confidence wasn't exactly the right word. *Death by Violet* had given her—

Elodie jerked to a stop as a set of white shoes turned the corner and almost smacked into her own. Her gaze traveled up, up, up to mossy green eyes and a curly black mohawk.

"You should watch where you're going." The guy grunted and unzipped the top half of his orange suit, tying the arms around the waist of his fitted blue scrub top. "You could've run right into me."

"Sorry. I was thinking about—" She bit back the words before she accidentally spilled her darkest secret. "Stuff. Thinking about stuff and not paying attention."

"You don't need to apologize. I'm the one who was just an ass. I wasn't paying attention either." He rubbed his hand across his dark brow. "Got a lot of stuff to think about too."

Elodie brushed a damp curl from her shoulder as the familiar scent of earth and pine swirled around her. "Well, have a good one." She double checked her map, and, with a quick and awkward wave, resumed her trek to the medi-pump station.

"You didn't happen to run into a door this morning, did you?"

Elodie stiffened as his words pricked her back. She knew she'd recognized his voice and that evergreen scent. Unfortunately, she couldn't run away this time. There was nothing in this hallway except for the doors he'd just emerged from, and she didn't want to go anywhere near room forty-four and its biohazard symbol. Especially if it spit out frazzled employees half-dressed in biohazard gear.

She turned slowly, hoping that in the time it took her to face him, she would somehow disappear into the bright lights of the hallway. "It wasn't my finest moment."

His grin lit his entire face. "But it was pretty funny."

Her cheeks heated. "For you!"

"You're right." He cocked his head, a crease forming across his smooth brow. "Your hair is wet." He dragged his fingers along the shaved side of his mohawk. "*Still* wet is more accurate. I noticed it, you know, before." His orange suit crinkled as he crossed his ankles and leaned against the wall. "You took a shower. A real one."

Elodie's chin tilted skyward as she folded her arms across her chest. "I did."

And since she couldn't go anywhere or do anything without someone commenting, she was never going to do it again.

He picked at one of the orange sleeves tied around his waist. "I thought I was the only one who took water showers."

"Oh." She tucked another half-dry strand behind her ear. "It's a thing I do sometimes." She stood a little taller, pleased with how nonchalant she seemed.

He practically leapt away from the wall. "Have you ever taken a bath?" he blurted.

Her shoulders relaxed. "Every day. Light baths are practically mandatory."

"No." He stepped closer, tightening the suit arms hugging his lean middle. "I mean in *water*."

"Of course not." Her laughter echoed off the sterile walls. "I don't want to sit in dirty person soup."

He nodded as if it was his first time considering the fact, which would have made sense. It was the first time for Elodie.

The blinking light flashed in the corner of her vision. "Sorry, but I'm in a bit of a hurry." She pointed down the hall before resuming her quest.

His sneakers squeaked as he shuffled after her. "Where are we headed?"

She glanced up at him. "You're coming with me."

The ends of empty sleeves flopped against his legs with each step. "Unless I'm being uninvited."

Elodie couldn't help but grin. "Were you ever *in*vited?"

He tilted his head as he cracked his knuckles. "Technically, no, but you never know when you might need a guy with a biocontainment suit."

Elodie eyed the shiny orange suit, its arms flapping limply at his waist. "What do you do down here that you need one of those?"

Again, he tightened the arms around his waist. "ELU stuff."

Reflexively, Elodie widened the distance between them. She'd never met anyone who worked in the End-of-Life Unit. Cerberus was most contagious upon death, when people would collapse, their bodies bursting like raindrops against the pavement. Even though she worked in the MediCenter, she never worked with the deceased. No one did. The second someone was declared, the ELU was called, and everyone else went back to work on people they could actually help. Now that she thought about it, Elodie didn't even know what a real dead person looked like. Probably like her patients, but deader.

"Gross." Her brow pinched. "The *morgue?*"

He clapped his hands. "That's exactly what I said."

No wonder he had taken so many water showers. She'd had one VR experience and wished she could shower again. Each day he probably had dozens of real life situations that clung to him like a second skin.

Elodie glanced at the map, transparent across her vision. "I'm going to the medi-pump lab," she said, changing topics. "Hey, you're from down here. You wouldn't happen to know how to change out the tubes, would you? Or is that not part of your job description?"

His dark skin glowed deep brown under the lights. "Not that I know of, but it is my first day. I'm also not *from down here*, like some mole person living in those sealed up tunnels under the city." He tapped his chin. "Shanghai Tunnels! Knew I hadn't forgotten the name."

Elodie's lips quirked. "Shanghai Tunnel mole person?"

"Yeah like if some guy got bitten by a radioactive mole and became the world's first tunneling, night-vision mole man. Or, at least that's how I assume he would have become a mole man." He shrugged. "What do you need in the pump lab?"

"Long-Term Care Unit nursing business." She returned his shrug with one of her own. "It's kind of a long story." The map flashed as she closed in on her destination, and Elodie cleared the screen from her field of vision. "But I'm here now, so . . ." She stretched the word as he followed her through the open door and into the narrow room, busy with bots.

He held up his hands as he backed through the Violet Shield that coated every entryway within the MediCenter. "Say no more. I get when I'm not wanted." He glanced at his cuff. "I've gotta go anyway. But I'm always up for a good story, and I'll be down here for, you know, ever." He tossed her a sparkling smile before disappearing around the corner.

Elodie nearly tripped over the bot loading color-coded tubes into their corresponding receptacles as she craned her neck to watch him leave. "That was . . . *strange*." She glanced at the bot as if it cared about or was even aware of the encounter she'd just had.

"Water baths and mole people. Super weird." Her cheeks heated as a grin lifted her lips.

Elodie dug through the crate of glass tubes the bot had attached to its front until she located the bright yellow cylinder labeled Propofol. She stared at the large grid of boxy receptacles and flashing lights until she located the row of tubes for the eleventh floor and the flashing yellow rectangle. She rolled the glass cylinder of medicine between her hands before reaching up and exchanging the empty tube for the full one. A few mechanical clicks and the yellow light ceased flashing.

Elodie's heartbeat ticked up a notch as she made her way back to the elevator. Yes, she was nervous about Patient Ninety-Two's state when she got back to her unit, but tremors of excited anticipation ran beneath the anxiety.

Maybe she would see the ELU employee and his curly, dark mohawk again. Whoever he was.

The elevator opened and Elodie requested her floor. She clenched her fists by her sides in an attempt to regain control of her nerves as the metal box carried her back to the unknowns of her own unit and Patient Ninety-two. What would she do if Aubrey was still awake, crying, pleading for her mother?

The doors opened and Elodie stepped into the LTCU.

Aubrey's door was open, her room empty, and the unit ablaze with violet.

XIII

Lieutenant Commander Sparkman raced down the fifteenth-floor corridor. Her knuckles drained of color as she gripped the gurney's metal sides and braced herself. Her decades of military training hadn't prepared her for this, *couldn't have* prepared her for this. They had nearly arrived at the lab. Its gleaming metal doors were only two turns ahead. Two hundred paces to the first turn, seventy to the second, and a final one hundred and fifty to the lab. Four hundred and twenty paces until they reached the place where all of this had begun. It was the only place Sparkman could hope to fix what they had done—what the *Doctor* had done.

The gurney jerked to the right and then left. Sparkman's strawberry blond braid slapped her cheek and her fingers cramped as she took the first turn and the gurney careened into the wall.

Aubrey Masters was waking up. Again.

Sparkman grunted as she regained control and guided the gurney away from the wall and the small dent and gray streak that would, no doubt, be fixed by the end of the day. Instinctively, Sparkman glanced over her shoulder. No one would come running. The Doctor would make sure of that.

Sparkman's nostrils flared as she blew out a breath. Only three hundred paces.

She stared down at the little girl she'd been tasked to kidnap from the Long Term Care Unit. *He* had told her that it wasn't kidnapping. It was taking back what was rightfully his.

Aubrey's delicate features twisted and she let out a pained whine as she pulled against the plastic binding her wrists and ankles. Sparkman's heart surged up her throat. She had seen a lot in her years as a Key Corp military officer. Humans, the depth and breadth of their capacity for cruelty, no longer amazed her. But Patient Ninety-Two was different. Aubrey was innocent. An eight-year-old girl. A child. How could the Doctor do this?

Aubrey's whine grew piercing, a clarion call that rattled Sparkman's bones. The Lieutenant Commander squeezed the metal bars until her hands ached and took inventory of the container of prefilled syringes she'd brought down with her. She'd started with five. There was only one left.

Aubrey's high-pitched squeal ended as suddenly as it had begun. Then, nothing. No jerking movements so powerful they sent the gurney careening and Sparkman struggling to keep up. Instead, Aubrey Masters went silent, motionless. Her expression placid and serene.

Sparkman's braid slid down her shoulder as she, too, relaxed. She flipped it back behind her and maneuvered the gurney around the second corner. The lab was at the end of the hall. The last door on the right. One hundred and fifty paces ahead.

Aubrey's chest lifted and her stomach puffed with air. Her

small feet twitched and her tiny hands gripped the bedding as she sucked in ragged breath after ragged breath.

Adrenaline ripped through Sparkman's veins and she took off. The one hundred and fifty paces flew beneath her and the gurney in a blur of white tile. She halted just before the entrance to the lab and squeezed her boxy frame between the gurney and the door. As she slid her cuff under the scanner and waited for the door to slide open, the hairs on the back of her neck bristled. Sheets rustled behind Sparkman, and Aubrey's breathing changed. It now slipped out of her as smooth and easy as the ocean swept against the shore.

Sparkman pressed her fists together, cracking each of her knuckles, as she turned. Aubrey's plastic handcuffs hung limply from the bed as she sat at the head of the gurney, knees pulled to her chest and secured by thin arms. The neck of her hospital gown sagged down around her bare shoulders and she shivered as she buried her chin against her legs.

Sparkman's jaw slacked and her stomach clenched as Aubrey blinked up at her. A band of violet ringed the girl's pupils.

"Tell the Doctor," Patient Ninety-Two lifted her chin so as not to muffle her words. "Tell the Doctor they're coming."

The door hissed open behind Sparkman as Aubrey Masters collapsed against the gurney.

XIV

Preston Darby had gotten to Blair. Strike that. *Cath* had gotten to Blair. Gotten under Blair's skin when she said that Council Leader Darby could come after Denny.

Blair tapped the pointed toe of her pump against the corner of her desk and bit down on her fingernail. A jagged chunk tore free and she clenched it between her teeth.

Cath had been getting under Blair's skin for more than a decade. Blair's adoptive mother would toss out a small idea that stuck to Blair and festered and festered until she could feel it moving and breathing within her.

He can make your life more difficult. And Denny's.

Those two small sentences now had lives of their own.

Blair bit off another chunk of her nail, wincing when she drew blood. She forced her hands into her lap and put pressure on her pulsing nailbed.

"Holly." She cleared her throat and sat up a little straighter. The hologram wasn't a real person, but Blair didn't trust that a conversation with Holly would always only be between the two of them.

"Yes, Ms. Scott?" Holly materialized in front of Blair's onyx desk, her hair and clothes and smile all perfect where she stood on the plush throw rug.

A twinge of jealousy clawed at Blair's chest. Envying a computer's flawless, human-made image was illogical—Blair knew that— but envy reared its green head nonetheless. "Call my brother. When he answers, put the call through to my office comm system."

"Right away, Ms. Scott." Holly's eyelids fluttered as she contacted Denny.

It wasn't that Blair was opposed to using her own personal comlink to reach her brother. Since the update, the tech was more user friendly than it had ever been. She just didn't particularly like people talking in her head. She had enough to plot and sort through without the extra chatter.

Blair pressed her palms against the cold onyx slab and stood. Her shadow spilled onto the black surface of the desk, and the vase sitting on the edge, and pooled onto the rug and through Holly's feet. *Through* them. Because, no matter how much Blair's eyes tried to fool her, Holly's being was nothing but ones and zeros. Her "mind," however, all the secrets Holly held, that's what Blair should truly envy.

Holly's eyelids opened slowly, evenly. "Unfortunately, I'm unable to contact your brother. I've attempted to reach him three times and received an error message each time."

Blair's heart skipped and she lowered herself onto the edge of her chair. She stammered and pressed her hand against her chest. "What could cause this type of error message?" She released calm and steady breaths. Preston Darby couldn't act without cause. Blair's brother might not be as driven as she was, but he was no trouble-maker. He was her sweet little Denny. Everyone who met him loved him. And if they didn't, Blair Scott would burn them to the ground.

"The error is most likely a result of an incomplete chip update." The ends of Holly's perfectly styled hair brushed her chin as she spoke. "This malfunction has occurred in"—another rapid blink—"approximately four percent of Westfall's citizens. Would you like me to submit a work order to the IT department on your brother's behalf?"

Blair's free hand slid limply into her lap, leaving the sweaty ghost of a handprint on the desk. She'd gotten herself worked up for no reason at all. Denny was at his job, safe and secure. He couldn't be reached because technology, no matter how awe-inspiring, always possessed a flaw.

Blair leaned back in her chair and narrowed her gaze on Holly. "Leave me," she said with a flick of her wrist.

Before she'd finished the gesture, Holly was gone.

"Show off," she muttered as she turned her attention back to more important things. A gray box formed to one side of her vision before her messaging inbox appeared.

Maxine—

She thought, and the characters appeared instantaneously.

My office, immediately. We're going to make my brother a Key Corp soldier.

Blair paused and glanced down at her jagged nails before sending the message.

Oh, and get me everything you can on Preston Darby.

XV

The holoscreen activated, the floating rectangle blinking from sleeping gray to paper white as Dr. Normandy unlocked Patient Ninety-Two's chart. He stepped back a moment to take it all in.

What to look at first?

His weathered hands fell to the printed photos he'd lined up along the edge of the steel exam table under the translucent screen. His fingers blindly traced the edge of one of the photos. He liked the thinness of the printed pages, almost not there at all. It reminded him of his job—his world. Searching cells and sequences for the thinnest chance. A chance so small that anyone else would miss it. But not Normandy. Given enough time, he could find a single hair floating in a river the size of the Columbia. And he had been given all the time in the world.

Normandy opened Ninety-Two's most recent lab report before extending his arm to the holoscreen, pinching the digital paperwork that noted the previous day's test results, and plopping them into the empty space next to it. It had only been three weeks, and already a universe of changes bloomed to life inside of Ninety-Two. Although, he shouldn't be surprised. Didn't Christians believe their god created the cosmos in merely six days? Normandy was no god, at least not by those standards, but he was in the process of creating salvation. A completely germ-free, worry-free existence for all.

Squinting, he pressed his round glasses farther up the bridge of his thin nose.

Lieutenant Commander Sparkman let out a hiss of frustration as the door to Ninety-Two's room closed behind her and as she waited for the Violet Shield to complete its pass. "I thought you said the patient was stable."

"She is." Normandy flicked his bony fingers over the holoscreen and brought up the feed from Ninety-Two's room. "See for yourself."

The girl's slim, unconscious frame lay like a toothpick in the middle of the gurney. Or perhaps now Ninety-Two was no longer a *girl*. He would further dissect the tests Sparkman had conducted, but Normandy knew better than anyone that gender was more complex than genitalia.

Ninety-Two twitched, the sweat-soaked sheets rumpled like waves beneath her. The rise and fall of her chest had finally steadied along with the rhythmic beep of the pulse monitor. It had taken six hours and seventeen different combinations of tranquilizers, but Normandy had eventually figured it out. He eventually figured everything out.

"Then what the hell was all of that?" Sparkman's lab coat billowed around her waist as she stomped to Normandy's side. "We were supposed to be able to stick her up in the Long-Term Care Unit for the next three years at least! You said nothing would manifest until puberty." She gripped the edge of the table, her squared jaw flexing up to her gold-flecked temples. "That process doesn't start in eight-year-olds! And did you see her eyes? Purple, Doctor. They were *purple!*" The clean white lights overhead seemed to flicker in fear with each of Sparkman's shouts.

Fear.

It was one of the reasons Normandy had chosen the young Key Corp Lieutenant Commander. Sparkman could accomplish anything regardless of whether or not she possessed proper paperwork. And since Normandy had spent the last two decades on a task that those in charge preferred to leave untraceable, there often were no forms at all. That's when Sparkman's . . . *talents* came into play. She was a soldier, an enforcer, and no matter how many lab coats she donned, she would be nothing more.

Normandy removed his glasses, wiped them with the corner of his pristine lab coat, and slipped them back on. "We're dealing with something new, undiscovered, undocumented. I can tell you what I have calculated, but what we hope to achieve has never been attempted before much less seen to fruition, and our previous ninety-one patients were, as you know, failures. I shall explore the missteps in my calculations. You be grateful that Ninety-Two is still alive. Still human."

"Wait one second." Sparkman waggled her finger ferociously. "You're not holding me responsible for all of the other times you've fucked this up." Her long braid whipped the air as she shook her head. "I wasn't even here for most of them."

Normandy frowned at the smudged fingerprints Sparkman left behind on the photos. "You are here now. You are a witness and a participant in all of this."

When Normandy created his own version of Sparkman, a *better* version of Sparkman, he would remove this penchant for outbursts.

Normandy didn't value Sparkman's intelligence. He valued her discretion and her effectiveness in getting him what he needed.

His gaze fell to Sparkman's battle-worn hands as they again touched the fingerprint-clouded photographs. He would also minimize the oil output of Sparkman's skin by twenty percent.

A trench carved itself into the middle of Sparkman's otherwise smooth forehead. "But it's different now. What the hell are we dealing with?" Her golden-red brows arched. "All I know is that the patient burned through propofol so quickly that the entire tube was drained within an hour. Ninety-Two metabolized meds that were supposed to last an entire day in a *fucking hour.*"

Normandy resumed squinting at the screen. "There's no reason to be crude. I will review her tests. The answer is in there."

"Look, old man, I don't think you understand. If you did, you'd be as alarmed as I am."

Normandy took a breath and peered at Sparkman over the rim of his glasses. "What was to happen in three years took only three weeks. Thus far, Ninety-Two has been a triumph."

Sparkman's eyes hardened, and she brushed her hand across her smooth, freckled cheek, but said nothing.

"If you're no longer comfortable with what we're accomplishing, I can have you sent to Rehabilitation." The corner of Normandy's lips twitched with a grin. Before Ninety-Two, Rehabilitation had been his best creation.

"Fuck you," Sparkman spat.

Normandy pressed his hand against his stomach. "Your cursing, Lieutenant Commander. Your cursing. I cannot abide the foulness of your tongue. Perhaps that is something they can address during your Rehabilitation stay."

Silence burned through the lab.

Sparkman's broad shoulders slumped. "Everything's fine," she conceded. "The changes," she waved at the displayed reports, "they happened a lot faster than I was expecting, or even prepared for, but," she cleared her throat, "it's fine."

The threat of Rehabilitation guaranteed that Sparkman would never truly step out of bounds. That is, after all, why the Key had commissioned the program.

"I do have one question, though." Sparkman tugged on the stiff collar of her costume lab coat.

Normandy resumed tracing the edge of one of the photos. "You will not learn if you never ask."

Sparkman nodded toward the holoscreen and Ninety-Two's resting frame. "If she's transformed this much in so little time, what will she be three weeks from now?"

Normandy considered this as he again removed his glasses, folding them gently before hooking them onto the breast pocket of his coat. "More, Lieutenant Commander. Patient Ninety-Two will be more." The shrill, prolonged beep of Ninety-Two's pulse monitor grabbed Normandy's attention.

"Dammit, Normandy, she's flatlining!" Sparkman charged toward the door separating them from Ninety-Two—*protecting them* from Ninety-Two.

"Sparkman!" The soldier halted just short of the doorway as Normandy lifted his glasses from his pocket. "Wait."

Sparkman's fists clenched and unclenched by her sides. "She's dying!"

With one fluid motion, Normandy slid his finger down the volume control toggle, silencing the piercing electronic screech before motioning to the patient's brain wave monitor. The lines were flat. "She's braindead. Of absolutely no use to us."

"Let me get the bot." Sparkman moved her wrist toward the cuff scanner. "We can try to save her."

"The corporation does not need a strain that terminates its host." Normandy's fingers curled tightly around his glasses. The frames bit into the soft flesh of his palms. "She is not worth saving."

"But—"

"Enough!" Normandy snarled. Spittle sprang from his lips. "Leave me to clean up this mess."

Sparkman leaned forward almost imperceptibly before she dropped her hand from the cuff scanner, and her shoulders again slumped as she took a step back.

"I was close, Sparkman. This close." Normandy held up two fingers, separated only enough for a breath to pass through. "Perhaps if the patient is younger next time." He rubbed the earpieces of his glasses. "Ninety-Two was four when we started and lasted longer than any before her. Yes," he mused. "Age . . ." With the corner of his coat he rubbed small circles across his lenses. "We shall search for another suitable child. A male this time, perhaps."

Sparkman pursed her lips and nodded sharply. "You're the boss."

Normandy slid his glasses up his nose, glanced at Ninety-Two's ghostly pale frame, and smiled.

XVI

Aiden might end up being happy in the lab. Well, not *happy* necessarily, but content. No. No, not content either. Maybe *fine* was
the right word. He blew out a puff of air and weighed the innoc-
uous adjective. Yes, he could end up being very *fine* with a career
in one of the many End-of-Life Unit labs, or anywhere else in the
ELU that kept him out of Cold Storage or the incineration unit.
Tavi hadn't taken him there yet, but they'd walked by and Aiden
could imagine what fresh hell waited behind the shiny steel doors.

The lab, or at least the section of it in which he and Tavi
currently worked, was free of dead people, or anything else he
might need his orange garbage bag of a biocontainment suit to
protect him from. Tavi still hadn't allowed him to take it off.
Aiden was sure it was some sort of punishment for him acting
like, well, himself.

Even though the lab was better than where he'd been before,
there was no escaping the brilliant white light, so searing that it
could disinfect every surface of the ELU without the help of the

Violet Shield. Also, the glass walls made it a bit terrariumesque. On the bright side (pun intended), Aiden didn't have to do much as far as work was concerned. But greater than that was the fact that he could see straight into the no-nonsense science section of the laboratory, and, if he positioned himself just right, he could catch images displayed on the floor-to-ceiling holoscreen. People way smarter than he was took turns pointing at the images, looking in their fancy microscopes, and shuffling about in their orange biosuits like shriveled squash. It was wishful thinking, but maybe Tavi would decide that he didn't need to learn anything about any of the other sections of the ELU and could stay here indefinitely.

He adjusted the tight ring of rubber around his gloved wrist, snapping it for added effect before scooping up another tray of petri dishes and spilling them onto the waist-high metal table.

Aiden grabbed a few dishes and began stacking them on the table the way Tavi had instructed. His foot cramped from hours of standing in the same position. Maybe he could come up with another excuse to take a break. As long as he was throwing out possibilities, maybe he'd even see that wet-haired nurse out in the hall again.

Aiden leaned his hips against the table.

Now *that* was wishful thinking.

"Oh, Gods," Tavi said, "not like *that*. Like *this*." Propped up on a metal stool, she stacked her set of Petri dishes from biggest to smallest and pushed them to the edge of the spotless steel table. A bot motored up, scooped up the dishes, and puttered through the doorway's Violet Shield. "They won't come get them if the sensor doesn't relay that they're stacked correctly," she said.

Aiden understood that. He also understood how to stack round items from largest to smallest. But currently, he was having a hard time focusing on anything except the Long-Term Care

Unit nurse who'd been searching for the medi-pump lab, her round lips, and the way she pinned her gaze to the floor as if afraid that if she ignored its existence for too long, she would take flight and lose it forever.

And they'd had something in common. Showers. A strange thing to have in common, sure, but a commonality nonetheless. And there were shadows there, secrets. Aiden had gotten good at spotting secrets, and hers flickered in the depths of her black eyes. Intrigue swirled around him, clawing ribbons of curiosity down his back.

But had he really asked her if she took water baths? Shit. That was creepy. He was lucky she hadn't run away shouting for security. Maybe the weirdness of the ELU was already starting to rub off on him.

"And you don't need to worry about what's going to go in these dishes," Tavi continued, although Aiden had no recollection of how the conversation had started. "Your only job is to get them stacked so the bots can deliver them to departments around the ELU."

Aiden busied himself with more dishes. "Will I ever need to?"

Tavi blinked up at him, her lips stretched into a frown. "Need to what?"

He slid a completed stack to the pickup area on his side of the table. "Worry about what's going to go in these dishes."

She shook her head. Her pink-tipped hair helmet practically glowed neon under the lights. "I don't even know half the time."

"Then what's the point?" The quitter inside of him prodded, wanting to be set free. "And why isn't a bot doing this?"

"A bot normally does do this, but I'm *trying* to be a good instructor and have you *do* instead of *see*. It's better for learning and other brain development things." Tavi hiked her pointed shoulders. "At least that's what the handbook says." She balled her hands on her hips and glanced at the petri dishes Aiden had just begun stacking. "I don't know why I'm trying so hard. You clearly don't care." She cocked her head. "Or maybe you're just way dumber than I thought."

Aiden opened his mouth to object, but thought better of it. He didn't *want* Tavi to think of him as the guy who couldn't stack a bunch of glass dishes by descending size, but, at this point, there was no use in trying to change her opinion. It had been set the second he'd walked in late to the End-of-Life Unit.

"This seemed like it was the easiest thing to start with, especially with how you reacted to Cold Storage, but—" Tavi gestured toward the tubs of sanitized petri dishes waiting to be sorted. "Something tells me it's going to take you all frickin' day to get through the rest of those."

"Cold Storage is filled with dead bodies. And they all have those feet." With a shiver, Aiden held up his hands, miming two stiff, lifeless feet. "Anyone who walks in there and isn't, at the very least, grossed out, has some serious problems."

Tavi slid off her stool and glared up at him. "On my first shift, I worked in Cold Storage. *The entire day.* I didn't puke or run away crying or stare off like some stroke victim. My file says that *I* was a *perfect* trainee."

Aiden propped his elbow against the table. "Did you put in my file that *I* did those things?"

Tavi threw her hands in the air and let out an exasperated groan. "You are the absolute worst, you know that?" She held up a petite finger before he had a chance to speak. "I'm putting my instructor hat back on now." She closed her eyes and inhaled deeply. With the exhale, the vein that ran down the middle of her forehead disappeared, and a pleasant grin creased her cheeks.

The cheery pixie version of Tavi was more horrifying than the disappointed, annoyed-sister version he was growing accustomed to.

"How about we back off the hands-on lessons for a little bit? You can watch the containment protocol video while I figure out how to dumb down the rest of your assignments."

Ah, yes. There was the Tavi he knew. And at least now he'd set the bar so low, simply walking into work on time would earn him points.

Aiden followed Tavi out of the lab and into a room filled with rows of evenly spaced desks and the same uncomfortable chairs found in Cath Scott's office. Nearly everything in the MediCenter looked identical. The sameness of it all would have made it easy to get lost if he hadn't worked on every floor just long enough to learn their nuances.

Tavi pointed to the small student desk nearest to the instructor's broad desk, which sat at an angle at the front of the room. "Sit."

Aiden dropped into the chair. It was just as uncomfortable as he remembered. "You don't have to watch over me, you know."

Tavi squinted. "Sure I do."

She set down her holopad and typed for a few moments before turning her attention back to Aiden. She'd lost her bright and cheery instructor smile before they'd even left the lab. "I was going to ask if you wanted to take any notes, but I feel like it would be a waste of a good holopad."

Aiden cocked his head. "Actually, I prefer the age-old method of pen to paper."

She scrunched her face.

"What can I say, O Captain, My Captain? You've inspired me to be a better student." Aiden said with a dramatic flourish of his hand.

Another scrunch. "You are so frickin' weird." She scooped up her holopad and, eyes narrowed, watched him as she headed for the door. "You're up to something. I know you are." She paused in the open doorway. "Try not to do anything too terrible before I get back."

Aiden waited until the door to the classroom closed. The heavy doors leading back toward the reception area clanged shut before he kicked his feet up onto the small desk in front of him. "Hey, Holly?"

Haunting Holly flashed to life next to him, each pixel stacking on top of the one before until they'd formed a complete person. "Hello, Aiden. Octavia has bookmarked several lessons for you. Would you like to begin?"

"Not until the chief returns." He folded his hands behind his head and leaned back in his chair. "But I do need your help."

The hologram's smile was all teeth. "Sure thing."

"Can you bring up employee profiles for the Long-Term Care Unit nurses?"

He had probably scared her off, but if there was one thing Aiden had learned in all of his years of career hopping, it was that the only way to know whether or not you liked something was to try it. And hopefully the LTCU nurse was into trying new things.

XVII

The Pearl seemed to glide weightless down the street as Elodie stood outside the MediCenter. She glanced at her bracelet. Five minutes were left until its scheduled arrival time window, but it was only a block away. Astrid had been right about its punctuality.

It wasn't difficult to see how the automated vehicle got its name. Its round, opalescent shell alternated between gleaming white and muted swirls of rainbow in the patchy sunlight. Each Pearl added a level of whimsy to Westfall's otherwise serious palate of muted grays and aged whites. The only spots marring the car's pristine coating were two half-moon shaped windows on either side as if the zippy vehicle had freed itself from a tight pinch and had its glimmering sides sheared off.

The Pearl silently weaved around the clunky MAX train and paused for pedestrians with the intuitiveness of a human, but with the endless, split-second calculations of a computer.

Elodie leaned forward, then abruptly stopped herself. Astrid's text had said to meet the Pearl outside, but not to approach the

curb or the Pearl until it had made a complete stop and the door
had opened. It was part of the testing for the newer, smarter prototype, and Astrid, who hated using exclamation points because
they didn't feel "emotionally specific" enough, had used five.

The Pearl smoothly transitioned to the right lane, slowing as
soon as it reached the corner of Elodie's block. It eerily crept along
the curb. Its tinted window seemed to peer at the citizens entering and exiting the restaurant on the corner before it sped forward
and came to a halt directly in front of Elodie. It had stopped so
precisely that she only had to take a few steps to meet it at the curb.

A chime sounded from the Pearl, and Elodie's bracelet flashed
brilliant white as the back door swept open. She slapped the
passenger side window. Giggles burst from her lips as she waited.
She never was good at scaring anyone. Anyone other than herself,
that is. The window silently slid down. She'd expected to see
Astrid in the "driver" seat. Instead the front seats were empty.
Elodie bent over and poked her head inside the car.

Astrid's long legs and signature navy and green checkered
shoes were the first things Elodie saw.

"What's cookin', good lookin'?" Astrid leaned forward from
the backseat and winked. Her shimmery green eyeliner beauti-
fully accentuated the delicate upturn of her eyes. She clicked her
tongue and motioned for Elodie to join her inside.

"The Pearl was so accurate, I figured you'd be driving." Elodie
shrugged off her backpack and slid into the Pearl's plush interior.

Astrid's sleek ponytail brushed the headrest as she shook
her head. "Nope. Observing slash meeting my best friend who I
hardly ever see in the real. Work and play combined." She inter-
locked her fingers. "Throw a little bit of work in there, and every
hour becomes billable."

"I wish I could get paid for socializing." Elodie settled in to the seat and the door closed automatically.

"*You? Socialize?*" Astrid clutched her chest in mock horror.

Elodie shook her head and ignored the comment. "Well, I'm glad you did. A lot happened at work, and it's better to talk in person."

Astrid stretched her legs out in the open interior, toeing the seat across from her before crossing her long legs at her ankles and resting them on the fleecy carpet. "Real life meetups are highly overrated, and always seem to interrupt things."

"Gah. Thanks, Astrid. I'm so glad you could make some time for li'l ol' me." Elodie batted her eyelashes sardonically.

"Shut up. None of that applies to you. Just, you know, to . . ." Astrid tapped her black polished fingertips on the tinted window at the pedestrians briskly walking along the sidewalk. "Everybody else."

"You're only saying that because you get reclusey in that apartment all by yourself," Elodie commented with a little more brusqueness than she'd meant.

"Thea is crashing with me for a bit, so I'm no longer wild and free. You remember my sister?" Astrid didn't wait for a response. "Did I detect a hint of jealousy in there somewhere, Miss Elodie Grace?" She combed her fingers through her hair and settled back against the seat. "Gwen's on one again, isn't she?" She brushed the end of her ponytail against her cheek. "What am I saying? It's always something with *Gwendolyn Benavidez.*" Astrid stuck out her chest and lifted her chin in the same ostentatious way Elodie's mother did anytime she introduced herself to anyone.

Elodie let her hair down and massaged the tender spot where the rubber band had pulled at her scalp. She couldn't tell if the tight tie or the mention of her mother had made her temples start to throb with the first dull pains of a headache. "Don't get me started."

"Couldn't if I wanted to. A ride out to Zone Six wouldn't give us enough time." The apples of Astrid's highlighted cheeks lifted with a smile. "And this bad boy isn't charged up with enough juice for a trip like that."

Elodie blew out a long, lip-rattling sigh. "It's nothing new anyway. Same neurosis, different day."

And this day had truly been different from the rest.

Elodie pressed her hands against her thighs. "I met someone. He's really . . ." She bit her lower lip, pausing as she searched for a word that encompassed the mohawked stranger. "*Interesting.*"

Elodie flicked the zipper on her backpack as she replayed her encounter with tall, dark, and handsome while Astrid listened, her dark eyes widening with each detail.

Astrid stopped twirling the ends of her hair and sucked in a sharp breath. "So, he asked you if you'd ever had a *water bath*"—disgust pinched her features—"and then told you that he works in the morgue?"

Elodie hugged her backpack against her chest and pressed into the seat's milky soft fabric. "Yes, but not in a way that sounded as creepy as you just made it." At least, she didn't feel like what had happened was creepy. Strange, yes. But not creepy. Creepy implied danger and fear, and Elodie didn't feel threatened or afraid.

"It sounds creepy because that's really the only way it *can* sound." Astrid's inky black ponytail swished emphatically as she spoke. "When we talked about you being able to speak to guys, I didn't think you'd shoot so low. And I mean that both figuratively and literally since you found him in the *basement*." She rested her elbow on the armrest dividing the two bucket seats. "Although, I guess I should be happy that you talked to anyone at all about something other than work."

"I knew you could find the positive if you just looked hard enough." Elodie relaxed a little, letting her backpack slump into her lap. "And it wasn't super awkward. I managed to speak the whole time and everything."

"Did the whole 'Let me give you a bath in the ELU' conversation happen before or after you ran face-first into the door?" Astrid sucked in her lips to keep from laughing.

"Oh, don't remind me." Elodie groaned and slid down in the seat of the self-driving Pearl, tucking as much of her face as she could into the collar of her shirt. "He probably only spoke to me because he felt sorry for the weird girl who couldn't manage to enter the building correctly."

As the Pearl glided out of the city and into suburbia, the chunky gray freeway barricades ended, replaced by the blushing pink of flowering plum trees, brilliant green pines, and the steady thrumming of construction bots still working to upgrade the thousands of stores and homes that had made up the prepandemic suburbs.

"Possible, but I bet he wanted to talk to you because of how gorgeous and fabulous you are." Astrid held up her long finger. "Not that I am in any way rooting for or condoning an emotionally romantic liaison."

With how much Astrid obsessed over the rules, the thought that she would hope for something as torrid as an emotional liaison never crossed Elodie's mind. Plus, Elodie wasn't quite sure what an emotionally romantic liaison would even entail.

Astrid threw her ponytail over her shoulder. "Actually, if you ever encounter him again, tell him you're engaged to a Key Corp Major and then turn and run in the opposite direction before he has a chance to attack you with one of those End-of-Life Unit body carving bots."

Elodie zipped and unzipped the small front pouch of her backpack. "I don't think I need to worry about being attacked."

Astrid pursed her lips. "You say that now, but when you're lying face up on an exam table with bots waving their blades overhead and you hear creepy mohawk dude's maniacal laughter echoing around the room, you'll remember this conversation and wish that you had listened to me."

Comments like that made Elodie question whether or not Astrid had ever read one of the banned books she went on and on about having destroyed.

They passed by the faded orange Home Depot building stretched next to the freeway like spilled juice. Elodie held her breath. She'd seen a video of some kids who had broken into the abandoned warehouse-sized store not too long ago. It had been fifty years since the Cerberus virus first tore through civilization, yet blood still stained the concrete floors within.

Elodie drummed her fingertips against her knees. "Another *incident* happened today too," she said, changing the subject. She didn't want to think about Cerberus or let Astrid continue to destroy the only pleasant thing that had happened all day.

Astrid cocked her head and fingered the top button on her denim jacket. "Another scary real-life convo with a different creepy weirdo?"

The Pearl maneuvered off the highway and onto the nearly empty four-lane street that led to Elodie's neighborhood.

"No," said Elodie. "Do you think that your dad could use his connections at the MediCenter to get me an update on a patient?"

Astrid stilled in the way she did whenever she felt Elodie about do something she wouldn't agree with. "Why don't you ask for an update yourself?" Astrid said, her voice stony and low.

"I tried, but Holly still showed this patient as being in my unit." Elodie adjusted the hair tie around her wrist. "She'd just been transferred, so it might not have updated yet."

"Problem solved." Astrid clapped. "I'm sure Holly will have all the info when you go in tomorrow."

Elodie pressed her chin against her backpack. "Yeah, but there was something weird about the whole thing."

"Weirder than the guy you met in the basement?" Astrid waggled her sharp brows.

"Astrid, I'm serious. The transfer team came a lot faster than usual, and they didn't wait for me to sign off. And when I called their unit director, she said they'd never received the transfer order."

Astrid crossed and uncrossed her slender legs. "Then who came and got her?"

Elodie threw up her hands and glanced out the window, distracted by the holographic blue and orange MAX logo floating in front of the transit center like a human-sized button.

Astrid's brows pinched and she shook her head as if brushing away a thought. "I'm sure someone on the transfer team made a mistake and will come find you in the morning and have you sign off. No biggie."

The MAX red line pulled into the station and the platform was flooded in hazy purple orbs as the train doors opened and citizens poured into the suburbs of Westfall's Zone Two.

Elodie pressed her back into the seat. "It's against protocol to transfer a patient without a signoff."

"Then that person will totally pay for their mistake." Astrid resumed twirling the ends of her signature pony. "It doesn't seem like as big of a deal as you're making it. You're not the one who's going to get reprimanded."

Elodie let out a breath as she studied the lines of white stitching on the upholstered ceiling. Astrid didn't get it. People in the MediCenter didn't make those kinds of mistakes. There were protocols in place to make sure nothing fell through the cracks, certainly not entire patients. They were dealing with people's lives, not just making sure vehicles found their passengers without requiring them to walk to the curb.

Elodie chewed the inside of her cheek. That wasn't fair. Astrid worked hard and built tech Elodie could hardly understand how to use, much less create. Plus, Gus *had* slacked off and not refilled Patient Ninety-Two's sedation tube. But that wasn't nearly as big of a mistake as losing the girl completely.

The Pearl turned down a narrow, sunflower-bordered road, their round yellow-rimmed faces stretched up toward the sun. Elodie envied the simplicity of the flowers. Grow, grow, grow. Bloom. Drink in the light and the early morning rain. Return to the earth. They possessed no curiosity, no want, no need to experience something greater than what was laid out before them.

"Think about it like this." Astrid tucked her foot up underneath her and turned to better face Elodie. "What's the alternative?" She tilted her pointed chin. "That there's some big conspiracy going on that you know nothing about?" She snorted. "This is what happens when you read even a single page of a banned book. You make up all sorts of crazy shit in your mind instead of channeling that brain power toward productivity."

No, Astrid definitely wasn't reading anything unsanctioned.

Elodie twirled her finger into her scrub top. "You're probably right." She was beginning to feel a little silly. Gus had made a mistake, and so had the person who'd picked up Patient Ninety-Two from the Long-Term Care Unit. People weren't bots. They couldn't be expected to do everything flawlessly 100 percent of the time. When she arrived at work the next morning, Aubrey's chart would be annotated and everything would be completely normal.

The Pearl turned into Elodie's neighborhood and maneuvered down the main windy street that connected every cul-de-sac. Fir and big-leaf maple trees skirted the road, nearly hiding the one or two houses tucked back in each cul-de-sac. The original houses in the neighborhood had been built scrunched together with only a few feet and a sliver of yard separating one family from another. That design had died with most of the neighbors. Before Elodie was born, bots had come through and demolished the majority of houses throughout Zone Two and beyond. Now, where there had been four houses, one house remained, with an expansive front yard and backyard. Neither Elodie nor her friends had played outside much as children, but there was plenty of room if they'd made the decision to forego VR and meetup in the real.

"Now." Astrid bounced in her seat, jerking Elodie from her thoughts. "I have to tell you all about my VR date with Roxy. She's the chick from Madrid who I met at that lame worldwide tech ambassadors meeting."

"The one with the piercings?" Elodie had a hard time keeping track of all the adoring girlfriends who were as in love with the Fujimoto name as they were with Astrid.

Astrid shook her head. "That's Nadia. Roxy is the one whose hair is always a different color."

The Pearl stopped in front of Elodie's house, but she settled into the seat and hugged her backpack like it was a teddy bear and she was at a sleepover. Astrid always had the best VR meetups. Skydiving, creeking, cave diving. It was always something daring and fresh. Elodie didn't have the guts to try any of those things.

What if she splatted against the ground or got stuck in an underwater cave and drowned? Astrid had told her numerous times that dying in virtual reality didn't mean you'd die in the real, since one was actually happening while the other existed in a computer world, but Elodie didn't want to try . The word *reality* was in the name, and from what little she'd experienced of the VR update, it was as real as real life.

"You have to tell me everything," Elodie squealed. "But first, can we keep driving? I can't see her—yet—but I can feel Gwen staring at us."

Astrid pulled her holopad out from the storage pouch nestled inside the armrest. Her fingers danced over the screen as Elodie's gaze swept along the house and its ordinary mud-brown siding, brick steps, and flat green lawn. Soon she'd move into a house with Rhett. Into a house just as ordinary as this one.

The front door swung open and Gwen stepped onto the porch. Her long hair was swept up in a tight coiffure that didn't budge as she floated down the steps, her fingers dusting the air with each wave.

"Elodie, dear." Her practiced cheeriness passed through the window muffled and distorted.

Elodie's palms went clammy.

Astrid rolled down the window, stuck the top half of her body out, and used the door as a seat. The Pearl crept forward as Astrid drummed on the top of the vehicle and shouted, "Sorry, Gwendolyn. Your daughter and me got places to be."

XVIII

After another hour driving around the suburbs with Astrid, Elodie finally made it back to her house. The entire time they were out, she'd wanted to talk about the beautiful and exciting stranger from the ELU, but could sense that she'd be pushing Astrid past her limit. Her best friend could only handle a certain amount of curiosity before she shut it down completely and started talking about the facts, and facts weren't as exciting as the stories Elodie made up in her head.

Now that she was home, she would busy herself with a task more important than obsessing over an encounter with the mohawked mystery guy she would probably never see again, and shouldn't be thinking about anyway.

She would catch up with Vi.

As soon as she was in her room, Elodie tossed her backpack onto her bed, slipped out of her scrubs, and pulled on her comfiest pair of sweats. She folded herself under her weighted blanket and held her breath, listening for her mother's pealing laughter and staccato footsteps downstairs. Satisfied that Gwen was nowhere near her second-story room, Elodie cracked the spine of her textbook and propped it against her legs.

CHAPTER SEVEN

Love had always been at the bottom of Violet's priority list. Hell, if she was being honest, it hadn't even made the cut. Now, lust had been there, standing rock hard and at attention. But any itches she had, she scratched with her clients—scratched with the kills. That was, until she'd met Zane Cole. He'd made her itch in a way that only he could scratch. At first, she'd hated him—but wasn't that how all the best love stories started?

Zane's hair was black today. The flat, false kind of black that would wash out later, filling the tub with inky water until it disappeared down the drain along with the remnants of whichever character her wore for his most recent job. Finding a partner who understood the world Vi lived in was lucky. Most people in her line of work were terrible assholes. Zane was just terrible. But in a bad-boy-with-a-heart-of-gold clichéd type of way.

Incoming call from Gwendolyn Benavidez / "Mom."
Elodie groaned. The next time she started reading, she would have to remember to turn off her incoming calls.

"*What?*" she said, with a deep sigh and a roll of her eyes, thankful that her mother had opted for the comlink instead of the vidlink.

"I hope you had fun with your little friend." Gwen paused, waiting for a response Elodie wasn't going to provide. "Honestly,

Elodie, you take off with Astrid and now you're giving me an atti-
tude? That is no way to treat your mother, Elodie Grace."

Gwen had not only said Elodie's name twice, she'd added her
middle name for emphasis. She was more upset than her tone
revealed. Elodie clenched her teeth and drew a breath through her
nose as her mother continued.

"Hopefully you can reclaim your wits enough to tell me what
you think of this dress." Another pause. "The three of us will have
to go to the director's funeral, and I want to make sure we don't
embarrass your father. He's worked long and hard for his title, and
I wouldn't want us to do anything to put it in jeopardy."

Elodie's stomach soured with the mention of her father, and
she closed her textbook. "Mom, there's no way Dad is going to
lose his job because you're not wearing the right dress."

Through her comlink, she heard her mother's heels clicking against the new marble floor she'd just had installed in the
kitchen. Gwen always wore heels. Not because she was unsat-
isfied with her height (her statuesque figure came in just under
five ten), but because, as she always said whenever Elodie had the
audacity to lounge around the house in her sweats, *You always
want to look presentable. You never know who might show up unannounced.* Gwen had also told Elodie to wear a pantyliner at all
times in case she was ever involved in an accident so that, before
help arrived, of course, she could rip it off and throw it away and
have pristine undergarments. As a nurse, Elodie wasn't sure what
perceived vaginal hygiene had to do with the type of care one
would receive at the MediCenter, but, then again, her mother's
crowning achievement was that she had figured out how to make
and bake muffins from scratch in less than ten minutes.

"Then you won't mind doing me the favor of putting my

mind at ease," Gwen huffed. "Well, what do you think?"

Elodie twirled the frayed string of her sweatpants. "Of what?"

"*Of what?* The dress, Elodie, the dress. I swear . . ."

"I'm sure you look fine, but I can't actually see you." Elodie's pillow slid out from the perfect spot behind her head as she shrugged. "You didn't use the vid, just the com."

"Well, crumb. How do I . . .?" Gwen's strained words trailed off, and Elodie could picture her mother staring at her call screen, eyes pinched, tongue curled against her upper lip.

The gray box appeared with a bar of text: *Accept vidlink from Gwendolyn Benavidez / "Mom"?*

Elodie smoothed her hair and stiffened a bit before agreeing.

The box blurred and revealed Gwen. Her straight bangs brushed against her thick brows as she stared, eyes pinched, tongue curled against her expertly lipsticked upper lip.

Elodie couldn't help but grin. Her mother was predictable to the point of comforting. "Uh, exactly how fancy is too fancy for a funeral?"

The black lace dress clung to Gwen's curves like she'd been poured into it as liquid flesh. She turned in a circle, her coral lips moving.

Elodie leaned forward instinctually. "I can see you, but I can't hear you. Did you mute the call?"

Gwen's perfectly straight bangs shuffled against her forehead as she repeatedly craned her neck, birdlike. Besides Elodie's mother's faux blond hair, looking at her was like looking in a mirror. They both had the same smooth, full cheeks, perpetually pouty lips, square-tipped nose, and bronze skin. The only *real* difference was their eyes. Not the shape. They shared the same round eyes, the corners turning up like a sly half-smile. But unlike her mother's crystal blue, Elodie's were black and endless. Her father often said, *Puedo ver el mundo en tus ojos*, but Elodie could never remember what it meant.

Elodie's own vidlink was still inactive, but she waved her hands in protest. "You don't have to move your head around like that. There aren't any options to select anymore. The update made it so that you just think about unmuting, and it'll unmute. It's way easier than it's ever been."

Her mom's cheeks puffed with a sigh, her blue eyes narrowing with frustration. "Elodie, I can't figure out how to make this damn thing work!" Gwen's shout carried from the kitchen, up the stairs, and slammed into Elodie's closed door. "Come help your mother!"

Damn was as close as Gwen came to cursing, and without fail technological updates pushed her to that point.

"Gwendolyn." Determination hardened Elodie's tone and forced her to call her mother by her complete first name. "I won't be living with you forever," she yelled from her room. "You're going to have to learn how to do this without me rushing in to save you. Plus, you have Holly. Ask her for a tutorial."

For as long as Elodie could remember she'd been telling her mother that she'd have to figure out new tech features on her own, but *I won't live with you forever* had always seemed so far away. Then Elodie had been matched to Rhett, and now she was engaged. She'd be married in a few months, and was sure Rhett would not agree to them living in separate homes once they were wed. But living by herself for a little while would give her a chance to finish *Death by Violet* without being chastised for wearing comfy pants. Elodie shook away the thought, and, for the second time that day, reminded herself that there was no point in thinking about something that would never happen.

Another shout from downstairs. "I apparently did not do a

very good job raising you if you won't just come down here and help your mother figure this out."

With a sigh, Elodie slid her book into her bag and pushed herself out of bed. Repeatedly referring to herself as *your mother* was another one of Gwen's annoyed tells.

"Be right there." Elodie ended the call.

The ears on her fuzzy bunny slippers flopped side to side as she descended the stairs. She hadn't grown that much since her thirteenth birthday, when her father had surprised her with the slippers and an e-vid from the Key announcing that she'd be entering the Long-Term Care Unit's nursing program. Even though the rest of her wardrobe had matured, and her mother continued to make comments about them, Elodie had kept the slippers. They were a memory wrapped in fuzzy pink fluff, and she wasn't in the habit of throwing away memories.

The staircase opened to the kitchen, where Gwen impatiently drummed her fingers as she leaned against the rectangular island in the middle of the vast space. Elodie had to admit that the new flooring did look nice, or *expensive*, as one of Gwen's friends had commented. And, according to her mother, *expensive* was the best compliment one could receive.

"Oh, Elodie." Gwen stopped drumming and pressed her palms against her cheeks. "I would have insisted you stay at work and get yourself checked out if I'd known you weren't feeling well."

Elodie hid her hands in the sleeves of her sweatshirt. "I feel fine."

"Well." Gwen eyed her as she worried the high lace collar of her dress between her fingers. "I wish you would look a bit more," Gwen fluffed the air, "put together. What if someone were to stop by unannounced?"

Elodie glanced down at her bunnies partially swallowed by

her schlumpy gray pant legs. "I don't think that's something we have to worry about." She tucked her hair behind her ears. "Let's go to the living room so I can use the holoscreen. It'll be easier than trying to walk you through your comlink."

Elodie slid across the slick new marble floor till it ended at the living room threshold, where the pristine gray porcelain picked up, yawning into the expertly decorated living space. The flooring looked like wood—dreary, storm cloud–colored wood, but wood nonetheless—however, it wasn't. It fit their house. It fit with her mother, dressed up as one thing, but something else altogether.

Text from Astrid Fujimoto.

Elodie faced her mother as the gray text screen materialized:

Been thinking about Mohawk Man.

Elodie pressed her sleeve against her mouth to hide her smile as she replied.

AND . . .

With a strained chuckle, Gwen batted the air. "I suppose what's done is done." Pink cheeked and wide eyed, she stared at Elodie expectantly.

Elodie hugged her stomach. "Why are you looking at me like that?"

Gwen threw her arms into the air. "Surprise!" Her perpetual overpreparedness strangled the excitement from the word.

"There's my girl!" Rhett popped up from behind the kitchen island, arms shooting out like the points of a star.

"Rhett?" Elodie's stomach knotted. He'd been there the entire

time, listening as her mother went on about her father and the
dress and the comlink—all pretty typical for Gwen, but Astrid
had been the only other person who'd heard this side of her
mother. And even that was almost too much embarrassment for
Elodie to handle. "Wh-What are you doing here?"

He leaned against the island, his tight white tee and closely
cut white-blond hair blending almost perfectly with the row of
cabinets that stretched down the wall behind him like teeth. "You
said you wanted to see each other more. So here I am. You happy?"

What would you do if you weren't
already matched?

Elodie froze, guilt consuming her as her mother and fiancé
stood on the other side of the block letters etched into her vision.

Gwen's heels clapped against the floor as she hopped. "Oh,
Rhett, dear, she's excited. You just caught her off guard is all."

Like, would you want to see him
again? Meet up with him in VR?

Sweat popped against Elodie's forehead and she shook her
head and refocused, "From our talk earlier, you . . ." She picked at
a stray thread hanging from the cuff of her sweatshirt. "I thought
you were fine with the way things were."

With an annoyed grunt, Rhett folded his arms across his
chest. "Look, El, I can go." The hard angles of his jaw, his thick,
trunk-like neck, and the commanding timbre of his voice made
him seem much older than his twenty-one years.

Flapping her arms like a crazed goose, Gwen scooted behind

him. From her gestures, anyone else would've thought she needed medical assistance, but Elodie understood her mother's panicked waving. And Gwen was right. Elodie was being difficult yet again, which her mother understood would chase Rhett away. And no one, Elodie included, wanted Rhett to submit a request to have their match terminated. She'd be viewed as defective, and no one would want her then. Although, at times, that sounded divine.

"You're the one who wanted us to spend more time together," Rhett continued. "But if you don't want to hang out with your own fiancé . . ."

Or what about in the real? Would you want to talk to him again in real life????????

Elodie clutched her shoulders. Embarrassment licked hot streaks against her neck. "No, sorry. You did throw me off a little. I didn't—I just didn't expect to see you." She glanced down at her bunnies. The hopeless gray of the tile matched her mood. "I'll go get changed."

She headed for the stairs, pausing as Rhett said, "Where we're going is pretty casual."

Her mother clicked her tongue disapprovingly. "No place is *that* casual, Rhett, dear."

Blood surged to Elodie's cheeks.

Rhett scratched his smooth face, hiding his chuckle. "El, you, uh, might want to think about dumping those silly kid slippers while you're up there."

"My thought exactly." Gwen melted into a barstool uncomfortably close to the young soldier. "You know, you are so good for my Elodie. So wise and mature. And going places." She turned her ray of manipulation back on Elodie. "Don't I always say that Rhett here is going places in his career?" Her eyelids fluttered as she glanced up at him. "And that's really the most important thing."

Every year Elodie watched the bots make cotton candy at the upcoming Key Corp Rose Festival. Rainbows of fabric from nothing but sugar. She'd learned early on that it had to be protected or it would dissolve in on itself, turning the fluffy cloud into a hard, crusted lump.

Elodie balled her hands into fists inside the sleeves of her sweatshirt, bits of her disintegrating with each comment. She understood cotton candy more than anyone could know.

Is that a yes??????

Elodie's throat dried. She couldn't do both things. She couldn't talk about Mohawk and be with Rhett. There wasn't enough space in her brain—in this house. She would crack and bleed her guilty feelings all over her mother's new marble.

Fiiiiine. Don't answer

Hope you're knee deep in VR
adventure.

(Maybe with Mr. Mohawk?)

"You know, El, just today I received a personal call from Director Holbrook asking me to take care of the Eos threat." Rhett feigned casualness and rested his elbows against the island. "And with how ill he is? Oh, you must really be in his favor!"

Gwen swooned so aggressively, Elodie thought her mother might fall out of her chair and burst into the hundreds of pieces of plastic that made up her forty-year-old, newly adolescent appearance. And Elodie wouldn't even offer to sweep it up. "You're going to his funeral, yes, Rhett? This is what I'm thinking of wearing." Gwen hopped out of the chair and struck a pose before her heeled feet touched the floor. "Although, our Elodie has implied that it is a titch too fancy for such an occasion."

Elodie's groan was swallowed by the black hole of her mother's ego.

Rhett flashed his bleached smile. "You look stunning, Mrs. Benavidez. There's no way you can be too fancy for this funeral. He's the director, not a random nobody."

"Oh, Rhett." Gwen blushed, playfully clutching the strand of pearls against the dress's high collar. "*Ms.* Benavidez, please."

Elodie stiffened. "Mom! You're married."

Gwen waved dismissively. "Now, tell me. What do you think I should do with my hair?" She patted the blond waves piled on top of her head.

Elodie's toes dug into the warm fluff of her slippers. "I'll go up and change now." A smile burned across her lips. "I'll be back in a few."

"We don't need a narrated account of your comings and goings, Elodie, honestly." Gwen tittered to her captive audience of one, more than to Elodie. "Just because your wedding is coming up doesn't mean it's all about you all the time."

Pieces of Elodie seemed to flake away as she ascended the stairs. If she could've mustered the energy, she would have stomped her way up. But she was drained, too busy diverting fuel to make a new and tougher skin.

XIX

"Make sure you keep your eyes closed." Rhett was almost giggling. "No peeking."

Elodie's chest swelled with anticipation. The knee-high sock she'd tied over her eyes at Rhett's request inched its way down. She adjusted it until she was able to see the smallest sliver of pavement beneath her feet. Rhett had had her cover her eyes before the MAX had left the station. Since then, they'd switched trains, walked two blocks, and, from the lush green grass she currently trampled, they were now off-roading. She couldn't be expected to stay blind the entire time. She would have tripped and fallen before they'd made it to the second train.

"I'm not peeking!" She was, of course, but she didn't want to ruin the surprise. Especially after Rhett had witnessed the horror show that was her mother. He'd also participated a bit, hadn't he? Elodie's stomach knotted.

He was trying to fit in. Be a part of the family, Elodie told herself. *He just wants Gwen's approval.*

She couldn't think about it any other way. She *wouldn't*. She and Rhett were matched. There was no escaping it.

The warm evening breeze twirled through her hair and tickled the back of her neck. "I want to get there already! I'm so excited!" Concrete met her feet again as Rhett's clomping footsteps halted in front of her.

They were probably at a park. A real-life park. Elodie had talked about parks until she'd felt like a silly little girl, but Rhett had never shown interest in going. And, no matter how freeing it was to lean back in the swing and see nothing but your feet and the sky, it was no fun going alone. But now they were here. She could tell by the way the sidewalk framed the manicured lawn and the creaking of metal. *Swing chains!*

Not enough people played anymore. They were all so wrapped up in their careers and families, and they spent the little free time they had inside of a computer simulation. No matter how many times Astrid or Rhett or Gus or anyone else told Elodie that VR was indistinguishable from actual reality, it still wasn't real. In VR, rain didn't soak through her shoes and squish out with each step, snowflakes didn't cling to her lashes until her vision was rimmed in bright starbursts, and sunlight didn't paint her skin a deeper shade of golden tan. The way the planet enveloped them, played out around them regardless of their actions or plans—that was reality.

"Okay! Okay!" Rhett cheered. "Blindfold off!"

Elodie forced herself not to hop up and down as her fingers fumbled with the tight knot. She kept her eyes closed for a few moments after removing the blindfold. The wind tugged at the sock, twirling it around her arm.

I won't scream like a silly little girl. I won't. I won't. I won't.
Open.

"Oh." Breath rushed from her body like from a stuck balloon.

"Yeah!" Rhett crossed his arms over his chest and rocked from the balls of his feet back to his heels. "Frickin' awesome!"

Elodie stuffed the sock into the pocket of her jeans as she took in the six empty stalls stretched across the massive concrete slab in front of her. Each stall was a copy of the next, containing a green bench propped up on cinderblocks, a wooden stool, and, on the other side of the solid yellow line painted a foot behind the benches, two taller wooden stools.

The creaking sounded again and she swung her gaze to meet it. A metal pole was stabbed into the earth a few feet in front of a gray, windowless building. A wooden sign hung from the pole, its metal chains groaning with each listless sway.

Tuff's Gun Range. Real Guns. Real Life. Real Tuff.

Elodie balled the toe of the sock hanging out of her pocket. "An outdoor gun range?"

Rhett rocked again. A grin fattened his cheeks. "And only certain Key Corp personnel are allowed in, so," he waggled his brow, "you're lucky we're together. Without me you'd only be able to shoot in VR." He chortled. "Lame."

Elodie didn't want to shoot in VR, and she definitely did *not* want to shoot in real life.

Aside from the creaking, the range was dead quiet. "Where is everyone?" she asked as she followed him to one of the middle stalls.

Rhett whistled at the gun that lay in wait on the oddly shaped bench. "I rented out the whole place." He picked the rifle up, letting out a soft, pleased grunt, and tossing her a, "Just for us," as he weighed the wood and metal piece between his hands.

"Because you know how much I like guns?" Elodie said to the top of Rhett's head as he leaned over to wipe away an invisible smudge.

"Mmhhmm."

His anemic reply told her all she needed to know. This *date* wasn't for her or for their relationship. She was just tagging along while Rhett did what Rhett wanted to do.

"Feel this." Rhett's eyes were heavy lidded as he extended the rifle. She wouldn't be surprised if he started drooling.

Elodie forced her arms out, and he dropped the gun into her upturned palms.

Rhett's left eyebrow ticked up in amusement. "Heavier than you thought it would be, isn't it?"

No. She'd never thought about it.

"It's a *Kalashnikov*." He articulated the name as if teaching it to a child.

Human-shaped outlines glared at her from paper targets held in place by wooden frames a few hundred yards past the stalls.

"I can teach you to shoot it," he said.

Elodie couldn't keep her lips from peeling back in a revolted grimace. "Actually," she gingerly set the gun down on the table. Her hands snapped back to her sides as soon as they were free. "I think I'm going to sit this one out."

"That's probably for the best." His chest puffed and he waggled his left brow. "You'll want to watch the master at work for a little bit. Really get a feel for how it should be done." He picked up the gun and fit the curved box magazine into the receiver. "We might want to start you off with something a little smaller. You can't handle this bad boy."

Rhett unhooked a pair of earmuffs from under the table and handed them to her before tugging on his own. Elodie's smile was more a baring of teeth as she waved, slid the ear covers on, and backed away to the empty stool behind the yellow line of safety.

Rhett hunched around the gun and began shooting. Each bang of gunfire and hollow clink of empty shells made Elodie's stomach squeeze tighter and her bones rattle within her flesh. Seconds lasted an eternity as he loaded clip after clip, shredding paper humans.

"Fuck yeah!" he whooped when he had finally run out of ammo and magazines piled on the table like steel skeletons. "Whoo! What a rush!" He tugged his earmuffs down around his neck and dropped the gun onto the table.

Elodie followed his lead and slid her ear protectors off and dropped them into her lap.

"AKs are great, but nothing quite compares to the Fujimoto Fury. Wish Tuff's could get clearance to have one of those out here." He cracked his knuckles. "The Fury doesn't look like much, but it is a monster. A total beast. You slide your hand into this cannister, and it—" He held his left arm out straight, trying to demonstrate the weapon with sweeping gestures from his right. "I don't know, practically grows around it and morphs into this intense fire demon."

Astrid had talked about the Fury. It was one of the biotech weapons her father had created for the Key as a way to fund the civilian outreach projects he was most passionate about. Astrid had even hauled Elodie to a prototype demonstration. And what Rhett said was accurate. The way the fire had eaten up the mannequin, reducing it to ash in mere seconds, was something that fit right at home with the evil demon mythos.

She hadn't told Rhett about having witnessed it for the very reason that now stared her down. She didn't want this version of her fiancé. The man who pined after a machine that's purpose was annihilation. She wanted a different version of Rhett. One she had yet to discover.

"It does a perfect job of lighting up those Zone Seven abominations," he continued. "Turns 'em real crispy."

Elodie fidgeted in her seat. "Why do you have to go out there?" she asked, changing the subject. "Why can't whatever's in Zone Seven be left alone? The Zone barriers are protected. Nothing has gotten into the city in—"

"Nothing has gotten into the city because my team and others like us go out there and make sure those *things* aren't breeding and growing in numbers."

She frowned. Breeding was such a gross word. She'd learned about the process in her Preinfection World Studies class. It was all moisture and blood flow and thrusting. So messy and invasive. It was much better now. Eggs were harvested, fertilized, and the developing embryo was cared for in the lab until the fetus was ready to be harvested from the gestation bot and delivered to its parents with a caretaker bot that would stay with the family until the child's fourth birthday. All other *urges* that had encircled procreation were taken care of in sterile Release Pods at the MediCenter. Elodie had *never* used one.

She swung her legs as she sat on the stool. "But there hasn't been an attack in, like, a decade."

"Thanks to yours truly." Rhett gave a mock bow.

"You weren't even old enough to go out to Zone Seven when that attack happened. At least a few other people have had a hand in keeping the city monster free."

"Yeah, well," he blustered, "up until recently. But for the past three years or so, it's been all me. And they're not even the immediate threat. Eos, and Echo—"

"Echo?" Elodie asked.

"Don't worry. I got 'em both handled. Ask anyone." Rhett's chest puffed.

Elodie blinked long and slow to keep from rolling her eyes. How many times would she have to tell him how great he was?

"*And* guess who was hand chosen by Fujimoto himself to take Fury on its Zone Seven maiden voyage?" Rhett was so full of hot air, he might take flight.

"You were." Elodie meant to sound more excited, but the words spilled out flat and glum.

"Damn fucking right, I was!" He slapped his chest so hard Elodie winced. "And they're going to have a team out there filming to show the big guys at Key Corp. Key News might even be out there too." He sucked his teeth and rocked back onto his heels. "Your man could get pretty famous off this."

Elodie's feet stopped swinging. "Off killing?"

"My favorite thing to do." He winked. "Now, get over here and let me show you how to be a lean, mean, monster-killing machine."

Elodie slid off the stool, but her feet stayed glued to the pavement.

"I put in a request for unlimited ammo to go along with the Glock. It's lighter. Way easier to handle. We can stay here until you hit the target."

She crept forward, twisting the plastic-banded earmuffs between her clammy hands.

"El, can you imagine if we were out in Zone Seven together? Lighting shit up and wreaking havoc?" Rhett's eyes glazed for a moment before he blinked himself back to the present. "Controlled havoc, of course. Even someone as high up the chain as I am has his orders. Too bad, though. My team and I would destroy some shit real nice if I was in complete control."

Elodie was tired of listening. Tired of guns and death and destruction and who this brick of a man kept revealing himself to be.

"There's the bot now." Rhett rubbed his palms together,

pausing as Elodie extended a trembling hand and placed the earmuffs on the table. "You don't have to be scared."

"I'm not scared." She picked at the edges of her short finger-nails. "It's just that my career, everything I've worked for and believe in, is about protecting and maintaining life. Guns serve no purpose but to end it." She dragged her tongue across dry lips. "I don't like them."

"Gah, El, you're being such a girl about the whole thing."

There it was again. Her gender used as a way to patronize. Disliking guns had nothing to do with being a woman and everything to do with what she stood for and how she felt. Why couldn't he see that?

She stiffened. "It really doesn't have anything to do with—"

"You know, we had that talk this morning and I realized that I was being kind of stuck in my ways, so I come surprise you at your house, but you weren't happy I was there, and then I bring you out here—a place that civilians aren't even allowed—and you're totally unappreciative. I don't know what to do with you, Elodie."

She hugged her arms around her middle. All of that was true. She hadn't realized she was being ungrateful, but now that he'd said it . . .

Tears pricked her eyes. "I'm sorry. I'm not trying to be difficult."

Her relationship would be easier if she would stop telling Rhett she wanted something and then hate it when he delivered.

"El, hey, don't be like that. I don't want you to cry." Rhett scratched the back of his head. "How about this? I'll use your gun, finish up all the ammo the bot brought, then I'll take you back home. You can clean yourself up and later tonight we can meet up in VR like we usually do."

She brushed away a tear and nodded.

Rhett hooked his thumb through his belt loop. "Yeah, maybe we could go to ancient Rome and dress up in those bedsheets you like to nerd out in."

"Togas." She chuckled.

"Whatever." Bullets tinkled like bells as Rhett arranged the boxes of ammo on the table. "It's not my favorite time period, but you got a kick out of it last time we went."

It wasn't anyone's favorite time period. Most citizens hung out in futuristic VR realms, but Elodie was a sucker for the past. It also didn't hurt that the historic realms were sparsely populated.

"What about Paris?" She tingled with the thought.

He shrugged. "Whatever my girl wants, she gets."

A small, muffled part of her told her that was far from the truth, but she stuffed the voice back into the trenches of her mind.

"It's the city of love," she said with a sigh. "Or it was at one point."

Rhett lined up his shot, relaxed, and then lined it up again. "What is that supposed to mean?"

"It's romantic." Elodie traced the stitching along her collar. "Couples used to go there and climb the stairs of the Eiffel Tower or watch it twinkling at night. They'd even *kiss*," she whispered. "I'm pretty sure that's where that term *French kissing* came from."

"See, that kind of stuff is what was wrong with people from the past." Rhett adjusted the earmuffs around his thick neck. "They were all over each other, touching and hugging, smashed together traveling to work and wherever else. And since that apparently wasn't bad enough, they had to rub their disgusting, wet mouth holes all over each other too. They were out of control and practically begging to be wiped out." He slid Elodie's earmuffs closer to her.

Elodie pressed the squishy muffs against her ears and crossed back over the yellow line, flinching at the first round of gun blasts.

She wasn't asking to kiss. She didn't understand the need any more than Rhett and was fully aware of the risks involved. Mixing her saliva with Rhett's could very well spawn another pandemic and wipe out Westfall. All Elodie wanted was a nice, romantic adventure that would assure their arrival to romancia-landia, and Paris seemed like a great place to start.

"Survive that, you monster fuckers!" Rhett roared over the cracks of gunfire.

Elodie grimaced.

Maybe Rhett wasn't built for romance.

Sparkman swung her legs over the edge of the bed. Her boots hit the ground before her alarm had a chance to sound. She fastened the belt yawning open like the mouth of a single-toothed snake above her hips before pressing her fists together, each knuckle cracking. Her strawberry-blond braid brushed her shoulder blades as she stretched her neck, then her arms, and then her legs.

She always slept dressed. Ready to go. Ready for anything.

Her alarm finally caught up to her and blared through the one-room apartment, reverberating off the barren beige walls and the thin glass of the twin windows stretched against the far wall like eyes. She wasn't sure why she even set the alarm anymore.

The old-fashioned coffee pot gurgled to life, hissing and popping as the first drops hit the heated glass. Except for one space, Sparkman's place was low tech. No bots, no holoscreens or holopads, and, better yet, no Holly. All day Sparkman worked with computers, the MediCenter's Holly assessing and offering advice. Holly was a babysitter, Normandy's spy, and the old kook took pleasure in the fact that Sparkman knew it. All day Sparkman yearned for the quiet of her modest home and the peace that zipped up around her like a sleeping bag.

Sparkman fastened the blackout drapes shut. They were her only furnishings, if she was desperate enough to call them that, which she hadn't found in an alley or abandoned building.

She opened the door to the closet, or what should have been the closet, and leaned forward, resting her broad chin against the chinstrap worn smooth from repeated use. Orange light, the same orange of the rising sun, burst across her retina.

Three beeps sounded.

She was in.

Four holoscreens activated in succession, lighting the inside of the dark closet. Sparkman slid her only chair across the cracked linoleum floor and settled into it as four pixelated shadows each found their seats and did the same.

She twined her fingers and rested her hands against her lap before announcing herself to the group. "Sparkman, here."

"And Whiskey." The voice came from the first screen.

"Delta." From the second.

"Zulu." The third.

And finally, the fourth, "Echo."

The board members had each called out their sign. Their voices had been altered, with a robotic tinge, a kind of hollowness only perceptible to those trained to hear it. Only top-ranking Eos members knew each other's identities, as well as the identities of everyone involved within their sect of the organization. And Sparkman wasn't at the top.

"Sparky!" The first holoscreen flashed a little brighter as Whiskey spoke. "Tired of working with good ol' Normandy?" There was a drawl to Whiskey's voice. A kind of lilt Sparkman couldn't quite place through the filter. "We could sure use you here in my department."

For years Whiskey had tried to lure Sparkman away from Normandy, but she had to see this assignment through, for the good of Westfall's citizens or not. Normandy experimented on people. On children.

"He's looking for another one," Sparkman began without acknowledging Whiskey. "A child. Younger this time."

Whiskey's blurred squares bounced with a presumed nod. "Jumpin' right in, are we? Gotta respect a woman who gets down to business."

"Another child?" Echo's voice was whisper-soft. And when she spoke, everyone listened.

Sparkman's fingers clenched. "Yes, ma'am. Aubrey Masters, Patient Ninety-Two, passed yesterday afternoon." Only at the MediCenter did Sparkman call the men, women, and children strictly by their assigned numbers. In her home and in front of the faceless board members of Eos who she trusted with her life, the ninety-two souls weren't numbers. They were human beings.

"There is nothing we can do." Echo's screen lightened as she spoke. "It's terrible, but we mustn't intervene. We must allow Normandy to choose another."

Delta's screen flashed as she cleared her throat. "Echo's right," she said, clipped and clear. "We shut Normandy down now and they'll have someone in his place in a matter of days. The doctor might think he's irreplaceable, but I've seen many young people readying themselves to take over the Genetic Technology divisions. In a few years, Normandy will be obsolete."

But a few years wasn't now, and now was all Sparkman had.

She knew Eos had a plan. A grand, all-consuming plan to right many of the Key's wrongs, but how long would that take? How many children would she have to watch die?

Sparkman stiffened. "There's more. Aubrey was . . ." she paused, unsure of how to describe the remarkable little girl. "Different." Sparkman set her jaw, displeased with the vagueness of the word, but unsure of how to elaborate.

Echo's pixelated form shifted. "Different how?"

Sparkman had asked herself the same question. She pressed her fists together, cracking her knuckles. "The science behind Aubrey's changes is unclear. As Normandy gets closer to perfecting the serum, he becomes more secretive. What I witnessed yesterday was unlike anything I've seen before. She's a child. Even partially awake, she was stronger than I am. She seemed . . ." Sparkman focused on Echo. To sway the body, she needed the head. "*More than human.*"

Whiskey's screen flashed with a huff. "Fucking fuck. The Key let Normandy have free rein of the GenTech Unit and this is what they get."

"*Tell the Doctor they're coming.*" Sparkman interjected. "She woke up and said, *tell the Doctor they're coming.*"

Zulu's screen brightened. "*Who's coming?*"

Sparkman shook her head. "I'm not sure Aubrey even knew where she was."

"Your suggestions, Sparkman?" Echo was stern and soft and calm and confident.

Sparkman's braid grazed her back as she nodded. "We need Aubrey," she said, her gaze intent and unwavering.

Whiskey grunted. "You said she was dead."

"But she'll be in Cold Storage." Zulu spoke for the first time.

"If I can get her to my lab, I can work backward. Figure out what Normandy's been developing while the Key has had its head turned."

There was silence, all members instinctively awaiting Echo's response.

"Sparkman, you have a plan." Echo didn't phrase it as a question. She didn't need to. Sparkman was always prepared before she reported in to Eos. "I assume you'll need access to the End-of-Life Unit. We have someone who can get you in. Someone young and eager who won't be suspected."

Eos blanketed the globe with eleven total board members, soldiers in every unit of each MediCenter around the globe, and operatives within different careers. Sparkman had only ever spoken with Echo, Zulu, Whiskey, and Delta, the heads of the North and Central American factions of Eos. And those four were the only people out of the eleven to know Sparkman's identity. Layers of protection. That way it was more difficult for one person to bring down the entire resistance organization.

Once again Sparkman nodded and clenched her fists, cracking her knuckles. "As always, I will work with anyone you trust."

"Good," Echo said. "Let's get started."

XXI

Elodie drummed her fingers along the hard cover of the nursing textbook that hid her deepest, darkest secret. She'd pulled it out to catch up with Vi, but the bright empty space of Patient Ninety-Two's former room drew her attention like a flower to sunlight.

Elodie's toes tapped feverishly against the tile. Since she'd arrived that morning, she'd waited for one of the doctors to come tell her what had happened with Aubrey. Through Holly, she'd submitted four status update requests. It wasn't odd to follow up on transferred patients. Elodie had done it many times. Currently, she had update requests pending for each of her patients that had been transferred to different units in the blur of activity that had filled the previous day. It was comforting to know that some of her patients would eventually leave the MediCenter healthy and alive. It made her job worth doing.

But each time Elodie had checked Aubrey's status update in the queue, Holly informed her that it had been deleted. It wouldn't have been that big of a deal if they'd also been read before being deleted, but if that was the case, why hadn't Elodie been contacted?

She'd have to go about it a different way. "Holly, has there been any activity on Patient Ninety-Two's file?"

"Let me check." Holly's disembodied voice paused for a moment before continuing. "Yours is the final entry on Patient Ninety-Two's chart. Would you like me to read you the entry?"

With a groan, Elodie massaged the tightness in her neck. "How is it possible that mine is the last entry?" She chewed her bottom lip. "Holly, can you take down an email for me?"

"I'd be happy to." Holly's crisp voice rang out over the steady clicking and whirring of the LTCU bots. "Who would you like me to send it to?"

"The director of the MediCenter." Elodie held her breath. She was doing it. She was really doing it. She was going to jump over everyone and go straight to the one person in the entire city whose words could affect real change and get her real answers.

"While Director Holbrook still holds the title of MediCenter Director, he will soon be inactive, and therefore is no longer able to respond to any messages." Holly regurgitated the facts, her computer-generated emotions unable to harness the finality of the statement. "I can send it to his assistant; although, I cannot be certain that it'll be answered by or forwarded to the new director."

"Crap. I completely forgot about Holbrook. How could I forget something as huge as that?" Elodie dropped her chin against her palm. "Because I'm stuck in my own little bubble, so wrapped up in my own feelings that I'm oblivious to the outside world." Her cheeks heated. Had she really intended to send the director an email? She would have been demoted for sure, bringing something so trivial as incomplete paperwork to the attention of the leader of the city. Jeez, she was being unreasonable.

"Never mind, Holly. I'm going to get back to my job." Elodie leaned back in her chair, swiped Patient Ninety-Two's files clear from the holoscreen, and pulled up the care chart for her only current patient.

The elevator chimed its arrival as the doors slowly hissed opened. All of the *what ifs* Elodie was only beginning to tamp down roared back to the surface. They were finally here to tell her what had happened to Aubrey. Elodie calmly pushed her chair away from the control panel and stood. She wasn't the emotional young nurse who had almost made a spectacle of herself by calling in the director of the MediCenter. No, she was the cool and collected, mature lead nurse who cared about her patients and wanted to make sure they were doing well after leaving her care.

As she completed her about-face, Elodie took a deep breath, flipped her hair, and smiled. The elevator doors had closed, and no one was there waiting to speak with her.

"Hello?" She whirled around a little more frantically than she'd meant to. Her calm facade was cracking.

Still, no one answered. No lab coat–clad doctor or holopad-wielding assistant caught the corner of her eye. There was . . . no one.

Elodie gingerly lowered herself back into her chair. Her gaze remained fixed on the shiny elevator doors.

I'm losing my mind.

But elevators didn't travel to whichever floor they felt the urge to visit. A floor had to be requested by a person or a—

"Ouch!" Elodie jerked backward and grabbed the toe of her sneaker. She blinked down at the bot clicking and whirring and repeatedly ramming into the leg of her chair.

The familiar bot stilled, let out a hiss, and then resumed knocking its stumpy square body against the chair. The glass tubes in the bin attached to its front clanked with each repeated run in.

With a grunt, Elodie hefted the motorized cube. "You're from the medi-pump lab. You're not supposed to be up here."

It beeped in response and began vibrating as its wheels rapidly spun, searching for a solid surface.

"Okay, okay." A strip of white fluttered out from the bot's shiny yellow frame as Elodie lowered it back to the ground. She lunged forward and grabbed the paper before the bot spun around and headed toward the elevator. She had almost balled up the strip of paper and tested her aim by tossing it the long distance to the incinerator pail, when scratches of handwritten text caught her eye.

Salmon Springs Fountain. 4:30.
—Your Neighborhood Mohawked Moleman

Elodie squealed a high-pitched bleat of excitement. She clapped her hands over her mouth. This is exactly what Astrid had mentioned.

Would you want to talk to him again in real life?

Elodie had never answered the question; instead, she'd just reported on her horrible gun-filled non-date date with Rhett. She hadn't thought there was a reason to say anything about Mr. Mohawk, er, the *Mohawked Moleman*. When would she actually ever see him again?

Today. The word chimed between her ears. *Four thirty. Salmon Springs Fountain.*

Elodie placed the strip of paper on her textbook.

What would Vi do?

XXII

Elodie worried the edges of the folded note. No one had ever written her a note. Not a real one, using a pen and paper, that is. Actually, now that she thought about it, she couldn't remember anyone who had written anything down on paper ever. That's what Holly was for, and holopads, and, well, computers in general.

She flipped up the hood of her rain jacket and activated her Violet Shield as she passed through the automatic sets of glass doors of the downtown MediCenter building and onto the rain-slicked brick sidewalk.

The corners of the paper were furry beneath her fingers as she smoothed them over again and again. It wasn't technically an invitation, but who went around telling people where they were going to be for no reason at all? Then again, who wrote a note and taped it to a bot? It was like something out of *Death by Violet*—except for the bot, of course.

Rain fell in fat droplets and lapped against her boots as she splashed through shallow puddles on the five-block walk to

Waterfront Park. She slipped the note into her jacket pocket and balled her hands within the sleeves. She wasn't doing anything wrong. Elodie knew that for a fact. But if she wasn't breaking any rules, why did she feel so . . . *quaky?*

Elodie shook her head. She'd never make it to the fountain if she continued down that path. Plus, there would be plenty of time to assess where her current bout of anxiety had come from as soon as she was home.

Across the street, the stretch of grass that bordered the walkway along the river's edge sparkled vibrant green through the steady rainfall.

Okay. She was nearly there. She hadn't stopped or convinced herself to go on home. For all the losses she'd acquired at work that morning, she was finally winning at something.

Well, almost. She still needed to cross the street. And all sorts of things happened to pedestrians. None that she could actually recall, but that didn't mean getting flattened by the MAX or run over by a rogue Pearl wasn't a thing.

She chewed on the corner of her nail and searched the concrete benches that surrounded Salmon Springs Fountain as she waited along with a handful of other Violet Shielded pedestrians to cross the two-lane street.

There he was, mohawk and all, casually leaning against a tree, a lightweight jacket over a tight T-shirt, no violet orb around him, without a care in the world. Like he'd somehow been able to transfer all of his emotions to her. That would explain the terrible clenching in her chest and stomach.

He pushed himself away from the tree and waved.

The pedestrian light flashed white, and Elodie suddenly had no idea what to do with her arms or her face. At least her legs were busy carrying her forward, although she'd forgotten how to walk normally, and skipped over to him. Her insides knotted, and she wished she had her backpack to hide behind. She'd left it in her locker in case they were going to go do something.

But why had she assumed they'd go do anything? What if he was trying to return something she'd dropped when they'd met, both the unofficial and official times? Crap, had she *ever* managed to be a normal, functioning human being when he'd been around? Or what if he was a complete weirdo like Astrid had said? He did work down in the morgue. What kind of craziness did you have to display in your testing to make them assign you to a career dealing with dead people? Part of her knew he was a bit weird (he *had* attached a handwritten note to a bot), but that's what had drawn her out into the rain in only her Violet Shield, scrubs, raincoat, and boots, with the hopes of an adventure.

As she reached his side of the street, Elodie clicked the button on her wristband and the purple orb around her vanished. Rarely did anyone stray from the sidewalk that bordered the street and venture into Waterfront Park or take the path that ran along the Willamette River. Plus, it was always awkward to have a meetup with one person shielded and the other person not, and Elodie was already feeling awkward enough.

He jogged up to her, excitement stitched in the creases of his grin. "I wasn't sure you'd come."

"I was surprised when I, um . . ." Elodie watched the beads of water sliding down the tops of her rainboots as she fiddled with her jacket zipper. "When I got your note. The bot and everything. It was different."

His worn boots creaked as he shifted. A muddy shadow spread against the pavement where his foot had been before the smudge was pulled away by the steady stream of rainwater seeking out the nearest drain. "Different, huh?"

She couldn't bring herself to look up at him. "Not different in a bad way. It was just different in a different way." She winced. "I mean, no one has ever sent me a note before." Heat crept up her neck. "People have sent me notes before. I get them all the time." Warmth pricked her cheeks. "Not *all the time*, all the time. Just some of the time. Like, a normal amount of notes a normal amount of the time." Her mouth went dry and her tongue felt glued to her teeth. "Sorry, what I'm trying to say is that I liked it." A stray raindrop landed on her cheek. She brushed it away before it had a chance to sizzle and evaporate against her fiery flesh. "The paper and the bot. Very clever and unexpected." She sighed, and finally met his gaze. "It was nice."

His eyes searched hers, and she felt the sudden urge to zip up her coat and pull the bungees on her hood until only the tip of her nose was visible. She wasn't going to do it, of course. She'd already made enough of a fool of herself. Not to mention the fact that she had also criticized the very cute thing that he had done.

He was probably trying to come up with an excuse to leave.

He shoved his hands into his pockets. "There's nothing wrong with different." He rocked his head from side to side as if weighing the words. "At least, there shouldn't be."

Elodie exhaled completely for the first time that day.

"I'm Aiden, by the way," he offered as he turned and clomped back toward the grass. "Not that you can't call me Your Neighborhood Mohawked Moleman," he tossed over his shoulder as he motioned for her to follow. "I just figured you'd want something a little more"—he hiked his shoulders—"formal."

Soggy grass squished under Elodie's boots as she trailed behind him through the trees. "Elodie. Elodie Benavidez." She paused alongside him as he surveyed the expansive Willamette River.

"Benavidez. Is that Spanish?"

Elodie picked at her fingernails. "I think so. My dad used to try to teach me, but what's the point in learning a language that Cerberus took down with it?"

Aiden's gaze brushed over her. "To respect it, I suppose. I mean, it *is* a part of you."

Goosebumps popped along Elodie's arms. It was hard to think about the pieces that made up who she was when so much of the past had been gone for so long, weakened by Cerberus and put out of sight by the Key—to keep everyone strong, and safe, and the same, united. There was comfort in unity and comfort in knowing that only here and now remained. Only here and now mattered.

Aiden ran his hands along the faded sides of his curly mohawk. "This place is gorgeous." With a sudden jolt of energy, he jogged across the lawn past the trees and halted at the thick stone balustrade that guarded the abrupt drop off along the edge of the dark rolling sheet of the river.

The ground squelched as she closed the distance between them.

He rested his elbows against the gray stone. "Amazing, isn't it?"

Elodie tried to follow his line of sight, squinting as she looked up the river. "I don't think I'm seeing it."

"Sure you are." He pressed his palms against the rain-soaked rock and nodded toward the steady flow of gray water. "Sometimes I feel like no one looks at where we live. They see it, but they don't *really see it*. You know?"

The swollen droplets had ceased, leaving behind a cool mist on Elodie's skin as she watched the churning waters patiently carve out a home through the heart of the city. On the far shore, the tree-lined Riverwalk wound past sculptures and beneath bridges.

Elodie's hair began to curl in the constant moisture, and she tucked it behind her ears.

She'd lived in Westfall her whole life and had never stopped to look at what was around her. She'd been too busy constructing a life as empty and hollow as VR.

Aiden ground the toe of his boot against the pavement. "It probably sounds crazy—"

"No." And if it was, Elodie needed a little bit of crazy in her life. "You're right."

A grin plumped his cheeks. "Ever been skateboarding?"

She blinked at the sudden change in tempo. Or maybe it wasn't an abrupt shift as much as it was a snapshot of the way Aiden viewed the world, like everything could at once be appreciated and playful; understood, yet still a question.

Elodie shook her head. "I usually go skiing or climbing. I went horseback riding once, but it was before all the updates, so it was kind of lame."

"No, I mean, in real life?" He dug around the inside pocket of his jacket, pulled out a thick, black rectangle, and dropped it onto the sidewalk. The lone pedestrian quickly passing by didn't seem to notice when the box landed on the concrete with a loud thud. "Tap it," he said with a slight nod toward the box. "With your foot."

Elodie's toes squished together in the tip of her rainboot. "What will it do?"

He tilted his chin. "Guess you're about to find out."

With the quickness of a snake strike, Elodie kicked out her foot, tapped the box with the thick toe of her boot, and recoiled.

The box flattened against the sidewalk as it unfolded into a smooth concave deck with rounded ends.

"No way." Elodie's fingers flew to her smile as the board popped up off the ground and a set of chunky neon green wheels appeared on either end. "Where did you find that?"

"You can find anything if you're willing to look hard enough." Aiden's gaze, deep and warm and sparking with secrets, found hers. "Having a few engineer friends helps too."

Elodie's cheeks were hot again, and she pulled her attention to the skateboard. "Are you going to . . ." she shrugged and tentatively tapped the lip of the board with her foot. "Ride it, or something?"

"I'm not, but you are." He pushed the board in Elodie's direction. A leaf stuck to one of its neon wheels and deposited it at her feet as it rolled to a stop.

Elodie pulled her arms further up her sleeves. "I don't know how."

"I'll teach you." Aiden brushed his hand through his mohawk. Rain sprung from his tight curls and dusted the air like glitter. "You're going to step onto it like this and then push off." He said as he mimed stepping onto the board with his left foot and pushing against the sidewalk with his right. "When you start moving, pivot and bring your back foot onto the deck." Aiden shifted his feet and held out his arms like he was flying. "Easy peasy."

Before she lost her nerve, Elodie sucked in a breath, balled her hands in her sleeves, stepped onto the skateboard, and pushed.

"Make sure you're solid and balanced before you—"

Aiden's advice came a second too late. Elodie squealed as the board surged out from under her and careened, riderless, into the grass, and her butt smacked against the concrete. "Ouch," she groaned as she inspected her hands.

Aiden kneeled down next to her, concern widening his eyes. "Are you okay?"

"Yeah, sorry about that." Elodie grimaced as she got to her feet. "I'm fine. My jacket, not so much." She offered her ripped sleeves as evidence.

"You sure you're okay?" Aiden asked as he stepped onto the curved tail of the skateboard. The board pointed straight up and he grabbed the nose.

The underside of the deck was the same neon green as the wheels, and littered with various scratches and divots. What drew Elodie's attention wasn't the proof that Aiden had taken similar, albeit far less embarrassing, spills. It was the beautiful, hand painted script that seemed to dance across the board's middle— *after the storm comes the dawn.*

"That's really pretty." Elodie motioned to the board.

Aiden dropped the nose and pushed the skateboard back onto the sidewalk. "The river's a few feet higher than normal. Want to go to the pier and check it out?"

"As long as I don't have to get there on that thing." Elodie smiled.

Aiden caught up to the board and gave it another push. "Are you saying that *wasn't* the funnest thing you've ever done?" he asked, his eyebrow arched.

Elodie joined him, kicking the skateboard as they neared it. "It comes in second, right behind running face first into a glass door."

"You know, I've heard crashing into a door is a wild ride." Aiden angled the board toward the pier and gave it a final tap before he strolled onto the dock. Wooden slats creaked and groaned as he headed toward the edge and stared out at the water.

Like Aiden had done, Elodie stepped on the end of the skateboard and lifted it by its nose before joining him on the pier. "Did you always want to work in the morgue?" She sat down with the board stretched across her lap. Her legs dangled over the edge of the pier as she absentmindedly traced the board's fancy lettering. "I mean, unless you don't want to talk about work." She shook her head and moved the skateboard behind her. Of course he didn't want to talk about work. People didn't leave work to then keep talking about work. Rhett never wanted to hear about her day and, most days, she didn't want to tell him about it anyway. "Sorry, I shouldn't have asked."

Aiden sat down next to her and tapped the toe of his boot against the river's rippling surface. "You apologize a lot."

"Sorry." Elodie pressed her teeth against her bottom lip. Could she be any more predictable?

"Have you thought about saving them?" He dipped the toe of his boot into the river and flicked up a splash of gray water.

Her brow creased at the question. "Save my apologies? For what?"

"They're heavy, apologies. At least they should be. And meaningful."

Elodie shrugged. "They're just words."

"But words have power." He lifted his foot. Water rolled off of his boot and rained back into the river. "That's something Echo tells me all the time."

Elodie smoothed the ends of her hair between her fingers. "Who's Echo?"

Aiden plunged his foot into the river. Water sprayed around his boot. Elodie jerked backward and yipped when the cold splash found her.

He clapped his hand over his mouth. "Shit! I did not think it would reach that far!" he exclaimed, the words muffled between his fingers.

Laughter shook Elodie's core and she collapsed back against the wooden slats. The clouds had cleared and left behind a pale blue sunlit sky.

"Seriously, that was a total accident." He joined her on his back. "I completely miscalculated."

Elodie shielded her eyes and stared into the endless blue. "Don't even think about saying you're sorry," she said through a final bout of giggles. Her cheeks ached as she lay there, still smiling, river water soaking her pants. It was nice, just being there with Aiden. There were no expectations or harsh judgments. There was only freedom, room to be whoever she wanted to be, room to find out who exactly that was. "Sometimes," she began, "I feel like this planet is the entirety of outer space. Like, the beginning of Zone Seven is the edge of our atmosphere, and it's just black nothingness until the next city or country. I mean, no one can survive in or beyond Zone Seven, so from our Zone Seven to the next city's Zone Seven is . . ." Elodie tossed her hands in the air. "Emptiness."

Aiden sucked in a breath like he wanted to speak but remained silent.

She shivered, suddenly aware how cold her wet pants were.

Aiden finally broke the silence. "Who told you no one can survive in or beyond Zone Seven?"

Elodie shrugged. "School, I guess. But no one actually *had* to tell me. It's a fact." She rolled onto her elbow. Her breath stuck in her throat as she looked down at him. He'd laid down *so close* to her. She cleared her throat and attempted to wiggle away. A jagged slat caught her raincoat and held her in place.

He rolled toward her and propped himself up on his elbow, mirroring Elodie's posture.

She stiffened and again attempted to move away. Her sleeve

made a distinctive ripping noise and she stopped. How was Aiden okay with being so close to her? Maybe he *wanted* to be close to her. She swallowed. Her cheeks were hot again.

His brow furrowed. "No, I get it. We're told that Zone Seven and beyond are monster-filled wastelands, and those notions are reinforced throughout our entire lives." He scratched his chin. "I guess I asked the wrong question."

"What's the *right* question?"

"I'm not sure."

"I have a friend, actually she's my *best friend*, who would say that you sound like one of those kooks who believes there's actually something out there," Elodie motioned toward the distance. "Between the cities."

Aiden sat up and grabbed the skateboard resting near her head. "Well, what does the myth say?" He spun one of the wheels before setting the board back down and rising to his feet.

Elodie's raincoat ripped a little more as she yanked her arm free. The torn piece of her jacket flapped in the breeze. "The one about New Dawn?"

Aiden nodded and stepped onto the board with one foot and pushed off with the other. Each wooden plank clicked under the skateboard as he cruised toward the pavement. "It's rumored to be an oasis outside of Zone Seven," he said, "that was built by some of the founding members of Eos before the Key cemented itself as the all-powerful corporation it is now, right?"

Elodie's insides rattled as Aiden clicked by on his board. "If you believe a rumor Eos started." She tucked her legs up under her and rose to her feet.

"Even if you don't," Aiden dragged his foot behind him before he hopped off the board. "Isn't it a little unbelievable that all the land between the four New American cities is some sort of apoc-alyptic zone? That's thousands of acres just, what . . ." He flipped the skateboard up and caught it with one hand, flashing the hand-painted script at her. "Inexplicably decimated?"

Elodie leaned against the railing. She'd never really thought about it like that. She'd never had the chance. Astrid would have told her she was being crazy, and Rhett . . . Elodie chewed the inside of her cheek. Well, she wouldn't talk about something like this with him. She didn't need to in order to know what he would say.

The Key orders its soldiers to torch Zone Seven, to keep a barrier between Westfall and the monster-infested wasteland that encom-passes the space between cities. Safety Precaution 101, El.

Elodie hugged her arms around her middle as Aiden stared at her expectantly. "I believe the Key." She opened her mouth to say more but decided against it. Something was wonky at the Medi-Center, but that didn't mean the Key was *lying*. Elodie tightened her grip and bit at the raw spot forming on the inside of her cheek.

"Yeah," Aiden brushed his hand along the closely cropped edges of his mohawk. "Totally." He set the board down and pushed it toward Elodie. "Want to try to make it back without any spills?" His cheeks ticked with a smile.

Elodie stepped on the board as it clunked by. "I'm blaming that fall on my teacher." Holding onto the railing, she maneuvered along the pier and toward the pavement. Her heartbeat picked up as she neared the end of the railing, and Aiden. She braced herself, pushed away from her crutch, and pivoted back onto the deck. Aiden whooped as she cruised by, and her heart leapt in response. She tilted her head back and watched the leaves blur past in vert clumps. She was doing it—by herself, and in the real.

XXIII

Blair arranged the five pencils resting against the rim of the gray vase, their finely sharpened tips pointed toward the vents in the ceiling blowing out crisp, sanitized air. Each pencil was labeled with a different phrase: Chance Taker, Trend Setter, Fear Slayer, Rule Maker, Patriarchy Smasher. She'd have to find out where Maxine had found these treasures that so completely summed up Blair.

She had been flattered. So much so that she had almost been speechless upon opening the gift.

Almost.

The severe points of the pencils matched the sleek angles of her pristine office. Six months ago, mere moments after her latest promotion, when her cuff had been updated with ownership access to the office space, Blair had sent in a work order to have every piece of drab, cookie-cutter furniture removed. She wasn't like any of the other MediCenter employees no matter their titles, and she certainly wouldn't work from a cloned office. Plus, her office doubled as a living space since she spent more time here than her Zone One downtown high-rise apartment.

It had taken Blair less than a day to choose her new furnishings, complete with black velvet chairs and a sleek silver chandelier that hung over the center of the room like the blade of a guillotine. One of her former assistants had compared her decor to a fortress—Blair had overheard him talking about it after she'd let him go. He'd stomped around melodramatically, braying about the peaks and points of the black and gray furniture Blair surrounded herself with as a metaphor for her fortress-like personality. But another word for *fortress* was *stronghold*, and Blair was most definitely strong. She'd taken it as a compliment.

The door hissed open. Blair yanked her nub of a fingernail from her mouth and flattened her hands against her lap as Maxine's kitten heels tap-tapped against the sleek tile and quieted when she stepped onto the plush throw rug. "I got your message," her assistant said, "Did you want to stream the mission live or would you like to start from the beginning?" Maxine blinked expectantly at Blair, her brown eyes glistening in the sharp overhead lighting. Unlike Cath, who seemed to soften in the shadows, Blair bristled with the mere thought of being in the dark. She needed her space to be so brightly lit that it was practically on fire.

"The beginning." Blair folded her hands across the smooth top of her uncluttered onyx desk, and expertly kicked off her shoes without moving the top half of her body. "I want to see everything as they saw it. It's ridiculous that you even have to ask me. I should have been here, ready and waiting to stream it live, not in a mind-numbing meeting."

The tip of Maxine's pink nose wiggled with a sniff as her fingers fluttered over her holopad. "I agree."

The Key's red logo seemed to envelop the wall as it unfurled across the expansive holoscreen that hovered opposite Blair's desk.

"Can you believe they had me travel all the way across the river on the MAX for that Eastside marketing meeting," Blair said, "like I'm some kind of cube worker whose thoughts are so small that it takes dozens just like me to come up with one idea good enough to use?" Blair still wasn't sure what had offended her more. The fact that someone with a higher title within the corporation considered her just another face in the crowd of zombie cubicle workers, or the fact that the Key hadn't provided her with a complimentary Pearl ride.

"Someone has to lead the regular people." Maxine sucked in a breath, her lips tightening into an O.

"Tell me." Blair nodded encouragingly, already able to read Maxine. The independent, decisive, and competent assistant was a lovely change of pace. It wasn't until Maxine that Blair had realized how much time she spent fighting or calculating her next battle strategy with her previous assistants. She was never truly at ease, and she never would be as long as her relationship with Maxine was tethered to the MediCenter, but Blair appreciated the possibility that they could maybe one day be friends. For now, there was only one person on the planet who could get Blair to release her guard completely. But she'd been so busy clawing her way up the MediCenter ladder that she hadn't spent quality time with her brother in months and, until Denny fixed his comlink, they also wouldn't be chatting anytime soon.

Maxine settled into the black chair opposite Blair. "Well, you didn't hear it from me, but the marketing pod has been totally uninspired lately. To the point that there have been talks of reassignment within the department." Her arched brows shot toward her hairline. "All the way up the chain."

A soldier clad in Key Corp tactical gear stood frozen in the still image that appeared on the screen behind Maxine. Tree trunks wider than the man himself shot up from the ground on all sides.

Blair crossed and uncrossed her legs. She *was* already late to the videocast . . .

"*And* have you heard who's in the running for the head position?" Maxine continued, excitement driving her delicate eyebrows toward the deep widow's peak of her short blond hair.

Head of marketing wasn't the title Blair had her eye on. But a title was a title. Besides, all of her titles thus far had been like ill-fitting pants, kept on long enough to prove they weren't right, and cast off for a better fit.

Blair silently set her jaw and reclasped her hands while her toes tapped under her desk.

"Well, I've heard who it's *not*." Maxine tucked her holopad under her arm and sniffled. "And it's not you."

If Blair were the violent type, she would have snatched one of those pointed pencils and reached across her desk and given Maxine something to sniffle about. Instead, she cleared her throat and planted her bare feet on the plush rug. "Good. I don't want the position anyway."

Red.

"Of course." Maxine settled against the high back of the velvet chair. "I can't picture you over on the Eastside. You belong at the MediCenter." Her lips again tightened into that gossipy little O. "But I can't say that I wasn't curious as to the reason why anyone would not consider you for a titled position. So I looked into it."

Blair bit down on the inside of her cheeks.

"I don't know if you knew this . . ." Sass tacked itself to Maxine's tone. "But the MediCenter director can't hold any other titles."

Blair squeezed her fingers together so tightly her ragged nailbeds drained of color.

Maxine scooted to the edge of her seat. "You're on the board's list of candidates!"

Copper pooled against the sides of Blair's tongue as she carved slivers in her cheeks. "Of course I am."

She'd expected to be considered by the board. More than that, Blair expected to be the next MediCenter director. But expecting something and it coming to fruition were two different beasts. She'd learned that early on, made adjustments in her thinking, and now had her own office and troop of cube workers looking to her for guidance.

Maxine tucked her hair behind her ears. "You knew?"

Blair's expression was flint. "Yes."

Black.

"Well, I apologize for unnecessarily taking up your time." Maxine shuffled stiffly in her seat and freed her holopad from under her arm. "And I will do everything in my power to assure you're appointed."

"Maxine," Blair said, as the petite blond stood and turned to face the holoscreen. "I do love to know all of the buzz, so if you would . . ." Her pulse increased and her palms grew clammy as the confirmation tunneled through each section of her brain. She ran the tip of her finger across her bottom lip. She'd made it to the final round. She, Blair Iris Scott, was being seriously considered for the head position of the Westfall MediCenter. It had always been possible, and everyone knew she'd sacrificed her life for the opportunity, but this was real. This wasn't in her head or tacked on the vision board she kept in her private virtual meditation chamber. This was actually happening.

Momma and Daddy would be so proud.

Her throat tightened with the thought, and her body heated as she fought back the memories thundering behind her eyes.

"Blair, I will always let you know what I hear. Even if it means you're hearing it twice." Maxine's lips sharpened with a smile.

Blair nodded her thanks.

Maxine understood Blair. Perhaps she was a stronghold too.

"So, just a quick note before I leave you to catch up on current events." Maxine's perfect Key Corp–red nails clacked against her holopad as she flitted to Blair's side. "The production team on the Zone Seven raid video tried to get a statement from Dr. Scott, but she declined to comment."

"Of course she declined to comment. She's the director of Career Services. I'm sure she has nothing to say about Zone Seven raids." They should have come to Blair. With her history, she had more than enough to say. "Unless . . ." Blair's gaze snapped up to Maxine. "She's another one the board is considering, isn't she?"

Blair sounded surprised, although she wasn't in the slightest. Cath *should be* up for consideration.

But Blair should win.

"Yes, but don't worry." Maxine winced. "Not that you are, or anything. I only meant that Dr. Scott won't get very far if she's unable to type up a simple statement about the raid. That's not nearly as difficult as the live speech you had to make the other morning."

Blair's chest puffed slightly. She hadn't stopped criticizing herself for all that she could have done, but she supposed she *had* done better than most.

With a flick of her wrist, Maxine threw Blair's calendar from her holopad onto the holoscreen. "I already contacted the head of the production team. You have an on-camera interview between your meetings tomorrow."

Blair didn't know what to say. Between this and the color-coded and expertly researched file Maxine had given her on Preston Darby, Blair was . . . *pleased?* Whatever the feeling was, it was rather strange.

"Unless you'd rather I call and cancel . . ."

"Absolutely not. This is my chance." Blair wet her lips. "My chance to inform our fine citizens of whatever the corporation deems necessary." She smiled to herself. Truly a Cath-like recovery.

"Maxine, you and everyone else know that Cath and I are *very* close." She paused to add emphasis to the statement as she folded her hands in front of her the same way Cath did when she explained something serious. "And I do appreciate your excitement and ability to seize an opportunity—but she is the closest thing I have to a mother. We mustn't forget that." The corner of Blair's lip itched with a sly grin. "While still working to claim Holbrook's title, of course."

Maxine nodded.

"And get a new card for Holbrook's widow, what's-her-face. I should sign it myself this time." Blair huffed. "While you're at it, go ahead and have my funeral attire dyed black." She'd wanted to standout as much as possible while also appearing respectful, but perhaps she'd have a better edge if people thought she was grieving as much as Cath. The board was clearly comparing them, so she had to try harder to embody everything everyone loved about Cath, while maintaining her own ruthlessness and persistence. It shouldn't be too hard. She'd been pouring herself into different molds for as long as she could remember.

"I'm on it." Maxine tapped out notes as she headed to the

door. "And Holly will play the feeds whenever you're ready. I loaded both the version that we'll show the public as well as the actual footage." She scanned her cuff and the door closed noiselessly behind her.

Blair settled into her plush velvet seat and crisscrossed her legs underneath her. She stretched, brushing the top of her chair with her fingertips. She'd told the designer that she wanted a throne, and he had delivered.

"Holly, play the version that's been approved for citizen viewing." Blair trailed her fingers over the metal-studded armrests as the holoscreen image changed, replaced again by the Key's vibrant red logo.

"To health. To life. To the future. We are the Key." Blair said the words along with the version of her own voice that she'd had programmed into Holly.

"Good afternoon, citizens." Vaughn Kelley stared into the camera. His expertly maintained caterpillar eyebrows twitched with each inflection. Blair often wondered if that had been taught, a sort of signature he'd perfected over the years of being Westfall's go-to news anchor, or if it was natural, if his brows and his vocal cords had been stitched together since birth. "We have reporters on the ground in Zone Seven to bring you live, up-to-date information on the current raids and how they are impacting the safety of our community." Vaughn flicked his attention between the cameras as the studio bots changed angles. His tailored blue blazer matched the intense aqua of his eyes and stood out in stark contrast against the white backdrop beaming behind him.

Live, up-to-date information . . .

Blair didn't stifle her eye roll.

One of the many false truths the Key fed to its citizens. Black lies of necessity. Protection and safety and helpfulness wrapped into an easily digested nugget of censor-enriched truth. That may sound confusing to some, only because some people had too much faith in what citizens would do if given the whole truth and nothing but the truth. And Blair, more than anyone, understood how facts created monsters.

Only real emergencies or causes for celebration were reported in real time. This video may not go out for days. And, up until the Eos attacks, there had never been a *real* emergency in Westfall. *Real* emergencies had occurred overseas and in other New American cities where Eos cells had been active for years, but Westfall had seemed immune. Apparently, no city was safe from Eos.

Vaughn's eyebrows twitched as he snapped his gaze to another camera. "Now, over to Chad Sandhar, reporting live from Zone Seven."

Flames seemed to engulf the wall of Blair's office as the view switched from Vaughn's sterile newsroom to the fires blazing throughout Westfall's outermost zone.

The corner of Blair's mouth curled with a grin.

The camera steadied and zoomed in on a row of Key Corp soldiers, their black, flame-retardant uniforms rising from the charred and barren field like so many more lifeless husks. The black earth and withered trees told the story of the Key's previous voyages to the wooded forbidden zone. Soldiers would be deployed to Zone Seven and beyond again and again until the fingers of the Key stretched black and charred throughout the land. And, if—No, *when* Blair was appointed director, the land surrounding Westfall would be the first thing up in flames.

The camera swung around to Chad Sandhar, reporting on scene, decked out in red gear. The thin paper face mask loosely hanging from his ears was streaked gray with soot, and tears carved clean tracks down his smudged cheeks. "What we're seeing now, Vaughn, are our very own brave and dependable Key Corp soldiers torching the Zone Seven area behind me so no bacteria, viruses, or germs can develop and mutate or hop species, like the bird and swine flus that plagued our ancestors and led to the mutated Cerberus strain." Chad waved the camera away as a bout of dry, hacking coughs overtook him.

The camera panned to the right and slowly zoomed in on flames licking nearby treetops.

"Vaughn," Chad continued, a hoarseness clawing at his voice. "I'm out here in flame retardant gear issued by the corporation and specially made to withstand these conditions. And, I have to say, I am having a hard time maintaining my cool." The view widened to again encompass the reporter as he brushed a gloved hand down the red Key Corp zip-up suit. "These soldiers, *our* soldiers, are out here protecting our community while wearing at least fifty pounds more than I am. I do not know how they're able to handle it. It's—" Another cough. "It's mighty impressive. If you see one of these amazing people in the street, give them a big thank you. It's the least we can do for what they're doing to protect us."

A crack splintered the smoke-filled air.

"Look out! Look out!" a soldier shouted over the flames as he ran up to the reporter.

The camera jerked as the soldier herded Chad and the cameraman to the safety.

The view went blurry for a moment before the camera stabilized and refocused on the flame-filled field behind them. The charred carcass of a two-story tall tree slammed to the ground, spraying fiery black bark into the air.

"I didn't see—man, that—close." Chad's voice cut in and out as he adjusted his microphone. "Thank you."

The camera expertly swooped back to the reporter as he regained his composure and turned his attention to the helmeted soldier. "What's your name, soldier?"

"Major Owens." He holstered his flame thrower and adjusted the straps of the large square pack hooked over his shoulders. "Rhett Owens," the soldier said, looking past Chad at the line of flames behind them. The once brilliant red stripes streaking the arm of Owens's uniform were now the same stale, muted red of dried blood.

Chad motioned to the faceless man. "Major, we'd be on our way to the MediCenter if it wasn't for your quick action."

"It's my duty." The helmet bobbed with a nod. "And I'm proud to serve Westfall and the Key." Sweat streaked through the soot plastering his neck.

"Can you tell me what these duties mean to our community? Our citizens would love to hear firsthand." Chad dragged a gloved hand across his own forehead before adjusting his facemask.

Rhett removed his helmet and secured it under his arm. "Leaving this zone and the lands beyond to grow wild would only result in another outbreak. We have all heard the term *concrete jungle*. Cerberus nearly eviscerated our species because of the wildness of the concrete jungle in cities like Westfall. This"—he lifted a gloved hand toward the ferocious flames burning brilliant orange and yellow and red behind him—"would be a true jungle where Cerberus and who knows what else would thrive and mutate. We are lucky enough to have great minds within the Key Corporation, who have recognized this threat and who send teams like mine all over the globe to ensure these wilds—concrete or nature made—will never get so far out of control that they again threaten us." Rhett's golden amber eyes bored into the camera. "We truly do have the Key to thank for our continued survival."

Blair's lips twisted into a satisfied smirk. "Well, well, Major Owens. Perhaps we should chat." An assistant, even one as skilled as Maxine, could only help a woman like Blair reach a certain level of power. There were some things—so few Blair could count them on one hand—only a male protégé could provide. Like a spider, Blair had left many dried-up, shriveled husks of men in a trail behind her.

The "live" footage ended, seamlessly transitioning back to Vaughn in his light-drenched studio. "I don't know about you," the anchor said, "but I for one am supremely grateful for the Key and soldiers like Major Rhett Owens who risk their lives to keep us safe." The camera angle changed, and Vaughn shifted his attention without missing a beat. "And our gracious Key Corp is hosting the annual Rose Festival at Waterfront Park this weekend. We'll report live and cannot wait to see you there, where we all will show our gratitude."

The image froze on Vaughn and his overly active eyebrows.

Blair tented her fingers and swiveled her chair away from her desk to look out her windows. Soon, she would own this city. She'd earned it, and, more importantly, she'd burn anyone who got in her way.

XXIV

If Elodie hadn't read ahead in her nursing textbook (the real pages, not the pages of Vi hidden inside), and learned all about coronary events, she'd have thought that she was about to keel over from a massive heart attack. The muscle inside of her chest had never beat as hard as it beat now. She sucked air through her nose and released her breath through pursed lips.

Why was she so amped? It wasn't like Aiden would be waiting for her when the elevator opened to the Long-Term Care Unit. They weren't meeting in VR until after work. Her heart seemed to skip a beat. Elodie couldn't wait. She was more excited than she had been the first time she'd toured the MediCenter, and she hadn't thought anything could top that.

Since their skateboarding friend get-together, she and Aiden had communicated through handwritten notes attached to delivery bots. It was sweet and cute and mysterious and left her feeling like she was breaking the rules. In short, their new friendship was already frickin' amazing.

The elevator reached the LTCU and Elodie nearly bounded over to Gus and the control panel.

"What's got you so chipper this morning?" Dandruff swirled off Gus's shoulders as he pulled on his rain jacket in his usual speedy effort to leave the moment she arrived.

Elodie dropped her backpack onto the floor and practically wiggled in place in an attempt to tamp down her excitement. "Just happy to be alive, I guess."

Gus groaned heavy and deep. "That makes one of us." He flipped up the collar of his jacket as he shuffled toward the elevator. "Everything's been the same. Checked off all my duties." He scanned his cuff and the metal doors opened immediately. "Oh, you got another one of those paper notes." He motioned toward the folded slip resting on the corner of the control panel. "You do know what all this tech is for, right?"

Elodie plucked the note off the glass top and didn't bother to answer Gus as the elevator closed and whisked him away to be a dark cloud over someone else. No matter how much he tried, Gus couldn't ruin her mood. Nothing could make—

Something came up. Not going to be able to make it to the VR meeting. ☹

—MM

Aiden had done it again, canceled on her just before they were supposed to get together.

Elodie dropped into her chair.

It was weird that she and Aiden had sent so many notes but hadn't actually seen each other since the Waterfront. Elodie saw each of her other friends nearly every day. Sure, that list really only included Rhett, who had been chosen for her, and Astrid, who she'd known since grade school—but still, either through vidlink or VR, they were never out of contact for more than half a day.

After she and Aiden had their in-person meetup, Elodie had suggested a VR date—a simple friend get together. Where didn't matter. She just wanted to see him again. In a totally innocent, building-a-friendship sort of way. But Aiden had no-showed each scheduled meetup, leaving Elodie and Astrid (eager to meet the note-writing oddball) to wonder whether or not he was truly as nice as he seemed.

Every morning at work, Elodie would arrive to a disgruntled Gus, and a sealed note with a perfectly reasonable explanation as to why Aiden wouldn't show up. If they'd first met in VR instead of in person, Elodie would have thought that he'd hacked his avatar and altered his appearance, which would explain why he didn't want to meet in the real. But they'd met in person first, and there's no way Aiden could have faked those long lashes, emerald eyes, or sculpted arms.

She shook her head.

Why was she thinking about how great his arms looked under his slightly too tight T-shirt? She was engaged. Although, as Astrid had told her many times, engaged wasn't married. And she was pretty sure that her rule-abiding friend was referring to the way Elodie's mother talked about Rhett as Elodie's husband, since the second they'd been matched. Plus, Astrid had no room to comment on the subject. The only reason the Key hadn't matched her was because of what the Fujimotos could produce for the corporation, which didn't yet include Astrid or her sister Thea settling down to add to the world's population.

But none of that was the point.

The point was that if anyone should have wanted to flee after their utterly embarrassing real-life meetups, it would have been her, not him. She'd been the one to run into a closed door, and to fall on her butt the second she stepped on a skateboard. So what the hell was his problem?

She surged to her feet and stomped toward the elevator. Her hands snapped to her hips and her foot tapped as the metal box took its sweet time.

Had she done something to make Aiden want to only speak to her through written messages? She shook away the thought as she entered the elevator and headed down to the End-of-Life Unit. The notion that any of this could be her fault was ridiculous. The only thing Elodie was guilty of was meeting his level of enthusiasm and friendliness.

The elevator opened, exhaling a cloud of annoyed anticipation along with Elodie.

This was a much better line of thought than swooning over the way the rain had shimmered against his dark umber skin.

With the memory, her hands slipped from her hips.

"Stop it, Elodie!" she scolded herself aloud, and glued her fists back on her sides as she wound through the brightly lit bowels of the MediCenter.

The End-of-Life Unit's glossy metal doors loomed ahead.

Holly blinked to life in front of the Violet Shield that covered the doors. "Hello, and welcome to the End-of-Life Unit. Only authorized citizens and MediCenter employees are allowed entry. Please scan your cuff." With a sweep of her holographic arm, she motioned to the scanner next to the door.

"Oh, no, I don't have authorization." Elodie tucked her wavy hair behind her ears. "I'm just here to see someone. An employee, not a—you know." Elodie swallowed as Holly's unseeing eyes blinked down at her. "A dead person."

"I'm sorry. You'll have to contact the Unit Lead to gain authorization." Holly's still smile never reached the pointed corners of her brown eyes.

"Actually, is there any way that you—"

The Violet Shield flashed and Holly vanished as the metal doors slid open. Aiden rushed out, his tennis shoes squeaking against the floor as he halted in front of her.

"What a crazy coincidence!" Elodie nearly shouted as the doors closed behind him. She needed to get a handle on her excitement. There was a reason she was here. "I didn't realize until after I'd come all the way down that I'm not actually authorized to enter. Who knew it would be so hard to get into the morgue? It's just full of dead people." Her laughter clanked in the space between them. "I mean, like, somewhere in my brain I knew that I couldn't just walk in, but that was buried pretty deep under a lot of other useless info. Not useless for everyone. You obviously need to know who can and cannot enter your unit." Another bout of strained laughter. "But, yeah. It's a good thing that you came out."

Aiden's usual pine scent barely pierced the bleach tang in the hall. A thin line creased his sweat-dotted forehead as he stared blankly at her.

"So, ta-da." She could have crawled away and died of embarrassment.

Aiden shoved his fists into the shallow pockets of his pants. "What are you doing here?"

Her heart quavered beneath her ribs. "Thought I'd visit. Figure out face-to-face why it's so difficult to meet up." She rubbed the collar of her shirt between her thumb and forefinger. "Plus, you said

I should come down sometime. We work the same shift. I mean, it's not like it was a special trip or anything." But it had been a special trip. With the passage of every floor, she'd nearly told Holly to stop the elevator and take her back up to her unit. This was Elodie's foray into spontaneity, and Aiden was sucking all the air out of it.

"Who's watching your unit? Is Gus or someone up there?" Aiden shifted, peering at the empty stretch of hallway behind her. "Don't you think you should get back to your patients?"

Anxiety gnawed at Elodie's back as Aiden glanced down the hall to either side, then continued to crane his neck to look behind her to where the corridor turned.

"Is everything okay?" she asked. "Did I do something to make you all weird? Well, weirder than normal, anyway." Another awkward chuckle tripped past her lips.

"Yes. I mean, no." Again, he studied the space behind her. "You didn't do anything. Everything is fine."

She whirled, seeing nothing but the empty hallway. "What are you looking at?"

"Nothing." He swiped at the sweat beading against his forehead. "Thanks for coming down. You should go back to your unit. I'll, uh, I'll meet up with you later."

"No, you won't." Elodie pulled her shoulders back and jutted her chin into the air. "That's the whole reason I'm down here. You keep saying that we'll get together in VR and then you don't show, and I'm left all confused and annoyed. It's stupid and I don't like it."

A droplet of sweat slid down Aiden's brow. "Seriously, Elodie. You should leave. What if something happens in your unit?"

She clenched and unclenched her fists. "Nothing is going to happen."

"Aubrey's dead," he spat.

His words smacked into her, and she took a step back. In one of her notes to Aiden, she'd told him why she'd been in the basement the day they'd met, and how she knew without a doubt that the file on the little girl, Patient Ninety-Two, hadn't simply been misplaced. But she hadn't thought, hadn't considered, that Aubrey Masters was dead.

He unhitched his gaze from the empty hall and it fell to the floor. "I could have said that a million different ways." His shoulders drooped. "That was shitty of me."

Elodie's fingers were numb. "How did she . . ." The final word wouldn't leave her lips. She squeezed her eyes shut against the memory of Aubrey's small, scared cries.

Had the girl been alone when it happened? Had she been crying for her mother?

"I'm not even supposed to know that much." He remained slumped, only lifting his green eyes to meet hers. "What I do know is that your patients need you. You should be in the LTCU."

"And you should stop trying to tell me what to do." Her eyelids snapped open as she threw the words at him. "Someone in there knows what happened—" Elodie's voice cracked and she sucked in a breath to keep from breaking. "Ask them. Find out!"

"Elodie—"

A boom thundered through the corridor. Elodie snapped her attention to the empty hallway behind her. Something crashed, unseen around the sharp turns. The MediCenter was filled with safeguards, and all employees took precautions, but lab accidents sometimes still occurred. Alarms sounded, and a crew would arrive within minutes for cleanup and to treat anyone injured in the blast.

But who'd be working with anything that volatile in the morgue?

Elodie stood in a sea of pure white, but the sterile lights

and bleach-scented hallway couldn't protect her from what was coming, couldn't save her from the boots slapping against tile just around the corner.

Her limbs frosted, and each blink, each breath came in slow, underwater motion. Maintenance couldn't be here this fast, and those did not sound like the shoes of a doctor echoing through the sterile chamber.

Closer. Closer.

Elodie remained fixed in the pregnant, panicked moment until Aiden's quick movements caught her attention—she'd forgotten he was next to her.

"Eos," she said, and the word rode on haggard gulps.

Aiden released his inhale, calm and slow. "I know."

"We can make it back into your unit." Elodie's whisper came out a quivering, rushed jumble. "Holly!" she hissed. "Open the door."

Holly appeared, cheerful and vibrant. "Hello and welcome to the End-of-Life Unit." Her jovial voice loud and grating against Elodie's need for sanctuary. "Only authorized citizens and Medi-Center employees are allowed entry. Please scan your cuff."

"Aiden, we need to get in!" Elodie's throat burned as sobs threatened to break free.

"Holly, leave!" Aiden said, and Holly's pleasant grin remained fixed as she nodded and blinked from sight. Elodie's stomach hollowed, and her heart knocked against her ribs. "What are you doing?" The question was a screech of fear. "It's Eos. They'll—" Elodie struggled to pry the words from her throat. "They'll kill us."

"You should be more worried about the Key." Aiden produced a clear plastic die from his pocket and rolled it on the floor beneath the scanner.

Elodie's inhale stuck in her chest as she stared down at the die. "Will that help us?"

Footsteps hammered closer . . .

"Trust me, Elodie." Aiden's throat bobbed with a thick swallow. "Let's go!" He darted down the side hall and disappeared around a corner.

Nerves exploded in Elodie's legs and she sprinted to Aiden's side, away from those echoing bootsteps, and pressed her back against the wall.

He'd asked her to trust him.

Boots thundered closer . . . closer.

She didn't have a choice.

A woman's voice called out, clipped and strong. "I can only divert Key attention for another five minutes."

Eos had arrived, just around the corner, at the ELU door. Tears scraped Elodie's eyes as she pressed herself against the wall in hopes that it would swallow her whole. These five minutes would be her last. "We're going to die down here. They'll set off a germ stack or—" A whispered sob escaped. "They'll shoot us. We'll end up in boxes in your unit."

"None of that is going to happen." Aiden peered around the corner before jerking back. "Eos won't hurt us."

Elodie shook her head back and forth against the painted white wall. "We're not going to survive." Her teeth clacked as fear pulled the glacial cold of the concrete wall through her uniform into her quaking bones. "*No one* survives."

Aiden pressed his palms against the wall, framing her head. Warmth rolled off him, and his breath caressed her lashes. He was too close. But every part of her clamored to draw him closer, fit him against her as a shield.

"I promise, Elodie." His moss-green gaze clung to hers. "Nothing is going to happen."

Her heartbeat quickened, and her palms glued themselves to the wall. "Aiden—" A breathy sob spilled from her lips.

"You're braver." His elbows bent, drawing him closer, wringing the air from the space between them. "Stronger than you think."

She sipped shallow breaths. The moment numbed her frigid, trembling limbs.

The telltale hiss of the ELU doors opening awakened Elodie from the blissful few seconds of confidence Aiden had gifted.

"In and out, gentlemen," the woman hollered. "You two, scan the halls."

The boots began again.

Closer. Closer.

Elodie hardened. "They're killers, Aiden. They're Eos."

Aiden stiffened as the soldiers rounded the corner. His hands slid down the wall as he pushed himself away from her and stepped in front of the Eos soldiers, their helmets the same golden orange as the rising sun.

"She's with me." Aiden fisted his hand, rested it over his heart, and bowed sharply.

The masked soldiers nodded and bowed, fist over heart. "After the storm comes the dawn," they chanted in unison, before turning and marching back to the ELU entrance.

Elodie clapped her hands over her mouth. The shriek seared her palms.

XXV

Elodie stumbled backward. Her hands smacked against the concrete wall as she used it to keep herself from falling.

Aiden was one of them. A member of Eos. Her friend. Her confidant. *Her* Aiden.

No!

The word screeched between her ears. It tore her to shreds. She could feel it—pain pooling in her gut. She clutched her stomach and tried to run, but her body betrayed her. It always did when she was with him. It told her she should trust him, care for him, *like him.*

Hot tears distorted her vision. She pinched her eyes shut and swiped at her face.

Her body had deceived her. And Aiden had deceived her too.

"Elodie." Aiden stood there. In front of her. He'd gotten so close to her so quickly. "I can explain," he said, though his words were slow and hushed, drowning under the thoughts that tore through her.

You are matched. You have friends. A career. This is what you get

for not being satisfied. For being greedy. Needing more, more, more.
You deserve this mess. You deserve this!

"*Stop!*" Elodie screamed at Aiden, at herself, at the world for allowing this to happen.

She backed away on wobbly legs, ricocheting against the wall as she tried to replace the image of the Aiden she cared for with the picture that had come to life in front of her. "Stay away from me!" The wall was her crutch, and she slid along it, using the cold concrete to carry her away from Aiden and Eos and any other monsters he had yet to reveal.

But the wall opened up behind her back and Elodie fell into a room filled with dizzying lights and beeps and whirrs.

Aiden's footsteps followed her and he was next to her in seconds. He reached back and scanned his cuff under a sensor and the door hissed shut behind him.

He'd gotten lucky. She'd corralled herself. And now she was trapped. Alone with—

She scrambled backward until concrete slammed against her shoulders. "Who are you?"

Aiden's breath caught. His chin trembled slightly. "It's still me. I haven't changed."

"You're one of *them!*"

A stumpy yellow bot zoomed between them, its crate filled with empty tubes. They were in the room that had started it all. Where she'd dashed off to when she'd felt brave and determined. Had that really only been a few days before? Now she was plastered against the wall, sweat slicked and reeling, her life as she knew it coming to an end.

Elodie forced her legs under her and hefted herself to her feet. "There are cameras, Aiden. People will know that I came down here."

As he stood, he cast a glance at the white orb hanging from the ceiling. "We have it handled." He thrust his chin toward the camera. "And Eos would never hurt you. *I* would never hurt you."

"Then take it back!" She was crying again. Waterfalls cascaded down her cheeks. She could flood this room. "Tell me you were lying!"

"I won't lie to you!" He clutched his shirt, over his heart. The fabric stretched under his grasp. He'd kept Eos in his heart, locked just under his fist. Is that where he kept her too?

"This whole time has been a lie." She pressed herself away from the wall. "You're a lie."

Now we're as healthy as the lies you told.

"That's not fair," he said.

Elodie would have laughed if her breath wasn't strangled in her throat.

Aiden inched toward her, palms up, and out. Despair painted pools in his eyes and knotted itself between his brows. "I was trying to keep you safe. *Us* safe."

And he had. Hadn't he?

She tightened her hands into fists and locked her body back under her control. "I should have known better." She eyed the closed door behind him. "You aren't interesting and fun. You're dangerous and deceitful."

Aiden set his jaw and stepped away from the door. "Get back upstairs before Key Corp soldiers head this way. You're safe with Eos, Elodie. Safe with me." His lips parted slightly and he whispered, "But I understand if you can't believe that."

Elodie's heart ached. "They're killers, Aiden."

He shook his head. "Promise me you'll take a real look at what happened here."

Elodie opened her mouth to speak, but her mind, her body, her heart, all yearned for different things. She couldn't make any promises. Not even to herself.

Aiden passed his cuff under the scanner.

The door slid open and Elodie raced out into the hall. The terrorists didn't give her a second look.

XXVI

Elodie had taken the stairs two at a time back up to her unit and arrived at her nurse's station just as the MediCenter's Emergency Violet Shield clicked on. Holly materialized in front of the elevator, hands folded against her pristine skirt now painted a light lavender as the Shield shone through her holographic form.

Goosebumps flashed across Elodie's neck and her heartbeat quickened.

"Hello, Elodie. Please gather your things and exit the building as quickly as possible. This is not a drill." As Holly spoke, the elevator doors opened behind her.

Elodie balled her trembling fists and attempted to calm her breathing. "What's going on?"

"The Key has received a threat from a known terrorist organization and Key Corp soldiers are currently addressing the matter." Holly tilted her head and smiled. "Please, do not be alarmed. The Key will keep you safe." With that smile, she could make almost anyone believe almost anything. "Please take the elevator to the lobby and exit the building."

Elodie slung her backpack over her shoulder and clutched her textbook against her chest. "My patients . . ."

Holly nodded and motioned toward the elevator. "Thank you for your concern, Elodie. The Corporation will look after your patients. The Key will keep all its citizens safe."

Normally Elodie would have argued, demanded to speak with whoever was in charge of looking after her patients in her absence, but right now nothing was normal. Elodie rushed past the purple-stained hologram and into the open elevator.

Holly turned as the doors began to close. "Don't forget to activate your Personal Protection Pod," she said, her perfect smile firmly in place. "And, remember, no touching today for a healthy tomorrow."

Encased in her own purple orb, Elodie wove through the surge of MediCenter employees all pretending to be calm as they made their exit. She couldn't be in the building another second. Her legs itched to break into a sprint and carry her to the MAX stop as quickly as possible. She needed to be home, buried under her blankets until this day was over and the rising sun reset her world.

Elodie pulled on her beanie and kept her chin tucked against her chest as the train lumbered up to the curb. The pristine floor of the MAX glinted through the purple haze that coated the inside of the car. Elodie perched on the edge of the seat against the back wall of the MAX. Her clammy palms seemed to stick to the slick cover of her textbook as she rested it against her lap. By now, everyone knew about Eos's MediCenter invasion. *Everyone.*

She flicked her gaze around the car and its Violet Shield encased occupants. Silence blanketed the MAX. The same thick silence that had invaded days earlier. But what happened at the MediCenter wasn't the same as what occurred at Tilikum Crossing. There was no violence. No people laying with Xs across their chests. This was different. Didn't they see that?

The MAX lurched forward, beginning its journey into Zone Two. Soon, Elodie would be home. She chewed the inside of her cheek. Was Aiden headed home too? Had he done what she had and left the MediCenter as if nothing had happened?

It's still me. I haven't changed.

Heat pricked Elodie's eyes and she pressed her lids closed. She couldn't think about him. She *shouldn't*. Tears forced back, she cracked open her textbook to the dog-eared page. She needed a distraction.

"Meet Tanner Kerns," Zane's boot-clad foot clanked against the marble tile as he gave his best squinty-eyed, pensive Marlboro Man impression. With his squared jaw, broad shoulders, and the featherlight creases around his eyes, he wasn't far off.

"Tanner Kerns?" Vi folded the Arts section of the *New York Times* and tossed it onto the velvet couch cushion next to her. "How does the Office come up with these names?"

Zane shrugged and his cowboy boots creaked as his weight shifted.

Vi ran her fingertips across her lips. "Those pants are ... tight."

Zane turned and wiggled his butt before completing his spin. "Nice, right? All that gym time paid off. Tanner has the firmest ass."

Vi reached out and grabbed Zane's hand. "And, right now, it's all mine." She yanked him down onto the couch. A wave of sandalwood and whiskey brushed against her as he cupped her cheeks and rested his forehead against hers. Goosebumps crested across her skin as she and Zane sat in a moment of sweet contentedness.

"Have I told you today how much I love you?" Zane's lips grazed hers as he spoke.

Vi closed her eyes and brushed her nose against his. "How much?"

Heat met Violet's lips as Zane pressed his mouth against hers. She relaxed against him as his tongue swept between her lips and explored her own. Vi didn't need his words. This was answer enough.

Too soon, the kiss was over. Zane caressed her shoulder as his hand slipped from her cheek. Having him close felt so good, so safe, so comforting. For as long as Vi could remember, she'd been looking out for herself. It wasn't until Zane that she'd learned what it meant to be taken care of, and she would never let the feeling go.

"We might have a problem, Zane," Vi said. A soft smile creased her cheeks as she twined her fingers with his. "I might be in love with Tanner Kerns."

The train car shook as it put on its brakes and approached its next stop, forcing Elodie's attention from the butterflies that Vi's romantic life had loosed in her stomach. Back when *Death by Violet* had been written, people spent so much time *touching each other*. Now, it was so wrong—*illegal*. Elodie smoothed her hand over her own goosebumps. But the thought made her breath hitch and her heart race, and not out of fear.

A bright beacon of sunlight had broken through the MAX's windows and shone directly through her protective orb and onto Elodie's textbook. She snapped the book closed. The light frayed her nerves and forced her to hide under her itchy beanie. She pulled it down past her brows to lock in the bomb of a secret ticking behind her eyes as the MAX's Helper Holly continued to make a sport of giving "up-to-date" and "real time" alerts of "Eos's attack on the MediCenter."

Promise me you'll take a real look at what happened here.

Had it been an *attack*? She'd seen no one harmed. As she raced back to her own unit, she'd seen that Eos had literally sealed employees in their offices and labs. If, as the Key continued to purport, Eos's sole purpose was destruction and the perversion of the safe and right way of life, they'd definitely missed their mark. More than that, Eos, the terrorist organization that always left behind bodies, had gone above and beyond to ensure no one was injured. Even the explosion they'd used as an entry point had been in an empty storage closet.

As she clicked off her Violet Shield and trudged up the steps to her front door, Elodie's hair stuck out from under the black fabric in sweaty clumps against her forehead. Her backpack thumped against her rounded spine as her shoulders sagged and she curled in on herself.

You're safe with Eos, Elodie. Safe with me.

The front door opened noiselessly. Elodie filled her chest and waited for the click of her mother's heels.

Nothing.

She closed the door behind her and let loose a relieved exhale as she freed herself from the sweltering cap.

Sharp clicks splintered her reprieve.

"Oh, Elodie, my darling, darling girl!" Gwen's high-pitched hysterics reached Elodie before her mother's pointed stilettos carried her into the foyer.

Elodie let her backpack slide down her arms and crash onto the porcelain. "Mom, I can't right now."

With a tissue, Gwen dabbed her own rouged cheeks. "I've been beside myself with worry. Simply *beside* myself." She pressed the folded corner against her dry lashes. "Thank goodness Rhett was here."

Of course he was.

"Everything's fine, Mom." Elodie's attempt at cheerfulness fell flat. She couldn't muster a fake smile. She barely had the energy to move forward.

Gwen wrung her hands, her bottom lip in a pout. "I was so nervous, Elodie." She lowered her voice dramatically. "*Eos was at your workplace.*"

"You don't have to whisper. They can't hear you." Elodie slogged past her mother, pausing before she reached the living room's plush sectional, spotless glass tables and clear view to the kitchen. To Rhett.

"How can you be so glib at a time like this?" Gwen's claws pinched her hips. "My only daughter was in mortal peril, and I couldn't reach your father." Her hands flew to the pearls draped around her neck. "You know how my nerves can get the best of me."

Through the doorway, Elodie watched Rhett's white hair, white shirt, and white skin ghost through the white kitchen on his way to the fridge. He disappeared for a moment behind the door before reemerging, thick hands full of snacks.

"Thank goodness Rhett was here," Gwen repeated. As if Rhett needed anymore propping up.

Elodie dragged the damp beanie down her face, wiping away the residue of her real emotions and replacing them with a tight, forced smile. "Rhett, thank you so much for coming over," she began as she mustered the strength to stride through the living room and meet him at the kitchen island. Gwen's heels clacked behind her like a stalking reaper. "But you definitely don't need to stay. I'm sure they're desperate for your help back at the MediCenter."

Rhett stuffed a handful of baby carrots into his mouth. "Gosh, El," he managed around the orange chunks. "I'm surprised you're doing so well."

Gwen rounded the island to stand next to Rhett. "But you do look dreadful," she told her daughter, "which is to be expected after the absolute fright you've endured." She plucked a carrot from the bag and rolled it between her fingers. "But it is odd that you're so—" She waved the carrot around. Her inflated lips pressed into a straight line. "Well, we know how *sensitive* you are."

Why did they keep saying *sensitive* like it was something to be ashamed of? Empathy was never a bad thing.

Gwen pressed the tip of the carrot against her lips, thought better of it, and set it back down on the counter. "But this time you have every right to be. The attack was right in your building. Merely floors beneath yours."

Elodie stiffened. "It wasn't an attack," she countered.

Rhett popped another carrot into his mouth. "Everything from Eos is an attack. An act of terror. That's what they do. It's their whole purpose."

Elodie's fingertips dug into the thick beanie limply hanging from her balled fist. "Then why aren't you at the MediCenter? Isn't dealing with Eos your whole purpose?"

Rhett stopped chomping. He and Gwen blinked at her, slack jawed.

Rhett pushed his plate away from the edge of the counter and brushed off his hands. "I was wrong. This has you shaken up more than I expected."

"I, for one, *did* expect this." Gwen wagged her finger in the air. "We watched the attack live. There were soldiers crawling all over the MediCenter. Rhett was expertly fielding calls, managing his subordinates from afar. The attack—"

"It wasn't an attack!" This time Elodie spat the words. She was tense and ready, armor coated.

Gwen slowly rounded the island. "You are in denial. You've been traumatized and your mind has blurred the entire event so you don't . . ." she waved her hands in the air like she was batting flies, "end up with a terrible mental disorder. You're not seeing this clearly." Her stilettos whispered against the marble as she cautiously approached her daughter. "You *can't* be. I know you are no sympathizer."

Rhett huffed. "Of course she's not," he said, each word punctuated by a crunch as he resumed eating. "She's confused. The whole mess has her rattled."

Elodie *was* confused. *Very* confused. But she knew one thing for sure—what she'd witnessed was not an attack. "Maybe neither of you know me well enough to know what I am."

Add that to the list of what she knew to be true.

"El—" Rhett began.

"No! I don't want to hear it." Elodie's heartbeat clapped inside her ears.

Gwen stiffened and opened her mouth to speak.

"From either of you." Elodie spun around and marched toward the stairs.

Gwen clicked frantically after her. "Elodie!"

Elodie stopped short of the top of the stairs and steeled herself before she faced her mother.

Gwen's eyes glistened with tears. Real tears this time. "I worry about you so much. I want to be sure you're safe. The Key is safety—the *right path*. Please don't disappoint me and turn down the wrong one. Think first, my darling. Think."

"Disappoint you?" Her mother's display of honest emotion would have been sweet, touching even, but Elodie saw the snake coiling just beneath the surface. "How? By having my own opinion?"

"Dammit, Elodie!" Gwen snarled and struck the bannister. "When your father and I made the decision to bring you into this world, the lead in the Gestation Unit asked if there were any traits we wanted enhanced or stunted. I told him to let nature run its course." Gwen climbed two steps at once, her long legs flicking out like a praying mantis. "Of all the things you've done, and you've done plenty, becoming a sympathizer is the one thing that will make me regret turning those natal programmers down!"

Her mother's words hung in the air, stifling Elodie's breath and eating away at her flesh.

Rhett leaned into the stairwell, still chomping away.

Elodie's soul retreated, curling into the depths of her heart. "I need to go change." Her legs were putty as they carried her up the final few stairs.

"I didn't want to say any of that, but someone had to tell her the truth," Gwen loudly whispered to Rhett. "You're naïve, Elodie," she said, descending the stairs, "but I love you. I'm trying to protect you." Her mother's voice echoed within her, far away and paralyzingly close at the same time. "I had to tell her, Rhett. I had to." Gwen's heels clicked on the marble as she slipped past Rhett and made a noble retreat to the kitchen.

At the bottom of the stairs, Rhett cleared his throat and flicked an orange chunk from his pristine white tee. "We can, uh, go someplace when you're ready, El. No rush."

Elodie's chest heaved a dry sob as she reached the second floor. She forced herself to walk in slow, even paces to her room. Tears breached her vision as she closed the door behind her and ran to the window. She threw it open and inhaled the sun-warmed evening. The branches of the pink magnolia tree reached out to her, its verdant leaves whispering with each gust of crisp air.

She couldn't go back downstairs. She wouldn't. But it would only be a matter of time before Gwen's impatient footsteps brought her to Elodie's door. Her mother wouldn't let those words stain her home. She'd wring her hands and click her stilettos and pout those lips until the need to cleanse the space overtook her desire to ignore the distressing blemish. Elodie had seen it over and over again between her mother and her father until the only things that proved he lived there were his clothes and the faint scent of cedar that haunted the hall outside of her parent's room.

Daniel Benavidez was in a constant state of leaving. Elodie understood the impulse all too well.

Rhett's laughter wafted into Elodie's room in muffled bursts. Her stomach soured, and she caught another refreshing breath of fresh air. Her fiancé had stood there, watching as her mother chipped away at her. Then he'd offered to take her someplace after she changed. And where was he now?

Elodie's eyes burned.

He was supposed to love her.

They were supposed to love her.

But this didn't feel like love.

The narrow peaks of distant pine trees pierced the sun as it drained golden orange into the horizon.

Someone had to tell her the truth.

The truth was a funny thing. Like a pond during winter. Safe, stable. Until it wasn't. And the ground tumbled away, dropping you into an existence so cold the maw of death could look like a refuge.

Elodie wouldn't wait around for anymore of Gwen's truths. She had her own to determine. And from now on, Elodie would make sure her feet were always on solid ground.

Quickly, Elodie stripped out of her scrubs and pulled on her favorite pair of black leggings and a cotton tee before stuffing her feet into her tennis shoes. She shoved aside the row of rocks she'd collected on the banks of the Columbia and climbed onto the windowsill. She studied the tree's broad limbs, her cheeks puffing as she inhaled a large, contemplative breath and let it out slowly.

Violet Jasmin Royale would do it. Vi would leap out, spring-loaded, shimmy down the big magnolia, and be gone, vanish, never to be heard from again.

Elodie flexed her fingers and reached out. She grabbed the fat tree limb and pushed off the windowsill. Air squished out of her torso in a wheeze as her stomach hit the massive branch.

Not quite spring-loaded, but a leap toward freedom, however temporary.

Elodie swung her leg over and straddled the branch before shimmying backward down its sharp pitch toward the trunk. She winced as the rough bark clawed through her leggings.

She should have climbed more trees when she was younger. She should have climbed *any* trees when she was younger.

The trunk met her back, and she peered over the branch she straddled. When she'd looked up toward her window from the ground, the first of the tree's many branches had never looked *this* high. But now, sitting on top of it, she was pretty sure she was fifty feet in the air.

You're naïve, Elodie, and I'm trying to protect you.

She huffed.

"Your eyes are five and a half feet higher than your feet, so it's not actually as far as it seems. Stop scaring yourself and jump off the damn thing." Without another thought, she did just that.

Pain flared for an instant as her ankles complained, but she stuck the landing.

Elodie didn't give the nagging echo of her mother a chance to pull her back to the house. Instead, she jogged down the street along the same path she took every morning. The familiarity of the walkway and each house lining up between her and Gwen buffered a bit of the pain, but her mother's words were branded across her flesh, and no amount of *I love you*s would buff away the scars.

No one looked up as she leapt through the closing doors onto the MAX and skidded to a stop in the middle of the train car. Bursts of purple light from the other passengers bobbed around her. She looked at the button on her cuff.

Elodie had left the house without putting her shield up.

XXVII

Blair didn't look up from her holopad when Maxine entered her office. She continued to scroll through the mind-numbing bar graphs and various inpatient, outpatient statistics as her faithful assistant stood quietly, calmly, *respectfully* in front of the onyx desk.

Bored with testing Maxine's unwavering resolve, Blair tapped off her holopad. "You have exciting news, I hope. My last few hours have been supremely dull."

Maxine's features smoothed into an unreadable mask. The girl was actually quite pretty—which would serve them both well. "It's about your brother."

Bad news, Blair suspected, shaking back her curly mane. Good thing she could weather any storm.

Maxine flipped up her holopad, glanced at it quickly, and set it back against her hip. She nodded tightly before continuing. "I know you want him to be reassigned as an entry-level Key Corp soldier, but I am having trouble. The highest chain-of-command level I've been able to reach is just a standard *anybody* officer. Anyone with a higher title just referred me to one of the peons I had already spoken to. I'm sure I could gain a bit more traction if I told them this is for you—but I won't." Maxine's cheeks reddened as she let out a tight sigh. "I've exhausted all avenues, though. Without the truth, that is, and I refuse to tell the truth."

Blair settled back into her seat.

Maxine, my faithful little monster.

It was nice not being the one who ran around begging, *manipulating*, to get information. It was nice not being the bad guy, the fall guy.

Guy.

That was interesting. The way *guy* infiltrated everything. Or *man. Man* was the same. Repair*man*. Fire*man*. Other*man*. As if women were less than, an afterthought, or simply didn't exist at all. It was a problem that had plagued mankind—there it was again—since as far back as any historic text cared to remember. But without *woman*kind, there would be no *man*kind.

What had men been good for, anyway? A whole portion of the species who couldn't reproduce. Yes, there is something to be said for the sperm and egg meeting, and the genetic diversity that asexual reproduction can't provide, but wouldn't it be better not having to deal with complete dickheadedness? Perhaps she could only pose the question because she was a product of two different races, and, therefore more genetically diverse than most. None of this, however, made the male sex superior, it simply made suffering fools a part of Blair's destiny.

Maxine's allergy-induced sniffle drew Blair's attention back. "I would apologize," Maxine said, "but . . ."

"You don't feel you need to." Blair's brow lifted. "Good.

Apologies are weakness and I won't have that kind of filth floating around my workspace."

Maxine's spine straightened and her chin ticked up an inch. "You're so very right."

Blair was never quite sure how to respond to that statement. It was like stating that the sky is up above and the ground down below. Of course they were. And of course she was right. If she'd thought there was even a chance she could be incorrect, she never would have said anything.

"I am," she finally said.

Blair glanced under her massive desk as she stretched out her legs, admiring the way her slim calves delicately sloped before her ankles. With a sigh, she wiggled her bare toes in the fuzzy rug.

Although having Denny as a Key Corp soldier would benefit both her brother and the citizens of Westfall, Blair couldn't be seen advocating on behalf of young Denny. That was Cath's job as director of Career Services.

Director of Career Services. Blair chortled. Another example of a task she could perform better than her adoptive mother. Blair should really relax about the MediCenter directorial position. She was truly the best option. She might as well have been the only option.

But they could always give it to Cath . . .

Blair shook her head.

Denny. That's who this was about. Her poor lost little brother. The only man who'd earned her love, her trust. The one that all men should be fashioned after. Sweet, sweet Denny . . .

As always, Blair would have to pick up the slack.

She drummed her fingers along the metal-studded armrest and focused on the bare wall behind Maxine. Blair had created something from nothing before. She'd created herself, hadn't she? Sure, her parents' titles and Cath's titles had helped, but she'd done all the real work, all the hard work. All she needed now was that same tiny edge, just the slightest handhold . . .

Blair pressed her palms against her desk and pushed herself from her chair. "Maxine, did you see Major Owens in the Zone Seven video?"

XXVIII

Major Rhett Owens arrived at Blair's office twenty-two minutes later. His custom-made Key Corp–red officer's jacket accentuated the thickly coiled muscles and tapered waist that his fire-retardant Zone Seven uniform had swallowed up. Blair's gaze slid from the towering officer to her petite blond assistant and back again. The three of them could make quite the trio, two gorgeous blonds flanking her like porcelain bookends.

Blair leaned against the side of her desk and motioned to the chair across from her. "Would you like to sit, Major? Or were you planning on leaving us?"

Rhett strode over, unbuttoned his coat, and stiffly lowered himself into the chair. "Not at all. It's an honor. A real honor. When your girl, Maxie, reached out—"

"Max*ine*," the assistant corrected as she crossed her arms over her chest. "Or should I call you Maj Owe?"

Blair's eyebrow rose. "Ms. Wyndham," she insisted, after a brief struggle to recall her assistant's surname. Normally Blair wouldn't care whether Maxine was addressed by her first or last name. It was her assistant's name and therefore her assistant's decision. But this wasn't about Maxine's name. No, this was about power. About laying a strong, unshakable foundation. If Rhett was going to work for her, he would know who was in charge.

Rhett's temples flexed with a quick clench of his jaw. "When *Ms. Wyndham* called, I thought to myself, *You're finally getting the recognition you deserve.*"

Blair dragged her nails along her desk as she circled it, moving closer to Rhett. "And what if you were here to be reprimanded?"

Rhett snorted. "There's no way. I do everything correctly. By the book."

"Because . . ." Blair paused, lifting her eyebrows as silence spilled into the room. No, it wasn't a question. It was a test.

Rhett rested his elbows on the armrests and clasped his hands. "I'm not sure what you know about Key Corp forces, Ms. Scott, but we pride ourselves on following orders. I happen to be one of the few who gets to give them—"

Blair's toes dug into her pointed high heels as Rhett stuffed the pause with a tight wriggle of his square shoulders.

The corner of Rhett's thin lips twitched with a smirk as he continued. "But I do so with the Key in mind. Protecting the corporation and its citizens are numbers one and two in my book."

Paper rustled as Maxine flipped the page of the paper pad she busily scribbled notes into. As she'd mentioned before the Major's arrival, there were some things only Blair needed access to.

Precious little monster.

Blair perched on the edge of her onyx desk. "And special projects. How are you with those, Major?"

Again, his shoulders wriggled with self-importance. "None

too big for me, Ms. Scott. I can handle any assignment you can think to give. Or I know the right man for the job." He shifted slightly. "I make sure to keep myself available for higher-level assignments." He glanced over his shoulder at Maxine before he leaned forward and whispered, "I'm sure you know what I mean. There are some tasks that aren't worth our pay grade."

Blair's cuticles ached as her nails bit the lip of her desk. Rhett's smugness was a palpable grit that hung in the air around him like dust. "Well, Major, it seems that I contacted the right man." She peeled her fingers away from the desk and forced them, loose and relaxed, in her lap. "My brother. He's a bit—" Blair pursed her lips. Denny was a hard person to describe. Every time she thought she did an adequate job, the word *loser* floated in the air, and popped on the tongue of whoever she'd been talking to like an acrid bubble. Blair had fired the last person to call him a loser. Her brother wasn't a loser. Purposeless? Unmotivated? Uninspired? Yes, yes, and yes. But, with the right push, there was no reason Denny wouldn't be as successful as Blair was. And she knew exactly which buttons to press. "Denny is a little *unmotivated*. The Key Corp guard would be the perfect place for him to find his way. Plus, he's a Scott. Once he's on the right path, he'll be unstoppable."

Rhett relaxed back into his seat. "So his testing showed that he has an aptitude for the armed guard? That's great. We can always use new talent. Don't get enough of it, if you ask me. I'll be sure to teach him everything he needs to know. You don't need to worry about a thing, Ms. Scott. I make sure to keep my men busy." With a squint, he raised his hands and pointed them straight ahead. "Focused. As they say, idle hands are more likely to get caught up in Eos."

Blair forced her grimace into an empty smile. "I don't believe I've heard that one, Major."

"Echo scoops up anyone prone to . . ." Rhett waved his hand in Blair's direction as he chose his next word, *"wandering.* Brainwashes them and makes them a part of Eos."

Blair's brow creased and her stomach knotted. She could not abide this windbag knowing more than her. "Maxine, were you aware of an *Echo*?"

Without looking up from her diligent note taking, Maxine shook her head.

"Our intel names Echo as the leader of the Eos cell here in the New American West Coast. This Echo character tops the Most Wanted list." Rhett snorted. "Ms. Wyndham wouldn't have been privy to that kind of information."

Maxine ceased writing and stood. "Going back a bit, Rhett." She cocked her head and smiled at the Major as she would a lost child as she took a seat in the chair next to him. "May I call you Rhett?"

Major Owens opened his mouth, but Maxine continued, slipping into the space between breath and word before Rhett could utter a sound. "Blair's brother has an aptitude for the medical sciences, not the armed guard. However, as she stated, medical isn't the best place for him."

Rhett's brow wrinkled as his expression twisted into shock. "The best place for him is wherever the Key says he should be. My career is no joke, Ms. Wyndham. It takes a certain kind of man to do what I do. To see what I see and not be affected by it."

With a subtle wave of her hand, Blair shooed Maxine out of the chair and back to her corner. "I couldn't agree more, Major." Blair settled into the chair next to him. "A *special* kind of man. A *strong* man. An *intelligent* man. You are that man." Blair forced the sneer from her lips as Rhett's chest puffed. "Major Owens, you are the embodiment of who a Key Corp soldier should be."

Maxine opened her mouth and Blair lifted her hand, catching the go-getter before she spoke. There was blood in the water, and Major Rhett Owens had no idea he was the one hemorrhaging.

Blair wet her lips and continued. "I believe, with your immeasurable skill set, the fact that you are in command of your own squadron, and the superb way you perform under pressure, that you, Major, should have no trouble getting my brother a position in your ranks."

Rhett swiped the back of his hand down his cheek. "I don't think—"

"I need you, Major." The words stained Blair's tongue, tacky and bitter. "You'll be doing me a personal favor. And, more importantly, you'll be directly responsible for the betterment of the Key. Isn't that what you want?"

His temples pulsed. "Yes, of course—"

"Then it's settled," Blair said with a clap. "Major Owens, you and I . . ." She inhaled slowly, letting the lilting words further ensnare the brute. "We're going to be the best of friends."

"A powerhouse." Maxine added silk to the web.

Blair glanced at the sharp lead points jutting out from the vase on her desk. "Rule makers, Major. And wouldn't you like to make the rules?"

The bright amber of Rhett's eyes thinned as his pupils dilated.

Blair's stomach fluttered and her breath hitched as the air around her seemed to tremble. Rhett had stumbled into her web.

XXIX

Stars wiggled overhead as Elodie walked toward the river. Each inch, block, mile that the MAX put between her and Gwen had taken a piece of her with it. Not a bad piece. Not a piece of her foundation. Not a piece that left pain in its absence. The walk had smoothed away the hard edges left behind by her mother's chisel-tipped words. Elodie had even decided to text an apology to Rhett for leaving him at her house—but not just yet.

A group of girls laughed as they crossed the street in front of her. Their Violet Shields bobbed as the trio hurried to beat the orange light flashing at them from the crosswalk sign. Elodie finally activated her own shield. She wanted to blend, be invisible.

She didn't wait for the crosswalk sign to illuminate white. Instead, she darted across the nearly empty street, stopping only when she reached Salmon Springs fountain. The way the spray swayed in the breeze, each spout reaching for the next until they were one, until they were touching. How many times had she seen the arching waters and not noticed their beauty?

Sure she was alone, Elodie clicked the button on her cuff and the purple haze around her dissipated.

Elodie *was* blind to the real world around her. Aiden had been right.

Aiden.

Her heart clenched.

Boots pressed heavy against the pavement behind her. "What are you doing here?"

Elodie stiffened as the familiar footsteps, familiar voice, familiar pine scent, splashed against her back. She had escaped her house, fled to the MAX, to the core of the city, to find freedom and space and—

"Aiden." Her breath trembled as she turned to face him. The roaring fountain did nothing to drown out the heartbeat thrumming between her ears. "I needed to be alone." She blinked rapidly but couldn't keep the tears from spilling down her cheeks. Her numbness faded, and her armor fell in a battered heap around her feet.

Aiden took a step forward, stiffened, and retreated. "I'm sorry, Elodie. I—" He clenched and unclenched his fists. "I should have . . ." He sagged. "I'll leave you alone."

"Don't." The word flew from her lips in a sudden burst.

Aiden's gaze rested against hers. "I don't know what to say."

Elodie brushed the tears from her cheeks as she dropped onto one of the wide stone benches ringing the fountain. "The truth."

He took a seat next to her. A gust of pine caressed her as the warm breeze picked up and his jacket fluttered by his sides. "I only know pieces."

"How can you believe in Eos if you don't know the truth behind it?" She didn't try to keep her voice from trembling.

Aiden turned to face her, straddling the bench. "How much of what you think you know comes directly from the Key?"

"Facts are facts," she said too quickly.

"But whose facts?" He pressed his hands against the stone slab and leaned forward. "Who benefits?"

Silence pawed the air between them.

Aiden was a good person. Elodie knew that. She felt it in the way he spoke to her. The way he looked at her. The way he interacted with the world and the people around him. Kindness clung to him like skin. Not like Rhett and his pretentious, self-important ramblings, or the way he looked at her when she wasn't wearing the exact right outfit, or how he spoke *at* her instead of *with* her.

And then there was the way Rhett did nothing at all. Nothing at all when she needed him the most. Nothing at all when she needed a shield against the storm that was her mother. Rhett kept his career safe, his image safe, *himself* safe, but he'd never kept *her* safe.

No, Aiden was nothing like her fiancé.

But how could she place her trust in Aiden if he blindly placed his in Eos?

Elodie rubbed the collar of her shirt between her thumb and forefinger. "You said that words matter, they have meaning."

Of all the things you've done, and you've done plenty, becoming a sympathizer is the one thing that will make me regret turning those natal programmers down!

Elodie's throat burned with the memory of her mother's words. "What you don't say is just as important, Aiden." She forced back more tears as the image of Rhett standing silently, complacently at her mother's side flashed behind her eyes.

Aiden zipped and unzipped his jacket. "You're right." He

stopped zipping and dragged his fingertips along the metal teeth. "I wanted to keep you safe."

"I can keep myself safe." Elodie bit out the words more harshly than she'd meant to.

The streetlight haloed him in brittle white as his chin dipped toward his chest.

Elodie had a hundred questions, a million questions, but they stuck in her throat, bitter and barbed. Maybe she didn't want to know the answers.

She picked at her fingernails.

That wasn't true. She wanted to know everything.

Aiden broke the stillness, charging up from the bench. "Go somewhere with me."

Anywhere. Each fiber within her quaked.

She shook her head. "I'm not an Eos sympathizer." She winced. There Gwen was again like a bruise Elodie couldn't keep from pressing. Her throat tightened. "I can't be," she whispered.

Aiden stood in front of her, his hands stuffed into his pockets. "You can be whoever you want."

He made it sound so simple.

Elodie chewed her bottom lip, the very fabric of her identity fraying, unraveling as she yanked herself in different directions.

Explore. Conform.

Explore. Conform.

Moonlight glinted in the shallow pools of Aiden's eyes as he waited expectantly.

To health. To life. To the future. We are the Key.

And the corporation had kept Elodie on the right path since they'd intertwined her mother and father's DNA and grown her in the lab nearly eighteen years ago. But Elodie wanted so much more out of life than a predetermined path. She wanted to, *needed* to, let herself loose.

The endless black of the star-speckled sky pressed down on top of her.

Were Aiden's truths like Gwen's, thin and unstable and treacherous? Were they worth dying to uncover?

Elodie swallowed past the tightness in her throat.

Cool droplets dusted her cheek as the wind twisted and played between the spray of the fountain. "Eos kills people, Aiden," she said as she stood.

He took a deep breath and shook his head. "Eos is protecting people—*children*. The *Key* is hurting kids."

She threw her hands into the air before stepping away, packing more empty space between them. "And I'm just supposed to believe that?" His deep scent faded as she neared the street.

He walked closer. "What do you think happened to Patient Ninety-Two?"

A swarm of partially realized questions buzzed between her ears.

"The Key did something to her," he continued. "They used her . . ." He twirled the air as if trying to generate an explanation. "Ran tests on her."

Elodie's thoughts began to fall into place like tumblers in a lock.

Aiden shoved his hands into his pockets. "I only just found out, and don't really know anymore, but she's why Eos breached the ELU. They needed Aubrey's body to find out what the Key did to her so they can stop it from happening again."

Click.

Elodie sucked in a breath. "That's why no one would tell me where Aubrey was transferred, and why Holly said I didn't have access to her file."

Aiden's brow lifted with a nod. "Elodie, I'll understand if you still feel like you have to turn me into the Council." His soft tone was almost swallowed by the steady clank of the MAX as it lumbered down the street.

"I could never do that." She *would never* do that, sentence someone to death. Not for what she'd seen. Eos hadn't hurt anyone. And what Aiden said made too much sense. Aubrey's was the one case that didn't fit. That felt *wrong*. Elodie needed answers.

Aiden's jacket wheezed as he shifted. "Then let me show you what you're protecting."

With a shake of her head, Elodie jerked back. "I'm not protecting anything."

He shrugged. "By not telling, you're protecting me."

The air thickened around her. Doing nothing was never as simple as it seemed. The absence of an action, a decision, was a choice in itself. Rhett had taught her that.

She wished she had her jacket to hide in. "I don't want to do anything scary."

Aiden chuckled, a glorious fizzy pop against the stiffness of the night air. "You're braver than you think."

It was the second time he'd said that, and it still pressed against Elodie with the weight of a lie.

He brushed his hand through the air, motioning for her to follow. "It won't be scary. Promise."

Elodie hesitated. She wanted to follow. Desperately wanted . . .

But her mother's sentiment burned within her.

Aiden disappeared into the black curtain of shadows stretching between the trees, the light squish of his boots against the moist grass the only sign of him.

Elodie chewed the inside of her cheek, listening to him go.

She was doing it again. Making a life-altering choice by simply doing nothing.

Aiden's footsteps faded, swallowed whole by the dark.

She took a deep breath.

Life continued, dragging her around in its wake, shredding her like an unwanted doll. Elodie was tired of life happening *to* her.

"Aiden!" She charged forward, her eyes adjusting as she plunged into the darkness.

XXX

Elodie had followed. Aiden had been positive that she wouldn't. That he'd feel the last bits of their relationship, however it was categorized and shelved within each of them, evaporate with the evening mist as the space between them grew.

But she *was* following.

Aiden had thought he'd come to say goodbye to the river, the murky artery that pulsed through the city, bisecting east from west. He thought he'd sit on a cool fountain bench for one last time and toss a whispered *I'm sorry* into the water. For what? He wasn't sure. But remorse seeped into the hollow of his bones. Maybe it was because he'd dragged Elodie into a world she didn't want to or have to exist in. Aiden knew all too well that stepping into the light of Eos would bleach out the shadows from the rest of the world. Was Elodie ready to leave the darkness?

Had he given her a choice?

They'd been walking for nearly ten minutes when Elodie cleared the silence. "Where are we going?"

Aiden's boots scraped against the pavement as they crossed another street on their trek away from the river. It was a simple enough question, a fair enough question, but the answer was too big for mere words.

Each breath stuffed him full of anticipation. "You just have to see it."

At the next intersection they waited for the MAX to clank past.

"I don't like surprises." The crisp white light of the streetlamp glimmered in Elodie's dark eyes and illuminated the smirk pinning the corners of her lips.

Man, she was beautiful. What was it that they said? Beauty is in the eye of the beholder?

But that was only partially correct. There was a silently agreed-upon standard. There had been forever. There would be until the end of time. Participation wasn't mandatory, but categorization happened nonetheless.

Elodie was striking, noticeable. But her true beauty surfaced as her layers of protection flaked away and she unfurled, bloomed into herself.

Aiden hopped off the curb and continued their nighttime adventure to the disregarded industrial outskirts of Westfall. "You don't like surprises?" Aiden scratched his stubbled cheek. "You sure about that?"

The corners of her eyes creased as her smirk deepened and her shoulders hiked to her ears.

Elodie pinned her arms to her sides, her cheerfulness draining with the motion. "I'm not sure about anything right now." Honesty thickened her voice as she focused on the empty, warehouse-lined street ahead.

Aiden understood her uncertainty. He harbored his own.

He'd thought that the next time he saw Elodie would be at trial when the Key Council called her as a witness to his dealings with Eos. Even then, he wouldn't have blamed her.

Her shoes scraped against the sudden rises and falls of the cracked and weathered street. "I do have a question—*questions*, actually," she said.

He knew she would. He also knew he didn't have the answers. "About Aubrey?"

She was silent for a moment before releasing the flood-gates. "You said the Key was using her. For what? What kind of tests were they performing? Where is she now? Did Eos get her complete patient care chart? I'll need to see it and whatever Eos's doctors discovered. Do they have doctors, anyway?"

Aiden guided them into the dark alley between two unremark-able boxlike buildings. "Our doctors are Key doctors. Our people are Key people. Eos is kind of like Holly in that way—everywhere and nowhere." He took a right at the end of the narrow strip of battered asphalt and headed toward a glinting metal stair rail. "As for everything else . . ." He slowed before reaching the stairs and kicked a rock with the toe of his boot. "I don't have the answers, but I know someone who does. You aren't ready to meet her, but I'll get all the answers I can."

The nondescript three-story gray building Aiden stopped in front of looked the same as the last, the same as the next, and the same as the row of buildings across the street. At first, he'd thought Eos had chosen it for that reason, but had come to realize the location was a matter of convenience, not stealth. Eos needed somewhere centrally located for all of its Westfall members.

Elodie crossed her arms over her chest. "We'll get them together."

Aiden's lips quirked as he took the concrete steps two at a time before glancing up at the building stretched out like a cloud above him. "Might not look like much, but this is one of my favorite places."

Elodie remained at the bottom of the stairs, the toe of her sneaker grinding against the pavement with each twist of her ankle. "It's—" Her teeth grazed her bottom lip. "*Nice?*"

He looked up again at the front of the concrete square that spanned the city block and shrugged. "It looks like shit from the outside."

Elodie snorted as she ascended the stairs. "And very loomy. All big and sinister and foreboding."

Aiden considered this as he shuffled to the entryway and keyed his personal code on the panel outside the solid metal door. The first time he'd come here, he'd been so excited that there had been no space for nerves or second-guessing. And now that he knew what treasures grew within the warehouse walls, there was no way he could ever see the building as anything other than a beacon within the swirling red sea of the Key.

The deadbolt released. Aiden held open the door and motioned for Elodie to enter.

"Does your favorite place hold any of the answers we're looking—" Her hands clapped over her ears as she crossed the threshold. "*Ah!*" Pain folded her at the waist. An instant later she relaxed and looked up at him. She rubbed the spot behind her ear as she shook herself free of the sudden blitz. "What was that?"

Aiden winced. "I completely forgot about the tech shield. It neutralizes the implant in your head while you're within its boundaries." He grimaced. "Stings a little."

"*Stings a little?*" She twisted her neck and shook her head again. "Terrible thing to get used to."

Aiden pressed his fingertips against the star of scarred flesh behind his ear. He did have a few more secrets.

Aiden guided her down an empty corridor that ran between the front door and another set of locked double doors, where he entered a different access code.

"That's it for the sudden blasts of mind-numbing pain, right?" she asked.

"That was it." Aiden's heartbeat ticked up as his fingers curled around the knob, and he hefted the door open.

Heady sweet scents hit him before anything else. They lapped against his skin with playful newness before giving way to the spicy and intense waves of something deeper, something richer.

"That smell—" Elodie took a deep breath, her lids closing slightly as her chest filled. Her long lashes dusted her cheeks. "What is it?"

Black velvet drapes hung in front of them. Aiden brushed his hand across the soft edges as he found the opening. "Welcome to Wonderland."

XXXI

Elodie's fingers tingled as she brushed past the curtains. She'd never seen anything so beautiful. A rainbow brought to life and stretched before her in rows and rows of flourishing flowers and heavy buds—not in planters, but growing from the dirt floor of the warehouse. The thick and foreign notes greeted her and pulled her between the rows of blossoming color. Her vision spotted as she took deep inhale after deep inhale, trying to store the luscious scents within her chest.

The space had stolen her words, her thoughts, her worries. Trees blossomed pink and white and yellow along the sides of the warehouse. Their grace and beauty formed a protective, nurturing wall that surrounded the oasis. Jade-colored vines and tall, greenish-yellow stalks stretched toward the warm and gentle lights glowing above. The artificial sun and the small vine-covered shed sprouting from the middle of the space were the only obvious signs of human interference.

This is nature. Real *nature.*

"It exists," Elodie said aloud.

"It does." Aiden was behind her twirling his fingers between the leaves of a plant she'd never seen before, his rich pine scent in harmony with the complex and candied perfumes of the nearby blossoms.

She delicately brushed her fingers over a soft puff of powder-blue blooms. "How?"

"Eos," he said matter-of-factly.

Elodie thought about that for a moment as she sank her nose into the sweet center of a bloom so orange it looked ablaze. "*This*," she swept her arm over a group of flowers that waved gently in her breeze. "This is what Eos does?"

"One of its many functions." Aiden wandered deeper into the multi-colored rows. "The Key likes to take things, natural things, and distort them. Turn them into something else." Elodie followed as he explained. "Like corn." He paused near the tall yellow-tipped stalks. "The corporation took this plant in its pure, natural form,"—he grazed one of the stalk's pregnant pods—"and changed it."

Elodie tilted her chin. "Or did the Key make it better? They made just one of those plants able to feed one hundred people." She shrugged. "That's progress."

"That's perversion."

Her arms snapped up to cross over her chest. She'd never heard anyone talk that way about the corporation that had saved their species from extinction. They owed their lives to the Key. And their continued health. The Key was the only thing between humanity and another pandemic. Didn't Aiden understand that? Didn't Eos?

He broke off one of the pods and brought it to her. He peeled back the green covering and brushed away the shiny hairs, letting them fall to the dirt. White-and-yellow buds the washed-out color of a cloud-covered sun nestled inside.

It was familiar and nice, but in the way VR was familiar and nice—close enough to what she already knew to make her comfortable, but not exactly right. Elodie shook her head. This wasn't the corn she knew. Corn was bright, vibrant, electric, sunflower yellow. She wrinkled her nose. "What's wrong with it?"

Aiden brushed away a few more hairs and examined it. "Nothing. This is how nature intended. That's what I'm trying to tell you. This is what it looks like when we're hands off." His thumb grazed the swollen kernels. "Want to try it?"

Before she had the chance to answer, Aiden dashed into the plant-covered shed. He reemerged with two slightly burnt corncobs. He handed her one before peeling the charred husk away from his. The kernels squirted as he took his first bite. "Real corn is so much better than that genetically modified stuff." He jabbed his cob in her direction. "Try it."

Elodie shucked the rough papery husk. Golden hairs clung to her fingers and she shook the cob and her hand free from the soft strands. After a few attempts, she gave up and brought the warm cob to her lips. She loved corncobs, but had never seen one like this, fresh from the stalk, still trailing silk. If she hadn't watched Aiden, she wouldn't have known what to do with the green covering.

Again, Elodie's thoughts flashed to Vi and her no-nonsense bravery. Elodie could be that brave. Aiden already thought so.

She bit down. Flavor washed over her taste buds, and she couldn't help but close her eyes as she took another bite. It was so much more than what she'd tasted before. Those flavors had been enhanced, but the true taste of corn was better than the saccharine sweetness of what she was used to. It was dynamic and juicy and sweet and pure and utterly delicious.

She opened her eyes.

Aiden's gaze lifted from her mouth. How long had he been watching her mow through the corncob?

"It's good." His words were thick and sweet. "Isn't it?"

She swallowed and brushed the back of her hand over her mouth. "It's amazing." She was breathless despite standing still.

"You still have a little . . ." His hand split the air between them, hovering inches from her lips.

It was happening again. That feeling that rocketed to the surface from deep within her core. It radiated out, seeped into her legs, and turned them to quaking bags of mush. Elodie licked her aching lips as her breath locked itself within her chest. Dizziness swirled her thoughts and her heart clamored within her chest.

Suddenly, Aiden cleared his throat and backed away.

Her breath released with a rush and no words came out as she tried to thank him. She could only smile as she wiped her fingers across her mouth while her heart calmed and the ground steadied beneath her feet.

A bee, its fat, puffy body yellow with pollen, flew drunkenly between them.

Elodie forced a swallow down her dry throat. Too many silent seconds had passed. What should she say? She tugged at her collar. What had just happened?

Aiden tossed the cob into a bin marked *Compost* and brushed his hands off on his pants. He opened his mouth to speak but closed it just as quickly. His smile was strained as he tugged at one of the curls of his short mohawk.

Elodie cleared her throat. "The corn was great." She dug the toe of her shoe into the dirt. Everything was so . . . *awkward.* She turned back to the rows of flowers and crops, trying to buy herself enough time to formulate a sentence "So, Eos keeps all of this so they can . . ." She picked at the hem of her shirt. "Do things with it, then."

She winced, glad that her back was to him. Could she really not come up with anything more articulate?

Aiden passed her on his way back through the flowers. "The hope is that one day they'll be gifted to the earth. But that would mean that the Key would have to stop lighting it on fire."

Elodie sucked in a breath. "You think Eos is going to venture out into Zone Seven?" She jogged to catch up with him. "Citizens aren't allowed out there for a reason. It's filled with monsters. *That's* why they keep burning it down."

He whirled to face her. Pink and blue and orange petals reflected in his eyes. "Have you ever seen any of these monsters?"

"In pictures and feeds." Her shoulders hiked. "Just like everybody else." She bit down on her lip as she thought about everything Rhett told her about Zone Seven.

"Some of us have seen them for real. Been face to face." His throat bobbed with a tight swallow before he turned and headed back to the front of the warehouse.

"You've seen one? When? How? What was it like?" The questions flew out of her.

Aiden stopped sharply as the black velvet curtains flew open and two coverall-clad women stepped into the greenhouse.

Elodie peered out from behind Aiden at the woman wearing gloves and carrying a bag labeled *Fertilizer.* Her slick black hair, long legs, and pointed chin were unmistakably Fujimoto.

"Thea?" Elodie left Aiden's shadow. "I can't believe—" She shook her head, trying to clear her thoughts. "Does Astrid know . . .?"

The red-headed woman buried the tip of her shovel into the dirt floor, blocking their exit, before she stepped in front of Elodie's best friend's sister.

Thea leaned out from behind the intimidating woman and waggled her eyebrows. "Did we interrupt you two?"

"Aiden," the woman with the shovel began, "this isn't a date destination where you can get handsy without getting caught by the Key." Her voice was steady, stern, familiar.

Handsy? Elodie bristled and shuffled away from Aiden.

"Nothing of the kind, Sparkman," Aiden said, raising his open hands.

Sparkman cocked her head. "Don't tell me your girlfriend believes that line about no touching today for a healthy tomorrow." She shook her head and faced Elodie. "If you're eating up everything the Key is serving, there are a lot of surprises about to come your way."

Elodie's jaw slackened and a dry squeak slipped past her lips. She should have questions, millions of them, but she couldn't think of one. "They're lying . . ." She wet her lips. Sweet corn still stained her mouth.

Sparkman's golden red temples ticked as she clenched and unclenched her jaw. "Have been for a long time."

Aiden held up his hands. "Look, Sparkman, she's just a new recruit," he said, tossing a glance at Elodie and motioning for her to follow. "And we were just leaving."

The woman's broad chin jutted forward as she leaned on the shovel, and her eyes bored into Aiden. "New recruits aren't permitted here."

Goosebumps rose along Elodie's arms. She'd heard that voice. But where?

Aiden settled back onto his heels. "Well, you'll have to take it up with Echo. I'm sure she'll be glad to know that Westfall's Lieutenant Commander is giving new recruits a hard time."

Sparkman's reddish-blond braid slid from her shoulder as she stiffened. Her eyes narrowed slightly and she gripped the wooden handle of the shovel.

Elodie chewed the inside of her cheek. She'd heard that name before too. "Who's Echo?"

Sparkman trained her heated gaze on Elodie. "Quit while you're ahead, recruit."

Elodie flinched as Thea leaned out from behind the strong wall of the shovel-wielding redhead and pressed her slender finger against her lips.

Aiden cleared his throat. "Like I said, we were just leaving."

Thea disappeared back behind Sparkman. "Split up when you leave," Sparkman said as she yanked the shovel from the ground. "After this morning, it's not smart to have two members out together."

That voice . . .

Elodie shuffled after Aiden as he marched past the women. Her breath slammed against her ribs as Sparkman stabbed the air in front of Elodie with the handle of the shovel, blocking her path out.

"I didn't catch your name, recruit."

I know that voice . . . Elodie's memories cleared, and she was back in that bleach-scented hallway.

"In and out, gentlemen." Boots marching closer, closer. *"You two, scan the halls."*

"Your name, recruit," Sparkman repeated.

Elodie's heart flapped wildly as she struggled to form words.

"Violet." Thea stepped forward. "Lieutenant Commander,

this is Violet Royale. I know her. She's—she's a friend." Thea's slender arm swept back the velvet curtain as her eyes widened with warning. "Be safe out there, Violet."

Sparkman lowered the shovel. "Welcome to the fold, Royale," she said with a nod.

Elodie hurried past Sparkman, through the curtains past Thea, and didn't exhale until she and Aiden were back out under the stars.

"That was my best friend's sister." Elodie stood at the top of the stairs above Aiden, her hands clapped on top of her head. "Thea is a member of Eos!"

Aiden charged back up the stairs. "Never say that!" His nostrils flared. "She wasn't here. I wasn't here. You weren't here. None of this happened."

Elodie's cheeks were ablaze. "Yeah, I know." Her arms dropped to her sides and she shook her head. "I don't know why I said that out loud."

"I get it. I just want you . . ." He motioned to the warehouse behind her. "All of us, to be safe."

"One more thing," Elodie dug her fingernail into the collar of her shirt. "No touching today for a healthy tomorrow. All of that is . . ." She swallowed and took a deep breath. "At one point, it was true."

Aiden shoved his hands into his pockets. "No one's denying that."

Elodie nodded. "We should split up." She peered up and down the shadowed street that stretched in front of the row of buildings as she squeezed past Aiden. "I can use Holly now. She'll take me to the nearest MAX stop."

Aiden's heavy footsteps followed her down the stairs. "We're good, though, right?"

Elodie didn't know how to answer him. Eos was more than, *better than*, she'd thought, but she still had questions—about Echo, Sparkman, Aubrey, the Key. And then there was Thea. She was a Fujimoto, and Elodie had been a part of their family for years. Thea wouldn't be involved in something sinister.

"Director Holbrook's funeral is tomorrow." Elodie let the words hang in the air as she rubbed the tiny X-shaped scar behind her ear and brought up a map to the nearest MAX stop. The same blinking light and 3D view that had led her down to the End-of-Life Unit, down to Aiden and this new chapter of her story, came into focus.

Aiden scratched his brow. "About that—"

"You know . . ." Elodie started, as she stepped into the street, her eyes firmly fixed on the cloudless night sky. "I think I'm good on new information today." She ran her fingers through her hair and released the ends to dance along the steady breeze. "We can start again tomorrow."

Right now, she needed to focus and tuck away all of her questions and worries. Once she got home, she'd experience another first—climbing up that tree.

XXXII

The moment Director Holbrook's funeral service was finished and the guests had been released to the celebration on the grounds outside of the Holbrook's palatial estate, Elodie faded into the throngs of people who'd shown up to pay their respects. Each shieldless person she passed was another barrier between her and her mother and the desperation that dripped from each jewel Gwen had adorned herself with. She'd tried to dress Elodie up the same way, opening her jewelry case and telling her daughter to choose *absolutely anything*. People would be watching, and she needed to make the right impression.

Elodie ran her fingertips along the delicate strand of pearls around her neck as she plucked a cup off the beverage table and took a sip. Lemon-flavored seltzer bubbled across her tongue. The light and cheery drink fit the sunny day and the distance that made Mt. Hood's snowcapped peak look less frigid and daunting.

Elodie found an empty cocktail table and set her drink down on the pastel tablecloth as she scanned the crowd. The number of citizens who had come to the funeral and who were staying for the celebration was shocking, especially since it was tradition to go without the Violet Shield to all funeral festivities as a symbol of unity and closeness with the deceased. All public events were streamed live through VR. Every single person in Westfall could be there without actually being there. Elodie herself would be at home with her headset on in the comfort of her sweats if her mother hadn't made such a big deal about her attendance. Staying home to spite Gwen had most definitely crossed Elodie's mind.

Now that Elodie actually thought about it, so many people had shown up not because they too had terrible mothers, although that might be true, but because Director Holbrook had been so important. As the head of the Key Corp MediCenter, he'd effectively run the city of Westfall, and no one wanted to be thought of as disrespecting their commander in chief. Especially since the next MediCenter director was guaranteed to be in attendance.

If Elodie gambled, she would have bet on Dr. Scott or her daughter Blair. They'd been seated at the service, front and center, practically on thrones. They'd also been the first to exit, followed by a flood of MediCenter scientists and doctors who would need the next director on their side. Elodie might not have a bunch of letters after her name, or need funding for a project, but she did need answers to a question that wouldn't stop gnawing at her. What had the Key done to Aubrey?

Out of the corner of her eye, Elodie caught the sizzling flash of Key Corp–red stilettos amidst a sea of black. She followed the long legs up to an impeccably tailored, high-necked dress, a mane of curls, and—

Elodie sucked in a breath and nearly knocked over her drink as the woman turned toward her. It was Blair Scott. And she wasn't alone. Dr. Cath Scott stood next to her, smiling and waving as the group around them continued to dissipate.

Elodie smoothed down her pleated skirt and tucked her hair behind her ears. As soon as the last few people walked away from Dr. and Ms. Scott, Elodie would have her chance.

But before she could take it, her gaze landed on Aiden, fast approaching in a black suit and those clunky boots, his brows pinched and a line of worry creasing his forehead.

"You have that look," she said as he got closer. "The look that says, 'I'm about to tell you something you don't want to hear.'" It was the same expression he'd worn when he'd told her about Aubrey. Elodie's stomach clenched. "I don't understand how you were able to keep the huge secret you kept with such a crappy poker face," she playfully chimed through the apprehension tightening her throat.

Then again, Thea Fujimoto had kept the same secret from her family without raising even the slightest suspicions. There was no way Astrid knew. If she found out, maybe she wouldn't tell the Council, but she'd at least tell Elodie. Astrid could never keep that huge of a secret, the kind that lived and breathed and eventually consumed its jailer. Elodie knew how it felt to hold such a secret. She now kept two.

Aiden unbuttoned his suitcoat and rested his hands on his waist. The tailored black suit expertly fit his lean form and made him look older than his nearly eighteen years. "It's nothing bad," he paused. "At least, I don't think you'll think it is." He dug the crusty toe of his boot into the finely manicured lawn. Those dirty things had to be attached to his feet.

Elodie spotted Blair's red heels coming their way with Cath Scott at her side. Elodie held up her hand to Aiden. "I know it's a funeral," she said, "but there are people here who can help us figure out what really happened to Aubrey." Elodie chewed her bottom lip. "This might be my only opportunity to talk to them."

And I have to do it before I lose my nerve.

Aiden surged in front of her. "Elodie, wait, I—"

She didn't wait for him to finish. Instead, she pushed away from the cocktail table and marched squarely in the path of Cath and Blair Scott.

You're braver than you think. You're braver than you think. You're braver than you think.

Cath cocked her head, but never lost her pleasant smile as Elodie planted herself in front of the duo.

For once, Elodie's legs and arms and face were all doing exactly what they were supposed to. "Hello, Dr. Scott, Ms. Scott. I'm Elodie Benavidez, Lead Nurse in the downtown MediCenter's Long-Term Care Unit."

Blair's lips thinned and she blinked at Elodie long and slow.

Elodie held her head with pride. Wallflower no more. She deserved answers. She deserved to talk to these women.

Blair pressed the back of her hand against her mouth as she yawned.

And Elodie deserved to talk to them no matter how annoyed or bored Blair Scott seemed. "I wanted to let you know how much I appreciate what you do. I love my job, and it's because of your unit's expertise, Dr. Scott, that I'm there." She'd decided, in the seconds it had taken her to intercept Cath and Blair, that she should start off slow. There was no reason to cause a scene or make a bad first impression.

Elodie's stomach flip-flopped. She was beginning to sound like her mother.

Aiden's earthy scent encircled them as he shuffled up behind Elodie. Cath glanced past Elodie's shoulder at him, her eyebrows arching and eyes brightening. "Miss Benavidez," she said, shining her smile back on Elodie, "meeting you is an absolute bright spot in my otherwise gloomy day."

Elodie blanched and shifted from one foot to the other. "Oh, yes, I'm so sorry about Director Holbrook. He was a good man." She hadn't known Holbrook, or even ever met him, but it seemed like the right thing to say. Especially because Cath, unlike the majority of the people in attendance, actually seemed saddened by the loss—the complete opposite of Elodie's own mother, who had practiced her Lines of Bereavement during the thirty-minute ride to the Holbrook estate.

A bot whirred by carrying drinks, and Blair leaned over and plucked a cup of sparkling orange liquid off the tray. "Ellie, I have to say, I am loving how bold you are." Her lips curled from behind the rim of the glass.

Elodie felt Aiden stiffen behind her. "*Blair*," he growled in warning.

Elodie's eyes went wide. "You can't call her Blair," she whispered sharply over her shoulder.

Blair cocked her hip. "Oh, Denny can call me just about anything. Can't you, Denny?" she teased.

Denny? Elodie's eyes ping ponged between Aiden and Blair. They had the same thick lashes, round eyes, and full cheekbones. Their lips were the same, too, the corners upturned in a constant state of mischief, although on Blair it felt a bit more like contempt. They looked so much alike, with their dark skin and tight curls. How had she not seen it before?

And how could Aiden not tell her that the women in his life were two of the most powerful people in Westfall?

With a sigh, Cath clasped her hands. "This isn't the play yard, you two." She offered a polite grin to the passersby gawking at the iconic Scott duo before casting that sunbeam of a smile back on Elodie. "I do hope I see you again soon, Miss Benavidez. Aiden doesn't bring enough friends around." She waved her goodbyes and headed over to a nearby cluster of beckoning attendees.

Blair tapped a taloned finger on her glass, her nailbed raw and red. "That would be because I"—she pressed her palm against the high neck of her perfect dress—"his dear sister, am Aiden's best and only friend."

Shock muzzled Elodie, sizzling against her tongue.

Aiden rolled his eyes and, with a smirk Elodie assumed only little brothers could pull off, said, "Good thing I feel sorry enough for you to be your best and only too."

A warm smile played around Blair's lips like a bee around a bloom. "Well." She sucked in a breath and it was gone so quickly it might not have been there at all. "If you'll excuse me, I'm off to find some munchies that won't make me bloat. I'm famished, but there's not an inch of extra room in this dress." Blair waved goodbye, her fingers twitching like spider's legs.

Elodie felt Aiden's gaze pressing against her, but she couldn't stop staring at the empty space the formidable Scott women had left in their wake.

He cleared his throat. "That's what I was about to tell you."

And if he had, maybe Elodie would have had the wherewithal to ask the Scott women her questions, instead of standing there like lawn furniture.

Aiden shifted uncomfortably. "What can I say? I have a successful family." He forced a chuckle and shoved his hands into his pant pockets.

"Anything else you think you should share?" Elodie threw out.

"El!" The familiar voice smacked against her back.

She stiffened. She'd completely forgotten to look for Rhett.

"There you are." Her fiancé's golden eyes beamed down at her, so much less hollow against the bright navy of his suit. "I was looking all over for you before the service, and then I ran into some of the guys, and your mom, and . . ." He trailed off, his steady gaze flicking to Aiden. "Who's this?"

Aiden's lips pursed. "Aiden. Aiden Scott." Had he taken a step closer to Elodie?

Rhett rocked onto the balls of his feet. "Scott? Like, Blair Scott's little brother?"

Aiden's chin tilted toward the sky. "Exactly like." If only he'd been so forthcoming with Elodie . . .

Another bot whizzed by. Elodie wished she could grab on and ride away from these men and this service and her unanswered questions—away from Westfall. "But Aiden was just leaving," she said, "so—"

"I'm Major Rhett Owens." He rocked to his heels and back to the balls of his feet. "Elodie's fiancé."

Elodie's teeth dug into her bottom lip. If she was lucky, the subduction-zone earthquake the Pacific Northwest had been waiting for would happen right at this moment and the ground would split and swallow her whole.

Aiden let out a strangled sort of grunt. "*Fiancé?*" His brows arched toward his mohawk. "Huh."

Rhett slipped on his most smug grin. "Actually, El, Gwendolyn was talking about showing you some flowers she saw during the procession. Something about table settings . . ."

Oh, great. Her mother and Rhett were now on a *Gwendolyn*

basis, the name her mother reserved for *special relationships*. Whatever that meant.

Rhett shrugged dramatically. "It's best to leave all that decorating nonsense to the ladies. Am I right?" He waggled a brow in Aiden's direction.

Elodie could have puked all over her new shoes.

Aiden went rigid. "I didn't realize you were engaged."

She clamped her chattering teeth as she searched for an explanation.

Luckily, Elodie didn't need her voice when Major Owens was around. "The Key came to me with the suggested match," he began, rubbing his hands together. "I thought about it, and, at the time, said to myself, 'Rhett, you're nineteen, she's almost sixteen. Good genetics, okay connections. She can't marry until her eighteenth birthday, but you should lock it down. Can't let her turn into an old maid.'"

Aiden's lips twisted and he glanced down at her, wide eyed, before turning his attention back to Rhett. "An old maid? Oh, gosh, no. Wouldn't want that."

Elodie tamped her hysteria with a sharp clap of her hands. "Rhett, I am *really* thirsty. Would you mind getting me a drink?"

Rhett aimed and fired a pair of finger guns in her direction. "You got it, babe." He bobbed his wide chin in Aiden's direction before heading off to find a drink, and, if Elodie was lucky, a different group to entertain.

"So, *El*," Aiden said, as he mimicked Rhett's rocking motion. "Anything else you think *you* should share?"

There was nothing to share about Rhett and her. Elodie grimaced. Just thinking of them together was awkward. She couldn't talk about this with Aiden. She could barely talk about it with Astrid. She needed an out.

"The fair started today," she blurted.

Aiden stopped rocking and tilted his head.

Elodie seized the moment of his confused silence. "To celebrate the Key and their success against Cerberus." She waved a hand toward the mass of people still meandering about the Holbrook estate. "Nearly everyone is here, so the lines should be short."

Aiden's brow twisted. "What does that have to do with the fact that you're engaged and didn't tell me?"

Elodie's stomach tumbled. "Let's go," she said, wringing her hands. "Let's just leave all of this and go."

Aiden studied her a moment before shrugging. "You know I'm always down for an adventure."

It had taken a lot for Rhett to forgive her for sneaking out of her house the night before, even though he had been called away to a clandestine work meeting. Guilt had led Elodie to make promise after promise. She promised him that he mattered. She promised she cared. She promised he was the sun and she the small planet orbiting.

Her promises were empty. Her promises were lies.

Now Aiden was behind her, his heavy boots crushing the grass, and for the first time, she couldn't care less how Major Rhett Owens felt.

Elodie was quickly trying, and failing, to come up with a way to flee the Holbrook estate and the discomfort of both Aiden's and her own most recent discoveries when Astrid Fujimoto's impossibly long, high ponytail lassoed her attention.

Elodie waved at her best friend just in time to stop Astrid from slipping into the Pearl's open door and escaping without her.

Aiden staggered at her side. "Whoa. She looks just like Thea."

And you look a whole lot like Blair. Funny how the whole sibling thing works. Elodie kept her snarky thoughts to herself. He wasn't the only one guilty of keeping a relationship a secret.

She chewed her bottom lip.

Who Aiden was related to wasn't a big deal. But being engaged . . . And to a guy like Rhett, who charged around saying whatever he wanted whenever he wanted . . .

Elodie's stomach squeezed.

But being engaged shouldn't matter to Aiden. Not if they were just friends.

Astrid leaned against the side of the Pearl, twirling the end of her ponytail. "El, I was literally just messaging you. I can't stay at this . . ." with her free hand, she motioned toward the guests still gathered on the grounds, " . . .Westfall show and tell." She tossed her ponytail over her shoulder and gave Aiden a once over. "You look familiar."

"Astrid, Aiden. Aiden, Astrid," Elodie offered.

Astrid straightened. "Like, *the* Aiden? I guess the mohawk should have given it away."

Aiden playfully hiked his shoulder. "Aw, you talk about me?"

Astrid crossed her ankles and resumed playing with her hair. "You're a Scott too." She fanned the ends of her ponytail and dusted them against her cheek. "I've seen your mom and sister at a zillion functions, but have only seen you at, like, one."

"He doesn't get out much," Elodie said, shuffling into the vehicle. "If no one is getting in with me, I'm stealing this Pearl."

Astrid slid into the seat next to her. "What got into you?"

Aiden crawled in and sat in the rear facing seat opposite Elodie. "I think it's more like what came out," he mumbled.

Elodie gripped the armrests. "Just need a change of scenery. Can you program this thing to take us to the waterfront?"

Astrid pulled out her holopad and began typing. "Sure, but the fair's happening right now, so—"

"Exactly." Elodie smiled. "We're going to the fair." She attempted a nonchalant shrug. "I thought it would be fun."

Astrid and Aiden both wore the same confused expression.

Elodie pressed herself into the seat. Maybe getting into a smaller space wasn't such a great idea. At least Astrid was there to break up the round of questions Aiden must be ready to fire. "Hey, Astrid. I'm sure Aiden hasn't been in an updated Pearl. You should tell him all about it."

As Astrid shimmied to the edge of her seat and began proudly explaining and demonstrating all of the new features she'd helped create for the plush ride, Elodie loosened her grip on the armrests and relaxed against the creamy soft upholstery when a line of text flashed into her field of vision.

Incoming call from Rhett Owens.

Elodie denied the call and turned off her comlink. She'd gotten lucky the night before. Gwen and Rhett had left her alone to *sort out her feelings*, as her mother had put it. But she didn't think she'd get that lucky again. Rhett would not be happy about being sent for drinks and then stood up.

Elodie pulled up the transparent gray messaging screen and sent a quick text to Rhett.

The funeral was so sad. I had to leave. Going to Astrid's. Call you later. Promise.

He wouldn't think twice about that. After all, his Elodie was the most sensitive girl in the world.

XXXIV

Energy sparked down Elodie's legs with each passing mile in the Pearl. It had been years since she'd gone to the fair. Two, to be exact. Which is also how long she'd been with Rhett. It wasn't a coincidence. Major Rhett Owens thought fun and playfulness were gateways to terrorism and malfeasance.

Elodie shook her head, clearing all traces of Rhett from her mind. She was with her friends, and she needed a little time off from dealing with the disappointing drama that was her fiancé. The current priority was dealing with the fact that Aiden had been so affected by the news that she and Rhett were matched.

Why hadn't she told him? It wasn't a secret. And the wedding was in only a few months, so Aiden would have found out eventually. Her mother would have insisted the entire Scott family be invited, and now she knew that Aiden would have been on the receiving end of her wedding invitation.

Aiden leaned forward and motioned to the holopad sticking

out of Astrid's seat pocket. "You mind if I use that? I want to get us some fair tokens."

Astrid pulled out her holopad and handed it to Aiden. "A whole afternoon on Aiden Scott." Her nose wrinkled with a grin. "I knew I went to that terrible funeral service for a reason."

Aiden's fingers skipped across the screen as he pulled up the Rose Festival's site and purchased tokens for the trio. "They should be in each of your accounts . . ." He tapped the screen a final time before looking up. "Now," he said, and passed the holopad back to Astrid.

Elodie slid her fingers along her strand of pearls. "Thanks, Aiden." There was a small scratch on one of the smooth beads and she rubbed her fingertip against it. Luckily Astrid was with them. No matter how many things Aiden paid for, this could never be considered a date.

Astrid tapped the screen a few times with her pointed, black-tipped nails before sliding it into the seat pocket. "You know, you could've asked Holly to get the tokens for you. She'd load them into each of our accounts." She extended a long, slender finger and pointed to Aiden's clear cuff. "And they'd push to our cuffs."

Aiden wriggled out of his black jacket and casually hiked his shoulders. "Either way I'm buying them and you're using them, right?" he asked, stretching his arm along the back of the empty seat next to him.

Astrid tapped her checkered shoes against the plush carpet. "It's your life, Scott. Just trying to make it a little bit easier."

Dirt flaked onto the floor as Aiden crossed his ankle over his knee. "That's what friends are for, right?" he said.

Elodie's palms went clammy. She brushed her hands down

the pleats of her skirt. *Could* Astrid and Aiden be friends? They were from completely different worlds.

Actually, that wasn't true. Not with what Elodie now knew. Aiden and Astrid were from extremely similar worlds of wealth and importance. The Key would do, and *had done*, almost anything for the Fujimotos and the Scotts. Astrid and Aiden were more alike, had more in common with each other, than either did with Elodie. And, in circles like theirs, Aiden's involvement in Eos would warrant a death sentence.

Elodie's fingers flew back to the small pearls ringing her collar. Why hadn't she thought about that before? She never should have brought the two of them together. Astrid said herself that she'd only seen him at one function. Aiden didn't have friends in high places, and, considering who he was, that had to be on purpose. The last thing Elodie or Aiden needed was the devilishly intelligent Astrid Fujimoto getting too curious about Aiden Scott.

Astrid stared at him for a moment as she tapped her fingernails together. Rhythmic clicks filled the space like a Newton's Cradle. "Yeah," Astrid offered with a quick shrug, her brow smoothing. "What the hell, Scott? We can be friends."

Elodie let loose the stale breath stuffed deep in her lungs. "That's saying a lot. Astrid's not really big on the whole *people-liking* thing." She forced a smile and added *Keep Aiden on Astrid's good side* to her growing to do list.

With a flourish, Aiden made his best attempt at a seated bow. "It's an honor, Fujimoto."

The Pearl slowed as the Key Corp's neon-red Rose Festival logo came into view, a massive steel sign hung from a system of bars stretched across the fair entrance. The sculpted red rose blossom, vibrant green stem, and fanning electric leaves were stunning even under the full light of the sun. Elodie was used to the neon signs and flashing lights. They were all used in holographic marketing. Nothing could be sold anymore without being packaged like the inside of virtual arcade. But holograms weren't tangible. The Key was smart for keeping the original steel Rose Festival sign. An antique like that had presence. It carried weight and occupied space in a way no hologram could duplicate. It was breathtaking because it was real.

The inside of the Pearl flashed violet, signaling the end of the ride, before the doors automatically slid open. Elodie stared up at the rose as she slid out of the vehicle. Goosebumps sprouted along her arms. She was doing what she wanted to do when she wanted to do it, taking charge of her time. And it felt good.

Unlike the years before, there was no line to wait in to enter the fair. Holbrook's funeral served as the day's main attraction. Elodie preferred it this way. No crowd. No mass of Violet Shields staining her view of what was ahead. The three of them could walk around the entire riverside festival without lines taking up their whole day.

Elodie glanced over her shoulder as Aiden jogged up to the entrance after her and Astrid hung back to use the Pearl's window to redo her ponytail.

Before the complications of Eos and the Scotts and Rhett, getting stuck at the fair with Aiden would have been a dream. Now, they were one awkward silence away from a heavy conversation.

Aiden cleared his throat and unbuttoned the top button of his shirt. "We really should talk about what happened."

Elodie gripped her pleats. "I didn't get to ask Blair what I needed to, but now I know that you can ask for me whenever you want."

"And now I know that you're matched."

Elodie's fingers again found the smooth pearls framing her neck. She swallowed tightly and swung her gaze to the street where Astrid lackadaisically shuffled up the entryway, tapping on her holopad. What was taking her so long? Couldn't she see that Elodie needed saving?

Elodie tucked a stray wave of hair behind her ear. "It really shouldn't matter, Aiden. You and I are just friends." As she said it, she knew it wasn't the complete truth. It was an oversimplification. A cutting jab to what she knew they had together—what they *could* have together if their circumstances weren't such a mess.

Aiden's hand fell to his side. "Still—"

Three loud claps shattered the heaviness shrouding Elodie and Aiden. "Holy shit," Astrid said. "You two know what we should do?" Excitement splashed pink across her sharp cheekbones.

Aiden shrugged and tossed a hand toward the brightly colored rides just beyond the entrance. "Go on a ride?"

"Only after we eat that giant fried dough thing covered in powdered sugar." Astrid mimed the heaping plate of sweet goodness. "Oh! And one of those pretzels the size of your face!" She bounced up and down a few times before taking off to the snack truck just inside the entrance.

Astrid's excitement was understandable. The only time of year Westfall had any food that was fried, covered in sugar, or the size of someone's entire face was at the Key's annual celebration. Every other day consisted of a plant-based diet tailored to each citizen as a way to keep everyone performing at their best. It was also a smart agricultural and waste management move. With predetermined diets, the Key only produced the amount of food that would be eaten.

Elodie trailed Aiden up to the snack cart. She couldn't think about eating. Not while her stomach worried itself into knots.

"Extra mustard," Astrid told the serving bot when Elodie approached. "Hey, El, they have those roasted corncobs that come on a stick. You love those. Want one?"

Elodie's heart fluttered and she couldn't help but pass a bashful glance at Aiden. Astrid had no idea. "I'm good," she said. Her cheeks heated as her eyes again found Aiden. He'd left his suitcoat in the Pearl and untucked his perfectly fitted button down. Now he undid a few more buttons, but with each movement the shirt still strained against his chest.

The knots in Elodie's stomach tightened.

When they'd been in the warehouse, had he felt the same rush of need that she had?

The excited drumming of Astrid's nails against the metal shelf of the food truck barreled through Elodie's thoughts. "I'm getting you a cherry limeade," Astrid said.

Good. Elodie needed to cool off.

"Hey, Scott, want anything?" Astrid tossed over her shoulder as she eyed the digital menu.

Aiden's mossy green eyes caught Elodie's and the corner of his mouth tipped in a sly grin. "Nothing that bot can give me."

Elodie's breath stilled in her chest as he continued to stare at her so intently she thought she might burst into flames. She tore her attention away and focused on the nearby rides. "Spooky tunnel ride!" Elodie snatched the sweating cup of limeade from Astrid, and gulped it as if she hadn't had a drink for days.

Astrid chortled around a mouthful of pretzel. "Yeah, right. You hate being scared." She swiped a napkin across the line of mustard running down her chin. "You especially hate things that pop out and scare you on purpose. That's the whole reason you wouldn't go with me to that kick-ass Halloween bash over in . . ."

She took another bite and waved her hand in the air. "Wherever it was."

Astrid was right. Elodie didn't like anything that was, by definition, designed to be frightening. But the idea of Astrid leaving her alone with Aiden, looking the way he looked in that tight shirt and those tight pants, was much more terrifying.

And Elodie had not actually *chosen* the terrifying tunnel ride. It was just the first one she'd seen. If only she'd been facing a little more to the left, they'd be getting on the teacups.

Elodie stabbed at the melting ice cubes with her quickly dissolving paper straw. "You know Gwen would have freaked if I was up in my room screaming because of some VR Halloween party. Besides—" Air burbled through the straw as she sucked down the last drops of cherry limeade. "People change."

Astrid popped the final bite of pretzel into her mouth. "I'll never say no to a good adrenaline boost." She grinned. "You in, Scott?"

Aiden nodded. "Scott is in."

Astrid wiped her hands on a napkin and threw it into the compost bin. The acrid smell of chemical-laced smoke drifted around them as the paper was sterilized and incinerated. "Well, then, *après vous, mis amigos.*"

Elodie dropped her cup into the bin and darted toward the creepy entrance to the one ride she had hoped she'd never have to go on. She scanned her cuff and waited for the admission bar to raise before she rushed into the last cart in the linked row while Aiden claimed the one in front of her, and Astrid skipped to the very front of the line.

"Hey, Scott," Astrid shouted. "How much you want to bet that Elodie screams within the first thirty seconds?"

Even though they were staying firmly on the ground, Elodie

clasped the cart's seat belt. "Ha ha. Very funny," she said, tightening the belt across her lap. She was definitely going to scream within the first thirty seconds. She'd probably scream the second they entered the tunnel.

Aiden stretched his arm along the back of his cart. "I'd never bet against Elodie."

Astrid stood so Elodie could see her over Aiden's tall frame. "You're only saying that because you know I'll win." She braced herself back in the seat as the cars began to inch forward. "Don't worry, El. I'm in front. I'll protect you." Astrid offered an exaggerated wink before the open mouth of the black tunnel claimed her.

Anxiety frosted Elodie's spine. She really did hate things that she knew were going to pop out and scare her.

The cold darkness swallowed Aiden before finally spilling across Elodie. Goosebumps rose on her arms. At least fear ensured she wouldn't think about the past few days.

Faint red lights illuminated the freakishly painted walls and cast a glow across the carts. A shadow moved toward her and she squeezed her eyes shut, bracing herself for the first of many zombies or ghosts or other ghoulish creatures to come screaming out of the darkness.

A weight plopped down in the seat beside her, and she shrieked.

"Totally would've won!" Astrid cheered from up ahead.

Crisp pine-scented air swirled around Elodie. "It's me," Aiden whispered.

He was next to her. *Right* next to her. Their legs an inch apart.

She scrunched herself into the corner of the cart, straining against the lap belt. "What are you doing?" she whispered back.

"We need to talk." Red illuminated his face, deepening his gaze. "I couldn't wait."

Elodie pressed her back into the side of the car, trying to increase the distance between them. "We can talk later."

"Do you love him?" Aiden blurted.

A ghost hurled itself toward their cart, its white sheet flowing in huge waves around its hollow eyes.

Her pulse thrummed behind her ears. "We were matched and now we're engaged."

Aiden searched her face. "But do you love him?"

What did he want from her? She and Rhett had been matched not only by their parents, but by the corporation. And, when it came to this, there was no defying the Key. At least, there wasn't for Elodie.

Elodie opened her mouth, but no words came out.

"You don't." He settled back against the cart. "Do you?"

Her eyes burned hot with unshed tears. "It doesn't matter."

An expression passed over his features that she couldn't quite place. "It's all that matters."

Up ahead, Astrid whooped with excitement as a zombie hurled itself from the shadows, reaching for the carts with mangled fingers.

Elodie's throat went dry as she hid her tears. "Aiden—"

He surged forward and reclaimed his name right from her lips, all of Elodie's words, her thoughts, lost within the softness of his mouth.

Rhett was a memory wiped clean as her eyelids slid shut.

Aiden was gentle. His lips brushed hers, tentative and sweet. Long-buried need sparked within Elodie and she parted her lips in surrender. Another gentle caress of his mouth against hers, like she was fragile, sacred.

But Elodie was not glass.

Desire exploded through her as she gripped his collar and

pulled him closer, deeper. Her hips twisted against the lap belt. Aiden groaned, low and eager, a trembling roar building within in as his arms encircled her and pulled her tight against his heaving chest. His hands tangled in her hair as her palms melted against the strong muscles of his back.

Elodie breathed him in, the forest after the rain. His tongue encircled hers, and heat bloomed within her, a thousand buds opening again and again.

Aiden was everywhere. *Everything.*

She dissolved into him. No beginning. No end. Just this moment. And them, diving into each other. In Aiden's kiss lived all the answers. In Aiden's kiss lived hope.

Elodie knew she didn't love Rhett, but she never thought she'd love the spooky tunnel ride.

XXXV

The screeches and screams of the creatures haunting the dark tunnel were reduced to a steady background hum as desire surged, molten hot inside Aiden. It crashed against the dam he'd built within his chest to keep this part of himself at bay. The part that *needed.* The part that *wanted.*

But now he was close to Elodie. Too close to keep the waves from roiling and striking through his inner walls.

"Do you love him?"

It was a simple question, but the way Elodie's eyes glinted in the dull red light and the absence of a swift *yes* told Aiden everything he needed to know.

The dam within him cracked. The rapids tore free. Every inch of him heated with wave after wave of desire. Aiden's mouth claimed hers and he pulled her closer. Needing more of her. Needing all of her. Elodie's lips parted in gentle welcoming.

She was everything.

Light crept in between his softly closed eyelids, but he refused to let loose the moment and give her back to the present. He'd found his place. He was home.

The sun's warmth poured onto Aiden's head.

"What the fuck are you doing?" Astrid's snarl tore through his world like a crack of lightning.

Aiden slammed back against the side of the cart as he jolted and Elodie pushed him away. His eyes strained to adjust to the brightness outside of the tunnel. The world tipped around Aiden as he tried to get his bearings and meet the heaven that was Elodie with the hell of the present, where the darkness from the tunnel no longer hid their kiss.

Astrid choked down a breath. "What the fuck is wrong with you?" she howled. Her tone was thunder, shaking Aiden to his core.

Aiden struggled to stand up inside the cramped cart. "Astrid, there are things you don't know."

"Things I don't know?" Her ponytail lifted and whipped the air with a sudden gust of wind. "Nothing you could say would make any of this okay. What you did—" Livid disgust sharpened her features. "You'll pay for this."

Elodie brushed against him as she struggled to free herself from the lap belt. "Astrid!" Finally free, Elodie leapt from the cart.

Astrid jerked backward and clicked on her Violet Shield. "Don't you dare touch me! I don't know what has happened to you. What *he*"—Astrid stabbed the air in Aiden's direction—"has done to you, but this is—it's unforgivable."

Elodie buried her face in her hands. "I know."

Aiden's heart froze within his chest. "You can't tell anyone, Astrid," he said, climbing out of the ride.

Astrid blinked and shook her head as if Aiden were a child

showing off a silly trick. "I have to. For your protection, for Elodie's, for Westfall. The Cerberus virus happened once before. It could happen again."

"A kiss won't hurt anyone." He could explain if she would only give him the chance. "I promise it won't."

Astrid took another step back. "Tell that to the billions of people the virus killed," she said. "I'm sure they felt the same way."

"Astrid—" Elodie began, but Astrid's cutting glance made her choke back her words.

Tears welled in Astrid's eyes. "How could you do this?" Sharply, she blinked them back before they had the chance to escape. "This isn't you."

"Please!" Elodie sobbed.

Aiden's chest clenched with each ragged burst. He'd caused this. And there was nothing he could do to fix it.

Astrid's hands trembled as she wiped at her cheek. "I have to go." She turned and sprinted toward the festival entrance.

Elodie lurched forward after her best friend.

Aiden grabbed her hand. "Elodie, I . . ." He didn't have any words. He didn't have any way to make up for what had happened.

Elodie studied their joined hands before looking up at him. Tears shimmered against her dark eyes.

With his thumb, Aiden traced slow circles against the back of her hand. "I'm sorry," he finally whispered. There was so much more he needed to say, but he had no idea where to start.

Elodie's throat tightened with a sob and she pulled away from him and took off after Astrid.

"Elodie!" Aiden leaped out of the cart and started after her, but a row of janitorial bots paraded between them, cutting him off from catching up with her.

Aiden brushed his hands through his hair and let out a curse. Elodie was always running away.

XXXVI

The best and worst moments of Elodie's life happened end to end. She should have known, should have sensed that although everything felt right, everything was wrong. The universe had lifted her up in order to slam her back down.

Elodie wove through the crowds of people outside the fair, exiting Pearls and getting off the MAX, still in their fine dress from Holbrook's funeral and all heading straight for the festivities. The scene of her crime.

She should have stayed at the funeral. Instead, she'd run away from one problem and crashed right into another.

Elodie's lungs burned and her arms pumped by her sides in rapid bursts as she raced to catch up to Astrid. Wind brushed against Elodie's cheeks and twirled through her hair, taking with it the deep forest scent of Aiden and his kiss.

Astrid paused at the intersection a block ahead. "Astrid!" Elodie continued to run, waving her arms over her head as she yelled. "Talk to me!"

Astrid didn't turn back, didn't wait. A Pearl stopped in front of her and she disappeared inside the opalescent orb.

By the time Elodie reached the corner, the Pearl and Astrid were gone.

XXXVII

The setting sun streamed in through Elodie's window and painted her bedroom door cheery orange. It was mocking her. It shouldn't be allowed to be all bright and happy while her life was falling apart.

She flopped onto her back and pulled the covers tight around her. "Go away," she groaned at the refracted rainbow spots dancing on the ceiling before she pulled the blanket up over her head and rolled onto her side. Any minute she'd hear her mother charging up the stairs to take her away to who knows where to pay for what she'd done. Astrid was right. Kissing Aiden was unforgiveable.

But maybe Astrid hadn't told. Maybe everything would be okay.

Yeah, right.

Elodie kicked off the covers and flew to her feet. She couldn't sit still. There was no possible way. What was going to happen to her? To Aiden?

"Ohhh!" she groaned again, wrapping her arms around her middle. Her stomach churned and bubbled in response.

Pacing next to her bed, she brought up the messaging thread she shared with Astrid. Elodie ignored the completely one-sided column of texts she'd started sending the second Astrid had left in the Pearl, and she began a new message.

Before Holly's update, each message had to be typed out letter by letter through a sophisticated system that tracked eye movement over the keyboard, until Holly recognized patterns and could autofill whole portions of the text. Now, with a simple thought and the slightest bit of concentration . . . *boom!* Text.

Talk to me. Please!

She hesitated before adding that line to the tower of panicked, pleading sent texts stretching in front of her vision. She needed to see Astrid and for Astrid to see her.

Would it change anything? It was worth a try.

She chewed her lip, wincing as her teeth dug into fresh skin. "Holly, vidlink Astrid." Elodie smoothed her hair behind her ears and clasped her hands in her lap to keep them from shaking.

Elodie's breath stuck in her chest as the ringing abruptly ceased and seconds of dead air hung on the line as Astrid's vidlink connected. Astrid had answered. She'd actually answered. As her face appeared, Elodie had to figure out what to say. Her heart fluttered against her ribs.

Astrid's hair hung in inky black sheets past her shoulders. She started to speak, then tucked one lock behind her ear before sucking in a breath and meeting Elodie's gaze. "I'm not supposed to talk to you."

Elodie's throat went dry and her teeth became an impenetrable wall holding back her words.

Astrid glanced down at something out of Elodie's field of view and her hair slid back to cover her right eye. "Something happened. Something I don't understand."

The wall crumbled and words tumbled from Elodie's tongue. "I know. I'm so sorry! I never meant for you to see that. I never meant to do it. Aiden was in the seat in front of me and then he was next to me and then he was . . ." Elodie sucked in a breath so deep she had to ground her feet to keep from floating away. "Everywhere."

A tear slid down Astrid's cheek, halting Elodie's words.

"Not that." Astrid's thin fingers trembled as she brushed back her hair. "That's something I—" A sob squeaked past Astrid's trembling jaw.

Elodie worried her worn cotton collar. "Astrid—"

Astrid's attention turned abruptly. Her father's sharp voice cut through the feed. "Your mother's made dinner."

Astrid's jaw tightened. "Yes, father."

"And wipe your face." He paused somewhere outside Elodie's view, and Astrid seemed to cave in on herself. Her shoulders slumped and her head hung low. "You don't want anyone to think you're upset. You'll worry your sister."

Astrid nodded almost imperceptibly before scrubbing the back of her hand down her tear-glossed cheek.

"And you mustn't say anything about what happened. I'd hoped I wouldn't have to mention that, but—" He let out a weary breath. "Here we are."

Astrid lifted her head. "I won't say anything, Father. You have my word."

A burst of dry laughter echoed from off camera. "Daughter, think about whether or not *your word* should mean anything to me."

The hiss of the door and Astrid's immediate deflation signaled his exit.

Astrid's father was usually nice, usually cheerful. The kind of dad who made Elodie wish hers was more than a picture on a mantle.

Elodie swallowed. "Is everything okay?"

Astrid chewed the sharpened tip of her polished nails. "Will you meet me tomorrow?" Desperation clawed at her voice in a way Elodie had never heard before.

Elodie nodded feverishly.

Astrid cleared her throat. "The sands," she said, her earlier vulnerability replaced with Astrid's normal matter-of-factness. "I have to go." Her mouth quirked with a failed attempt at a smile. "Dinner and everything." With practiced perfection, Astrid pulled her hair into her signature high pony, smoothed out the bumps, and twisted a clear tie around the base.

Elodie winced as her teeth again found the delicate spot of new flesh on her lip. "I'll see you tomorrow."

The feed went dark and Elodie exhaled, collapsing back against her mound of pillows.

Her ease was immediately interrupted by another wave of anxiety. Nothing was fixed. If anything, the situation was even more strange now. She and Astrid hadn't actually talked about anything. They hadn't *fixed* anything. And what was all that with Astrid's father?

Elodie dragged her hands down her cheeks. No, nothing was better. Somehow, she felt even more uneasy than she had before the vidlink.

Elodie rolled over and pressed her face into a fluffy pillow. Hot breath warmed her nose and mouth as she exhaled.

Nothing was ever going to be better.

Astrid had told. Elodie knew that for a fact. So what was the Key waiting for? Why weren't soldiers trying to pound down her door and take her away in chains? They should just do it and get it over with.

She sucked in a breath.

The corporation would send her to Rehabilitation. That's what they did with people like her. But she couldn't go to Rehab. She'd heard stories. The things they did to get citizens back on the right path . . .

She filled her lungs and pressed her face deeper into the mound of pillows. A scream tore from her throat.

"I CAN'T GO TO REHAB!"

The words were swallowed immediately by the thick fluff. Erased, like they had never happened. If only erasing time was as easy.

Clink.

Elodie lifted her head from the suffocating heat of her trapped fears. At some point, her eyes had teared. She wiped the moisture from her cheeks.

Clink.

There it was again. A tinkling against glass.

She popped up onto her elbows and craned her neck until her window came into view along with the river rocks she'd placed on the sill. The lace edges of her petal pink pillowcases quivered beneath her in the wake of her steady breaths.

Clink. A gray spot nicked the window.

Elodie pushed herself off the bed and crept toward the window.

Clink.

No, not spots. *Rocks.*

She threw the window open and peered out over the ledge.

Aiden lowered his arm mid windup and waved at her.

Elodie's pulse surged and her heartbeat thrummed wildly. "What are you doing here?" Her voice was hoarse and her throat scratchy from screaming into the pillows.

Aiden jumped and grabbed ahold of the thick tree limb above him before expertly pulling himself onto the next branch, then the next and the next until he was an arm's length away from Elodie's second-story window. She had descended that very same tree days before. Climbing down was much easier than climbing up, gravity made sure of that, but Aiden had sped up the massive pink magnolia like he had suction cups for hands.

"I wanted to see you," he said, a bit breathless as he closed the distance between them and sat on her windowsill. "I *needed* to see you." He brushed a stray leaf out of his hair. "Can I come in?"

"No!" Elodie hissed automatically. "You shouldn't even be here! You should have sent me a text. I could have met you somewhere else. *Anywhere* else!"

Aiden brushed away bits of tree bark from his shorts. "You never would have come to meet me anywhere. Not after what happened."

Elodie wrung out her hands. He was right. Aiden was what had *happened*. He was the only thing that had ever happened. But this one thing was big enough to swallow her world.

"Or I could stay outside and we can talk out in the open. *In front of everyone!*" He practically shouted the last bit as he leaned out the window and made a sweeping gesture that took in the empty sidewalk and street. But her neighbors were nosy, and Elodie never knew who was watching.

"Fine." Elodie slid the rocks on her windowsill into a pile in the corner before stepping aside. "You can't stay long or be loud."

As he crawled through the open window, Aiden looked

around. She had never had a guy in her room before. Not even Rhett. And she was wearing an old holey T-shirt she'd first gotten years ago from the New Americans for Wellness gala, one of her mother's many philanthropic causes. Elodie's stomach flip-flopped and her cheeks flamed.

Aiden ruffled his mohawk. His dark curls and rich brown skin seemed to deepen against the stark white of his tee. "Nice room."

Elodie balled her hands into the bottom of her oversized shirt. "I talked to Astrid."

Aiden faltered, scrubbing a hand down his cheek as he sat against the windowsill. "Elodie, I'm sorry. I didn't think—"

"No, Aiden, that's the problem. You didn't think. You just acted. You did something that has endangered both our lives." The panic returned, sending rivers of ice through Elodie's veins. "The Council—they could sentence us to death." It was a realization she hadn't been able to see before. The idea had been dormant, hibernating until she and Aiden were together again to jostle it awake.

Aiden surged to his feet and held up his hands. "That's not going to happen."

"What makes you think that? Of course it's going to happen. We broke a law. Not just *a* law, *the* law." Laughter bubbled up Elodie's throat. "We're traitors. That's what the Key does to traitors."

"No, Elodie. We're not. *You're* not."

"That's right. You have to make the distinction because you actually have committed treason." Her knees went weak as a last hiccup of laughter escaped her. "Eos." Elodie pulled the chair out from her desk and dropped onto the seat. "They'll find out about your involvement with Eos. That I was there . . ."

"Elodie, no, listen to me." Aiden knelt down before her. "The

Key won't find out about any of that. You're not going to tell them and I'm sure as hell not saying a word. We're the only two who know."

"We kissed, Aiden." Elodie's eyes flooded and her voice came out a whisper.

"And I'd do it again. *Will* do it again. A hundred times again," he said. "Next time we won't get caught. I'll make sure of it."

"*Next time?*" Elodie hopped up from the chair and paced between her bed and desk. "There can never be a *next time*, Aiden. I'm matched. To Rhett. I'm getting married in four months."

Aiden's head swiveled as his eyes followed her. "We don't have to be matched or married to be together."

Elodie stopped, her brow furrowed. "So what? I'm supposed to marry Rhett, but be with you behind his back? If you think that's something I'll agree to, you don't know me very well." She crossed her arms over her chest. "It was a mistake. The whole thing was a mistake."

Aiden stepped back like he'd been shot. "That's not how it felt. You were there. You kissed me back."

"I did not!" Her entire body sizzled.

Aiden threw up his hands. "Shit, Elodie. If we're going down for this—and we will—with who I am, who my sister and mother are, it won't be bad. Probation, career reassignment—" He took a deep breath. "We're going to get in some sort of trouble. *We* are. Both of us. That's happening, so don't you want to be honest about us?"

Elodie gripped the back of her chair to keep her bones from rattling loose. "It was wrong, Aiden."

"Then why did it feel the way it did? Like it was supposed to happen. Like it was *meant* to happen," Aiden said. "Maybe everyone else is living life wrong and we're the only people living it right."

Elodie sagged against the windowsill. "Or maybe we're just lying to ourselves."

A swift series of knocks cracked their conversation.

Everything within Elodie stilled as her wide-eyed gaze locked onto Aiden's.

Don't say a word, she mouthed.

"Elodie!" her mother shouted from outside her door. "I just received a notification from that neighborhood watch I signed up for. Says there's a prowler nearby. A young man. What kind of young man do you think would go prowling? And in this neighborhood!" The keypad on the inside of Elodie's door flashed red as Gwen tried to open it. "El, honey, your door is locked."

"Privacy, Mom! Jeez!" Elodie yelled through chattering teeth before she feverishly motioned for Aiden to move back toward the open window.

"El, sweetheart, let me in." The door panel again flashed red. "I'm starting to worry." Gwen's tone belied more threat than concern.

"Everything's fine! Just, uh, changing," Elodie called.

Another flash of red. "There's no reason to be modest. This wouldn't be the first time I've seen you without your clothes on."

Aiden had one leg out the window before he paused. "We can't stop fighting for what's right," he whispered. "There are things you still don't know about the Key. Things that, if they came out, would make everything different." He covered her hands with his and pressed his lips against her fingertips. "Things that would make *this* different. The way we live now isn't the way the world is supposed to work."

Elodie snatched her hand back. "But this is the way the world is, so . . ." she trailed off. "What's the point in trying?"

"Love, Elodie. Happiness, hope, freedom. Those all mean

something to you. If they didn't, we never would have found each other," Aiden said, pulling himself into the tree.

"Elodie Grace! You open this door right this second!" Gwen shouted.

Elodie gripped the edge of the window. "You have to go."

"Come to the warehouse tomorrow. I just—" He paused. "I want to tell you everything."

Elodie tugged the window down. "I'll think about it. Now, go."

Aiden slipped into the falling dark. Elodie noiselessly slid the window shut and hastily arranged her line of rocks on the sill until they looked perfect.

XXXVIII

Elodie sat on the sand-covered street, folding her legs up under her as she waited for Astrid at the base of her best friend's favorite building—the building Astrid had thrown herself off countless times, her webbed bodysuit threading from her arms to her legs like a human parachute. Loose strands of hair blew in front of Elodie's eyes and she pushed them back and squinted up at the glittering silver building. Its spire pierced the cloudless morning sky like the point of a needle through silk.

Astrid tested the limits with everything. *Almost* everything. When it came to the Key and its rules, there was no pushing for this rule-following Fujimoto. She was as rigid as the paved street beneath Elodie's feet, the same street she'd watched Astrid splat against as she tested the limits of her custom-coded suit.

Elodie couldn't help but wonder if sometimes Astrid hurled herself off the roof just for the sake of hitting the pavement, just to feel that second of nothingness between VR and real life. The cessation of breath before the next inhale.

The first time it had happened—the first time Astrid had died in VR—Elodie had almost puked. Astrid's body slammed into the replica Dubai street and dissolved into a pixelated mass of colors before sinking into the ground and disappearing completely. At least VR didn't leave a lot of corpses lying around.

Booted from the sim, Astrid had been back in Elodie's earpiece a moment later. "Did you see that?! What. A. Rush!"

Elodie had fallen to her knees. The blacktop sliced off a few centimeters of her bare kneecaps as the glitchy program struggled to interpret her sudden movement. "I thought you were dead!"

Astrid had scoffed. "You can't die in VR, El. It's not real." Even now, Elodie could practically hear her friend roll her eyes. "Wait right where you are. I'm logging back in and doing it again."

But this morning, Elodie would have done anything to know she was meeting Astrid here to talk like they used to. She'd do anything to have another chance at mustering the courage to jump from the high point of the building, following her best friend up, just to succumb to nerves at the last minute and ride the smooth elevator back down to the ground.

Everything was supposed to change when she married Rhett. Not now. Not like this. Why couldn't she live her life, experiment with it, have fun with it, without it all falling to pieces? Her life was hers. Wasn't it?

Navy and green-checkered shoes shuffled noiselessly into Elodie's periphery, tearing her from her memories. Astrid's avatar looked haggard, tired, like the stress from last night had seeped through and infected this fake world.

Elodie's ankle started to ache and she unfolded and refolded her legs beneath her. She stiffened. Her ankle *ached*. Since the update, she'd only been in VR to fulfill her nursing assignments. Within those programs, it was normal to feel temperatures and textures. Those aspects were programmed into all simulations. It's what made the virtual feel more real. But pain was different. Pain was new.

Astrid cleared her throat and scraped the toe of her shoe against the pavement. "Feels like it's been forever since we've been here together." She let out a weary sigh as she adjusted her tool-belt, another custom VR accessory covered in small silver boxes, and tucked her legs underneath her to join Elodie on the sand dusted blacktop.

Elodie brushed sparkling granules from her leggings, blinking frantically as the breeze picked up the sand and tossed it back against her lashes. "There's more sand than there used to be."

Astrid let out a dry chuckle. "It's always been the same. You're just used to watching me." She pointed at the blanket of blue above. "You're used to looking up."

"Change in perspective, I guess." Elodie felt the words so deep her chest ached.

Astrid grabbed a fistful of sand and let the golden specks drain between her fingers as she lifted her hand.

Elodie continued quickly. "I'm glad you decided to meet me."

Astrid remained silent. Her ponytail slid off her shoulders as her head hung from her neck like an anchor.

"Look, Astrid, I know what you saw—" Elodie began.

Astrid turned to face her, her upturned eyes red rimmed and awash in tears. "I'm sorry." She brushed her hands against her moist, pale cheeks, leaving streaks of sand in their wake. "*So, so sorry.*"

Elodie's fingers were numb. Her body cold, each cell frosted with fear. She couldn't breathe. It was all over. Aiden had said his last name would save them from any real consequences, but that wasn't true. His last name protected him, not her. Elodie would be shipped to Rehabilitation. There was no way Rhett would be there when she returned. The carefully planned lines of her carefully plotted life would be erased. New sharp edges and stiff cliffs penciled in over the ghost of what had been.

And Gwen.

Bile burned the back of Elodie's throat.

What will my mother say?

Astrid's chest heaved and she buried her face into her palms. "I shouldn't have."

Elodie finally managed to push words past her clenched teeth. "It's okay."

"I'm so, so sorry. So sorry. So sorry . . ." Astrid repeated again and again.

The muffled words tumbled against Elodie's ears until they'd lost meaning and became just another noise swallowed by the wind.

"Me too," she said. Elodie *was* sorry. Not for the kiss. Never for the kiss. Aiden was right. If that's how her story ended, she would do it all over again. A million times again. It was the only thing that she had ever *felt*.

At least she'd gone out in a blaze. A shooting star.

Elodie pressed her teeth against her bottom lip. "Want to know something?" she asked without listening for an answer. "I never stopped reading those banned books." If she was going to be sent in front of the Council to have her life rewritten, she'd go without any secrets. At least, she'd go without any secrets *she owned*. Other secrets—Eos secrets, Aiden secrets, even Fujimoto sister secrets—they weren't hers to tell.

Astrid's quakes calmed, replaced by short, hiccup-laden sniffles. "I got one. My first one." She peeked out above her hands. "My first banned book."

Elodie's breath stuck in her throat. Astrid's rigid rule-following was why she'd run from the fair without giving Elodie a chance to explain. It was why they were sitting in a made-up version of a real place that Elodie would never be able to visit. And not because her family couldn't afford air travel. No, it was now because her rule-abiding "bestie" had condemned her to a life much more oppressed than the one she'd tried to escape.

Astrid pulled a silver square from her toolbelt and set it on the ground, where it morphed into a slim black bag. Astrid was a VR-code genius. She pulled the bag onto her lap, dug through the outer pocket, and pulled out a book. Sinister clouds burned rusted orange against the cover of the worn paperback. "The image reminded me of the Zone Seven news reports."

Elodie held out her hand and Astrid passed her the book. Its weight shocked her. It felt as real as any she owned. The VR tech improved all the time. She smoothed her fingers over the cottony pages, soft from decades of wear. The color had worn off the embossed title, but the font's echo was still legible—*Poison Princess.*

Astrid inched closer. "It was my sister's. Can you believe Thea had a banned book?"

A knowing grin tickled the corner of Elodie's mouth as she slid her thumb down the book's spine.

Astrid reached out and traced the cover with her fingertips. "There's a sentence in there. Actually, it's the first sentence I read when I opened the book to skim through it. *Come, touch . . . but you'll pay a price.* It spoke to me in a way nothing has before." Astrid balled her hands in her lap. "How could that be dangerous?"

If Aiden were there, he'd have a million things to say. But Elodie only had one. "It's not."

"If I were you, I'd be pissed at me." Astrid didn't look up as she spoke.

Elodie dropped the book onto Astrid's bag. Her hands tightened into fists. Was the novel the reason Astrid had been so weird when they'd talked? Was this what her father was so angry about?

Elodie had nearly turned herself inside out the night before, agonizing over whether or not Astrid had told anyone about the kiss—and this is what Astrid had been dealing with? *A book?*

"So you didn't go to the Key and tell them about Aiden and me?"

"I did tell on you." Astrid's voice was tired and lost. "Both of you. That's where I went when I ran from the fair. Straight to the Council. What you did, Elodie, was so, so—" She shook her head. "I never thought I'd see anything like that." She stared down at her hands. "And I didn't think that the Key would do anything truly bad . . ."

"You didn't think they'd send me to Rehab?"

"I was busy thinking about Cerberus."

Elodie dug her fingers into the pile of sand that had blown up against her shoe. "The Key isn't telling the truth about that, you know?"

"Yeah, well." Astrid's voice trembled. "The Key isn't telling the truth about a lot of things."

Elodie blinked, her jaw bobbing as she gathered her thoughts. "You agree with me?"

Astrid's eyes flooded and her neck corded with tension. "Council Leader Darby." A sharp, ugly wail hacked its way out of her throat. "He sentenced you and Aiden. I knew last night, but I didn't know how to tell you."

Elodie's teeth ground together. "It'll be okay," she said, more to herself than to Astrid. "It's Rehabilitation. Aiden and I will get through it." She swallowed. "I'll get through it. It'll be okay."

"*Death*, Elodie," Astrid wailed. "Darby sentenced you to *death*!"

A bleat of panicked laughter escaped Elodie's chest. "No. He can't." She shook her head so vigorously her vision blurred. "The Council can't do that. The Key saves people." Tears leaked down her cheeks. "They won't, Astrid. There hasn't been a trial." Elodie sniffed and swiped her fingertips under her eyes. "You must have heard wrong. They would never. That's not an option."

Or had she just convinced herself it wasn't?

She and Aiden had broken *the* rule. The rule that the Key had used to maintain power. The rule that they'd said insured a row of tomorrows stretched on after today.

No one had ever broken *the rule*.

Or maybe they had, and the Key had wiped them out of existence before anyone realized they were missing.

Astrid braced her hands against the street and leaned in conspiratorially. "I went back. When I heard the sentence, I tried to recant." Her voice was hoarse, but she'd wrangled her sobs. "I even lied to my father and had him insist the Council needed to call an emergency meeting with me. I thought having him there would make them take what I had to say seriously." She pressed back into a crumpled shell of herself. Her ponytail brushed her shoulders as she shook her head. "Darby wouldn't listen. Wouldn't let anyone listen. He said that my words weren't my own and that I was being manipulated." Astrid inhaled a shaky breath. "My father is furious." She rubbed her puffy, red eyes. "The Key threatened his funding." Tears dripped from the quivering end of her pointed chin. "They're sending me to Rehabilitation. And when I come back, they're matching me, Elodie. They're matching me to a man. To create a *proper* family."

Elodie's heart melted into her veins. Her entire body pulsed with a rapid, deafening beat. Astrid was in front of her, all tears and pain and remorse and guilt. But to Elodie, she might as well have been another heap of sand.

"The Key is supposed to listen," Astrid said as she scrubbed the back of her hands across her cheeks. "They're supposed to help. They're supposed to be just! Why should I follow their rules if they won't?" She stared off into the distance. Her long ponytail, carried by a sudden gust of wind, struck the air behind her.

"I don't know what to do." Elodie felt the words leave her mouth, but wasn't quite sure what she'd said. Astrid informing her of her fate while in VR was fitting. They were together yet apart, anywhere and nowhere, doing everything and nothing. That had been Elodie's life—putting one foot in front of the other on a predetermined path, warmly cocooned in the illusion of choice.

The silver boxes on Astrid's toolbelt caught the sun as she bent her legs and rested her chin on her bare knees. "Can I ask you a question?" She paused. "You have to be real with your answer."

Elodie bit the inside of her cheek. Isn't that how all of this started? Her wanting, *needing* something real. She rubbed her hands up and down her goosebump-flecked arms and mentally shook herself. Maybe she and Aiden still had a chance. Astrid and her father had both stood before the Council while Astrid took back everything she'd said. That had to mean something. Maybe not to Council Leader Darby, but he wasn't the only Council member. It had to mean something.

Astrid dabbed the back of her hand against her nose. "What was it like?" She glanced at the sandy concrete beneath her feet. "The kiss." The words were whisper soft, as if she'd had to force them from her lips.

Elodie bristled. "Like we were magnets." She hugged her knees against her chest, folding herself in half as feelings too big washed over her. "I couldn't pull away." Elodie's cheeks were molten. "I didn't want to."

Astrid stared at her, wide eyed. "Did it feel . . ." She swallowed audibly. "Good?"

Elodie blinked. She had expected disgust, but she hadn't been prepared for curiosity. Embarrassment dragged its hot fingers down her neck.

Being lost and found and lost again. Bare and whole. Everything and more.

But that was too big, too much to lay at Astrid's feet.

"It was . . ." Elodie breathed in the crisp air. "The most amazing thing in the world."

Astrid opened her mouth and closed it as if testing the breeze before she spoke. "Sometimes I get this feeling . . ."

The space around them rippled, the very fabric of this virtual reality shaken out like a rug. For a moment, Elodie thought it was the power of the memory.

Astrid surged to her feet. "It's a hack. They're trying to get into our locked VR space."

Elodie stood. "A hack? But who—?"

The building behind them shivered before breaking apart into perfect pixilated squares and collapsing in a heap of flashing cubes.

Astrid stumbled away from the disintegrating landscape. "El, I'm exiting. Get someplace safe. I'll find you."

Shadows stretched against the sand as the sun waned and a deep unsettling black poured into the sky like spilled ink.

In the real, Elodie *was* someplace safe, tucked into one of the many hidden rooms of the Eos warehouse she'd discovered after running to Aiden at dawn. She needed to get back to him now.

Back to her body. Like she'd done a hundred times before, Elodie focused on exiting the program and bringing her hands, her *real* hands, to the headset resting against her ears.

There was nothing. Nothing but gusts of wind blowing sand through wild strands of hair.

Elodie tried again to exit. Her fingers scraped down her cheeks.

"Aiden!" Her voice quaked as the gentle blue sky succumbed to the black and the ground went soft beneath her feet. "Get me out!" Again and again Elodie tried to focus her panicked thoughts on escaping, on her body, on being anywhere but the haunting black, the sand stinging her face. But nothing changed. Her fingers dug against her cheeks, tangled in her hair.

This was real. The pain and the panic. The wind and the dark. *Too* real.

"Elodie! I can't get out!" Astrid was still next to her, *right* next to her. Arms and hands against hers. Skin searching for skin, for safety.

White light burned through the dark. Elodie winced, squeezing her eyes shut against the blinding spotlight glaring down at them.

Astrid let out a gasp as a line of gun-wielding Key Corp soldiers emerged from the dark. "Run!" she shouted.

Elodie took off after her. Her feet no longer sank into the sand as the dark enveloped them and they sprinted further into nothingness.

From under his visor, the lead soldier's voice boomed, "We have orders from the Council. Come willingly and we will not use force."

The soldier was just a few feet away, as if Elodie and Astrid had been standing still instead of running for their lives. He pulled a scanner from his vest and waved a red beam over Elodie's right side. "Sending Benavidez's last known coordinates now."

Astrid charged between Elodie and the soldier. "Your overlords let loose some code that has us stuck in here until what?" she asked. "We tell you where we really are? Then we'll each come out to find guards waiting for us? The whole thing is a little dramatic, don't you think?" Astrid nudged the tip of the soldier's drawn rifle. "I mean, what's the point in this? You want to prove you're a big man? Break the rules and bring in a weapon? *We're in VR. Hello?* This will hurt me about as much as falling off a twenty-story building—which I've done. Didn't make a lasting impact." She held up her hands and did a quick spin. "So tell whoever the fuck is in charge that they need to let us out of this freak show." She pressed her palm against the gun barrel and pushed.

Elodie's chin quivered. "Astrid, don't."

"It's okay, El." Astrid tossed a wink over her shoulder. "They can't do anything to us in here except turn off the lights. Right, boyo?"

The soldier's gear creaked as he stiffened. "You should listen to your friend."

Astrid crossed her arms over her chest. "Do you know who my father is?"

A smirk licked the corners of his lips. "Who do you think designed the hack?" He tilted his head and tapped the black visor that shielded his eyes. "And don't forget to smile big when I bring you in. I'm recording it all, and I'm sure Mr. Fujimoto would love to see those pearly whites."

Astrid hid her trembling hands behind her back, and with a dramatic flourish she stepped closer to the soldier. "Guess I should put on a show. Wouldn't want to disappoint dear old dad." Astrid reached for one of the silver boxes attached to her toolbelt. "See you on the other side, El."

With the swipe of her thumb, Astrid triggered the silver box's code. It morphed into a grappling gun. The hook gleamed as Astrid aimed it toward the soldier.

"Astrid—" Elodie's words were swallowed by the bang of gunfire. Warm liquid sprayed her face and copper flashed against her tongue as hands grabbed her biceps and pulled her back toward the shadows.

Astrid lay on the ground. Not a fading mass of pixels, but a heap of bone and muscle and skin. Astrid was still there. Still human. A pool of red spilled from her middle and glinted in the sharp light as she blankly stared at the grappling gun still in her hand.

"Get up!" Elodie felt herself screaming, fighting against the hands pulling her away from her friend. "Astrid! Get up!"

But there was no answer. Not from Astrid. Only soldiers scrambling, and blood pooling.

The grappling gun flickered in and out of focus before folding in on itself and turning back into a metal box.

The realization roared to life within Elodie and all she could do was surrender.

XXXIX

Blair wove her fingers through the high grass, silky seed tufts tickling her palms. This was her favorite time of day, when night pressed against the sky and the evergreens stood like shadowed guardians along the streets of suburban Westfall. The trees reminded her of their father. They reminded her of home.

"What are we doing out here?" Her little brother was only a head taller than the gently dancing grass. His beautiful dark skin glowed charcoal in the moonlight. "Cath will be worried if she goes into our rooms and we're gone."

Blair rolled her eyes. "Oh, Cath, smath," she mocked, with a flourish of her hand. The same kind of flourish, albeit a smidge exaggerated, that Cath did every time she lost her train of thought, which, as far as Blair could tell, was at least thirty times per day.

Denny laughed. A sound like bells chiming. And it was the best sound in the entire world.

"But for real, Blair," he said between giggles. "I don't want to get in trouble."

She slipped on a sly smile and cocked her head. "Don't tell me Big Denny Man is scared of a little tall grass and the dark."

He crossed his arms over his chest and lifted his chin defiantly. "I'm not scared of anything."

Oh, but little Denny had so much to fear. The Key could only protect its citizens so much. She and her brother had learned that the hard way. Denny was lucky he didn't have to rely on the corporation for safety. He had Blair. And she would spend her life keeping him safe.

Blair bent down, level with the young boy's sweet expression. "You know I'll always protect you, right?"

Denny's gaze dropped and he nodded slightly before looking back up at her, his eyes big and round and sparkling just as they had the day he was born.

The best day of Blair's life.

His eyes fell from hers. "I wish Momma and Daddy were still here." He was retreating, curling in on himself in that way he did when he thought about their parents and that monster that had eviscerated their mother and left their father in a lifeless pile on the kitchen floor.

Blair plucked a long blade of grass and brushed the soft tip against his cheek. "It's a lunar eclipse. I was going to tell you when we got to the clearing but—"

Denny stole the blade and lifted himself onto his toes. "Total? Partial? Penumbral?" The questions raced from him, each one punctuated by a swish of the grass. "What kind? What kind?" He saved her from guessing and took off toward the clearing before she had a chance to answer. Astronomy didn't interest her, but Denny loved it. Denny loved their father and their father loved—had loved—astronomy.

"You're gonna miss it!" Denny shouted.

Blair sped up, her boots sinking into the soggy ground as she reached the last row of trees framing the open space. Pine needles tugged at her tight curls and snared her shirt as she shuffled and twisted through the line of trees, their branches woven together like cloth. She'd read somewhere that Aspens were all connected underground. One living thing spanning acres and acres, sprouting up through the earth like hair. There was something to be learned from the power in that. The power of a single thing that made a forest.

A small rush of air slipped through Denny's parted lips. "Penumbral." He sighed wistfully, his chin tilted toward the darkly shaded moon. "Isn't it the best?"

Blair had rushed Denny through the house and into the backyard that night, months earlier when they'd lost their parents, their peace. She'd talked about the moon and how bright it was. How he had to look up even through the house. That if he looked hard enough, the light would shine through the roof. She didn't want him to know why his feet were wet. Why he slipped on the tile. Why they left behind red footprints.

Tears pricked her eyes. She shook her head slightly, willing them away. "I love you, Aiden."

He tore his gaze away from the sky to smile up at her. "Love you too, B."

Sunlight glinted off Blair's black desk, burning through her memories and leaving behind nothing but spots.

Something had happened to her brother. Something she'd missed. She'd given Aiden too much space to grow, trusted too many other people to keep him safe, and now her perfect boy was tainted. But Blair would fix it. She was the only one who could.

Blair pushed away from her desk, wincing as her fingertips made contact with the glinting onyx. She held her hands up in the thick bands of sunlight from the window. Each fingertip was raw pink, her nails chewed to stumps so short she'd made her nailbeds bleed.

How dare Darby pass sentence on a Scott. This was almost too much for her. But Blair was a fortress, an Aspen grove. Too bad Aiden couldn't be as strong.

What had happened to her brother? That innocent boy who ran to her when things were tough and times were bad? Now Blair had learned that he'd found a new girl to go to when he had nowhere else to turn.

Elodie.

Blair's teeth creaked with the tight clench of her jaw.

Compared to Blair, that girl had nothing. *Was* nothing. And the Council would make sure that her future was as empty as her past. The Key, the only thing Blair could trust besides herself, would save her brother from that scheming brat. Then Blair would deal with Darby's sentence.

None of it had been Aiden's fault. Blair was certain of that. He didn't know any better. How could he? They hadn't been raised in a traditional home with traditional rules. Sure, Cath was successful and kind, but she wasn't their mother. Not really. The misfortune that had made Blair stronger hadn't done the same for poor Denny. It had untethered him from what was important and made him an easy target for manipulation. This girl had seen that in him and used it to her advantage.

The office door hissed open and Maxine's determined footsteps clicked against the stained concrete floor. "I thought you might like these."

Blair lifted a pale blue rectangular box from Maxine's upturned palm and opened the lid.

"They're a prototype," Maxine explained while Blair removed the clear, paper-thin gloves from the box. "From the same lab that designs the skins for the caretaker bots."

The inside of the gloves was cold jelly that seemed to melt the second each finger slid into place. A sound like the release of steam and then a sharp prick on the back of each hand. Before Blair could protest, the gloves lifted like the scales of a pinecone before settling back against her skin. She could no longer differentiate the thin silicone from her own flesh. Or was it really *hers* anymore? Blair again brought her hands to the light. No crescents of red rimmed the tips of too short nails. Her nails were back, unpainted, unbuffed, but back. She turned her hands over and traced the thin creases in her palms. Her sense of touch was muted, but the image was perfection.

Maxine's shadow broke through Blair's awe. "Good as new."

Holly materialized in front of Blair's onyx desk. "Hello, Ms. Scott. Maxine requested I notify you when your visitor arrived." The similarities between Blair's own voice and Holly's was a constant reminder of her growing hold on Westfall.

With a huff, Maxine shook out her short hair and pressed her lips into a thin line.

"Maxine, before we welcome our guest, is there any more information about this elusive *Echo* person I knew nothing about?" Blair ground her teeth together. "A fact, I'm sure, Major Owens found quite pleasing."

Maxine sucked in her cheeks. "If I found something out, I would have told you."

Blair turned back to the window. "Then, show him in," she said, staring through her reflection at the city beneath.

Rhett's footsteps were louder than most employees'. Louder than they needed to be. As if his sharp cologne and the way the air went stiff and tense around him weren't enough to signal his arrival. How could this soldier ever sneak up on anyone? Then again, the stealthy ones weren't splashed across ads and featured in news stories. And that, she knew, was what Major Rhett Owens wanted more than anything. *To be someone.*

Blair shifted her attention to the Major's reflection as he removed his red dress cap and clasped it in front of him. "My men will have your brother to you by the end of the night. They're close to finding him."

"And the girl?" Blair sneered. Jealousy twisted her brow and burned hot against her tongue.

Rhett said nothing, his reflection stiffening almost imperceptibly.

Blair turned with liquid grace. "Major Owens—"

"Yes." Rhett bit out the word in a strangled grunt, his hands twisting his red Key cap.

Blair drifted like a feather into the seat next to the towering Major and motioned to the empty chair next to her. "Please, sit." She wet her lips. "And tell me what you know about Elodie Benavidez."

The name seemed to grip Rhett by the throat. Each corded muscle popped against his neck as he moved across the office. "We are matched."

Maxine sucked in a breath, her lips forming that distinct O as she waited for the salacious details of Rhett's tarnished romance.

The corner of Blair's mouth itched with a grin. It wasn't Rhett's pain that made her feel better, but the fact that this little girl wasn't ruining Blair's life alone. Misery loves company, and all that. "And you know the details of their . . . *impropriety?*"

"*Impropriety?*" Rhett snorted. "It's disgusting what they did. Barbaric!"

The hairs on the back of Blair's neck rose. "Rhett." She tented her new fingertips beneath her chin as he sat beside her.

"We are so much alike, you and I. We overestimate those around us. We expect in them the same traits that we possess. After all, it shouldn't be difficult to follow the path laid out before you. We did. And look at us now." Her sweeping gesture took in the marvelous expanse of her office. "In control. In power. But others, those we love . . ." Blair paused an extra breath to study Rhett, but he didn't waver. "Those we care for . . ." Another pause. Another impenetrable wall. "Those we possess . . ."

Rhett's fists tightened around his cap.

Blair clasped her hands and rested them against her knees. "I am not surprised this happened."

Rhett's brow creased. "Then you know something I don't."

"I know my brother. What I do not know, however, is how you were completely unaware that your match is such a trifling . . ." Blair twirled the air around her fingertips.

Maxine tilted her head. "Siren?" she chimed.

Oh, little monster. "Ah, yes." Blair nodded. "A word straight out of the history books."

Rhett shifted uncomfortably. "Now, I wouldn't go that far. Elodie has never seemed—"

Blair held up her hand. "Major Owens, most people are not how they seem. In your line of work, I'm sure you battle against that quite often."

Rhett puffed. "Who's to say you don't have it backward? That your brother—"

"I know him better than he knows himself!" With a deep inhale, Blair packed her rage back down her throat. "Do you not remember that I brought you here to guide him down the right path? Clearly, he is easily manipulated. I will give your vermin of a fiancée that much credit. She chose wisely."

Whatever Rhett was going to say, he'd channeled it into the cap he continued to twist in his hands.

Blair stood. She needed more space in her chest, more room for her lungs to expand and breathe, not to catch and quiver. She pursed her lips and dusted non-existent lint from her black pencil skirt "The next time I see you, you'll have my brother and that girl."

Rhett nodded and stood.

"And, Major Owens, I don't need to remind you that this matter is to be handled discretely." Blair dragged her new nails along the stone as she rounded her desk.

With a tight nod, Rhett smoothed out his cap and tented it against his white blond hair.

Blair gripped the back of her throne to keep from keeling over. Aiden was tearing her apart.

Maxine cleared her throat, widened her eyes, and pointed her chin in the Major's direction.

Blair bit the inside of her cheek. She needed to focus. She'd almost made a mistake. Men like Rhett Owens didn't like to be bossed. They liked control. They liked rewards. "Major Owens, this matter is personal and, I'm sure, affects you deeply. Know that after the dust has settled, I will make sure you are matched to a worthy woman. One of your choosing."

Rhett's Adam's apple bobbed with a thick swallow.

"Elodie." Blair scraped the tip of her tongue along her teeth. Just saying the girl's name left a bad taste in her mouth. "She did this to us all. And I trust you will help me right all her wrongs."

Rhett stood. "I would like nothing more."

Blair forced a smile as Maxine escorted Major Owens out.

The moment the door hissed shut Blair slid down the back of the velvet chair, dropping to the floor like a stone. Her body heaved and tightened, heaved and tightened. But no sick came up. The revelations about what the girl had done to her brother had already cleaned her out, leaving room for nothing except rage.

"Elodie!" Blair screeched. "I'm going to murder that bitch with my own hands! I'll kill them all for what they've done to him!"

Maxine was back in an instant, shutting the door behind her, mirroring Blair's posture, her fingers digging into the plush rug with the same white-knuckle ferocity as Blair. "You will deal with them. *We* will deal with them. But not like this."

Blair lifted her head and blinked through the swirl of tears.

Maxine's teeth clenched and her eyes narrowed savagely. "You are better than this," she growled. "*Stronger* than this. Stronger than them."

Maxine was right. Blair was no petulant child or stay-at-home wife. She was the definition of resourcefulness and determination. Despite this oversight regarding her brother, this *one* oversight. Her knuckles popped as she released her grip and settled against her heels. Blair had nearly forgotten who she was.

Her gaze swung around the room, taking in the tangible evidence of everything she'd achieved, before finally settling on the wall of windows. The rain had started up again and it slid down the glass like tears.

The first tears of many, she thought, her lips twisting into a sneer.

Blair fluffed the curls framing her face and dabbed at the moisture on her cheeks. "Maxine," she said with a final sniffle, "be a dear and fetch me a gun."

XL

Aiden struggled to pin Elodie's arms to the armrests as she thrashed and clawed the air.

"Get up!" Elodie screamed and kicked out.

Sparkman's reddish blond braid whipped the air as her attention bounced between the numerous monitors that served as their unit's main control center.

The saccharine scent of honeysuckles drifting in from the warehouse soured Aiden's stomach. There shouldn't be anything sweet about what was playing out in front of Elodie and on the screen just behind Aiden's head.

"Astrid! Get up!" she yelled. Tears spilled from Elodie's eyes and dotted her shirt with some of the only real-life evidence of the horror that had occurred.

Besides Astrid's lifeless body at home in her own VR setup, there was nothing except Elodie's tears to show that the murder ever occurred. And when questions were asked . . . Well, the Key had a way of turning fact into fiction.

Anguish twisted Elodie's features and Aiden blinked back the mist forming in his eyes. He turned his attention to Sparkman. "We have to get her out!"

Sparkman's fingertips hammered against the control panel. "Tech deleted her profile from the main servers. She'll be back in the real any minute."

Aiden swallowed past the lump in his throat. "Sparkman, I'm lucky you were here."

For a moment, Elodie stilled beneath Aiden's hands. Then, like she'd been struck by lightning, she jerked and exploded up from the chair. She ripped her VR headset off and threw it to the ground.

Aiden's heart squeezed. He knew better than anyone that there was no way to bring back the dead.

Elodie swiped her hand against her cheek. "She's gone!" It trembled as she studied her palm. "Astrid's dead." She offered her shaking hand as evidence. "There's no blood. No *nothing*. It's like it never happened." Elodie doubled over. Her sobs shook her so hard Aiden worried she'd splinter into pieces.

He crouched and cupped her face in his hands. "It doesn't feel like it now," he breathed, "but you *will* get through this." He'd said the same words to himself thousands of times over, but it wasn't until Elodie that he'd known that *through* was an actual destination, a reward after suffering, as opposed to a constant state of being.

Sparkman cleared her throat. A gentle signal that the world kept spinning even in the midst of tragedy. "You'll need to get through sooner than later. Tech informed me that those soldiers scanned her. They know our location. This place will be crawling with Key Corp troops in no time."

Aiden helped Elodie to her feet. "They can't *scan people* in VR."

Elodie let out a final trembling sob before speaking. "The Key can't kill someone in VR either."

Sparkman's strawberry blond brows arched. "The Corporation seems to be learning new tricks all the time." She cracked her knuckles and turned back to the bank of holoscreens. "I've given the order. Tech is powering us down and activating the light bath. We don't want to leave behind any fingerprints or genetic material they could use to track the rest of us." The image on two of the holoscreens pixilated before going completely black. "We need to move."

Aiden grabbed Elodie's hand and they followed Sparkman out of the office, running across concrete through the curtains onto moist earth, and into the light of the grow lamps and the rows and rows of plants. He ignored the thoughts writhing within him. All the living things in this building would die. The Key would make sure of it. He swallowed and tightened his grasp on Elodie. He had to make sure they were far, far away.

Another crack of her knuckles as Sparkman turned and sped through a patch of budding tomato plants. "We'll try to make it to the tunnels, but if anyone is arrested, we'll need an alternate plan. I'll send out a truck. It'll make one pass through this district at exactly twenty-three thirty. The Key soldiers will have cleared out by then. Protocol dictates that they immediately confiscate all technology." Her braid slid off her shoulder as she motioned back the way they'd come. "They'll return at first light to collect living specimens. They'll know what we know—this place is cutoff, worthless to us. We just have to make it worthless to them too."

They were fifty yards away from the hatch. Fifty yards away from the black depths of the tunnels that he'd been trained to navigate with his eyes closed. After all, that was how Eos operated—in the dark.

"Tech will also contact Echo." Sparkman continued. "The next—"

Aiden stopped so sharply, he jerked Elodie backward. "They can't notify Echo!" The idea that Eos would bring in Echo hardened his feet into anvils.

Sparkman's brisk pace widened the space between them as she neared the hidden hatch to the underground tunnels. "She's in charge of this region. More than that, she needs to know what's taking place. We have our own protocols that we must adhere to in order to survive." She reached her destination and brushed back the thick curtain that lined the walls of the warehouse.

Aiden shook his head. "But—"

"Aiden, there's no debate here. I do as I see fit and you follow. Especially now, when we are all in danger." The hatch beeped as Sparkman keyed in her entry code.

Elodie squeezed his hand. "We have to go. What those soldiers did to Astrid . . ." her chest heaved. "We can't be here when they get here."

Sparkman and Elodie were right. He would have to deal with Echo later.

A loud *boom* shook the warehouse. The lights flickered as another sounded. Aiden and Elodie bolted after Sparkman and toward the open hatch that promised safety. The sharp whine of caving metal forced Aiden's hands over his ears. His heartbeat raced inside his throat. He'd stopped and it had held Elodie back from reaching sanctuary.

He waved his arms, motioning for Sparkman to continue into the tunnel. "They didn't come for you!" he shouted.

Sparkman's chin lifted and her stance widened. "I won't leave anyone behind."

A root snagged the toe of Aiden's boot and he crashed against the dirt floor.

Another boom. Another flicker of lights overhead. Another screech of metal. And then something new behind them—marching, voices.

Elodie crouched next to him. Her red-rimmed and swollen eyes frantically swung from the front door to Aiden before settling on Sparkman.

"Go!" Aiden shouted, "We need you on the outside, not in handcuffs before the Council."

Sparkman nodded stiffly and pressed her fist against her chest. "After the storm comes the dawn!"

The hatch creaked closed and the velvet drapes fell back into place. Sparkman was gone.

The front curtains opened and a wave of gun-toting Key Corp red burst through. This was it. He'd known this day would eventually come, but he'd never imagined there'd be anyone by his side when it did. Aiden rose to his feet as the sea parted and a single officer marched forward.

Elodie shuddered and let out a strangled wheeze as the man removed his helmet and tucked it under his arm.

"So, I'm sent to find my fiancée in a fucking Eos stronghold." Rhett eyed Aiden for a moment before puffing up like a toad. "And with *Aiden Scott.* I'm sure your sister will just *love* that I found you here." He turned his attention back to Elodie. "Nice job making new friends, El." Rhett set his wide jaw and flicked his chin in the air. "Arrest them."

The soldiers overtook Aiden and Elodie. With sharp commands and prodding guns, the soldiers forced them to their knees. Aiden's jaw ticked and his chest tightened as handcuffs were bound around their wrists, complete with one lead rope for each of them. Air fled his lungs as he watched Elodie cower away from each rifle jab. Her hands quaked. Her eyes gleamed with tears. Her lips parted around panicked gasps for breath. He'd led her down this path, led her to a river of truths, but this was too much too fast. This was drowning.

A soldier jerked her to her feet. She let out a sharp howl of pain, but clamped her mouth closed just as quickly and tripped along the path toward the door.

Aiden couldn't watch her anymore, not while he was shackled and pulled from his favorite place on earth. He was useless. Just like he'd been a decade ago . . .

Rhett's white blond hair caught his attention and Aiden fixed his gaze, his fears, his rage on the Major. "What does my sister have to do with this?" Aiden grunted as he strained against his handcuffs and the soldier pulling him closer to the exit.

Rhett's lips thinned and stretched, wormlike, into a smirk. "You'll see soon enough."

The handcuffs bit into Aiden's wrists but he held his ground. "Tell me now!"

A dry laugh burst from Rhett's throat as he turned his back to Aiden and barked more orders at his sea of red-clad commandos.

Pain shot through Aiden's hands and he stumbled forward into black velvet curtains. His eyes burned, but he wouldn't let himself cry. Tears had never saved him. Another swift jerk of the leash and he was through the soft black. The curtains whooshed closed behind him as he was yanked from Wonderland.

XLI

Rhett stood next to the handcuffed traitors he'd forced up against the wall across from Blair's desk with Aiden between him and his erstwhile fiancée. Rhett, then Aiden, then Elodie. Blair wasn't sure whether or not he'd meant for them to be in height order, but they were. Like stairsteps, one leading down to the next. All leading to Elodie.

The girl was pretty. Not beautiful. At least, not as beautiful as she should have been to have gotten Aiden to betray who he was, to join Eos, and to commit the ultimate crime. Intercourse, the way it had been in the past, no longer existed. And in a perfect world, the world the Key was trying to create, a woman could no longer use her beauty as a tool to manipulate. But the world was far from perfect. Blair knew that firsthand. She'd used her beauty many times. It was just one part of her power.

Elodie fidgeted with the frayed ends of her plain T-shirt, which covered her plain brown skin beneath the lengths of her plain brown hair, which she shook away from her plain brown eyes. The girl might as well have been beige paint. So where was her power?

Not only had she manipulated Blair's only brother, she had also wiggled her way into the Fujimoto household and gotten Jasper Fujimoto's youngest daughter to recant her statement to the Council. Maxine's eyes on the Council had informed her that Council Leader Darby was certain the retraction couldn't be trusted. Astrid Fujimoto was, after all, one of Elodie's friends, and it was clear that Elodie could get anyone to do anything. Taking down Westfall's top families seemed to be Eos's goal, and they were using Elodie Benavidez to achieve it.

Aiden cleared his throat, snagging Blair's attention. "Blair, is all of this," he lifted his cuffed hands, "really necessary?"

Rhett's boots thumped against the concrete as he came to Blair's side. "They're Eos scum." His gaze hardened on Aiden. "Be thankful restraints are all you're getting."

"Rhett." Elodie's voice cracked. "You don't have to do this. I can explain."

Blair perched on the edge of her desk, her sleeveless top and her skirt matching the slick black Onyx. "Oh, please do. I would love to hear what sort of tales you weave."

Elodie sniffled, blinked, and sniffled again. "I don't understand."

Blair turned her attention to Aiden. If anyone was going to tell her the truth, it would be her Denny. "Is this how she did it? How she got you to join Eos? By playing the dumb girl."

Aiden's green eyes narrowed. "She didn't *get me* to do anything."

Blair dug her nails into her new palms. The synthetic gloves dulled the expected bursts of pain. "Don't defend her, brother!"

Elodie leapt from the wall. "I don't need defending!"

Rhett lumbered forward and forced his trifling fiancée back

to her place with the butt of his stock prod. "I know you haven't been yourself, but please don't make me do anything I'll regret."

Anything *he* would regret? How had this dull girl managed to subjugate both of these men? How could they not see her spoiled, volatile nature? Blair tossed up her hands as she slid off her desk. "And just like that, her switch has flipped."

Elodie was off the wall again. "Just like that?" she growled between clenched teeth. "I've been sentenced to death! My best friend was murdered in front of me! My fiancé put me in handcuffs! And for what? A kiss? At the end of this, the Key will have taken three lives and our kiss will have taken none."

"You destroyed my brother!" Blair snarled, spittle flying from her lips.

Rhett was there again with the safe end of his prod, shoving Elodie against the wall.

Elodie's pitiful brown hair swept her shoulders as she shook her head and fell back in line. "You don't know your brother."

Rhett returned the stock prod to its holster. "You couldn't possibly, Blair. If you did, you'd know this was mostly him." He crossed his sausage arms across his chest. "El and I had everything worked out. Then your brother comes along and has her acting like a total space cadet."

Blair's lips parted with a grin. "Men like you have been underestimating women for centuries."

Rhett's cheeks reddened. "Your brother did this. He recruited Elodie and filled her head with nonsense. We were meant to be. We were—"

Blair couldn't keep from laughing. It was the kind of hollow laughter that lived in her throat and leapt on wounded prey. "You really believe that?"

"I believe you shouldn't interrupt me when I'm speaking." Rhett's meatball of a hand rested on his stock prod. "Eos and your asshole of a brother broke my Elodie!"

Blair felt something deep within her click. Perhaps it was *her* switch that had been flipped. Her hand itched for the gun Maxine had promised.

The door hissed open and Blair's heartbeat quickened. Ask, believe, receive . . . Her hands grew clammy inside the gloves as she waited for the impatient stomps of Maxine's kitten heels.

Blair stepped backward, gripping the edge of her stone desk as Cath marched through the doorway. "You shouldn't be here." Blair clenched her teeth. "I have this handled."

Cath didn't look at Blair, didn't even acknowledge her adoptive daughter or that she had entered a private meeting in the office Blair had worked so hard to acquire. Cath only looked at Aiden.

Blair's stomach hollowed. No matter what she accomplished, Denny would always be Cath's favorite.

Cath brushed something from her cheek as she turned to face Blair. "Let my son go." The blistering light from the chandelier was somehow softer, more golden when it struck her.

Blair stiffened. Aiden was Cath's *son*. But Blair had always just been *Blair*. "I have this handled, Cath," she repeated without washing the coldness from her tone. "We don't need you."

Aiden lifted his wrists and his handcuffs rattled. "Mom, don't—"

Blair slapped the edge of her desk. "I said we don't need you!"

"Let my son go and take me instead." Cath pursed her lips and swallowed. "I'm a member of Eos. I'm who you want. Not Aiden, not Elodie—me."

Blair let out a throat-burning screech as she cast her gaze to the ceiling. "Don't lie, Cath. The girl needs to learn a lesson." She pressed her hands against her hips. "Plus, I can't let Denny leave. Preston Darby finally has a little bit of power and it's driving him crazy. He'll use this to destroy us."

Even amidst this circus of finger pointing and blame dodging, Cath's hands still rested gently clasped below her waist. "I'm afraid the lessons Elodie needs to learn are those you are unequipped to teach her." She frowned. "And I did caution you about teasing Darby."

Blair cocked her chin. "So this is my fault?"

Rhett ran his hand through his closely cropped hair. "This is getting ridiculous." He cracked his knuckles. "How about the three of us," he said, motioning to Cath and Aiden. "Go to *my* warehouse?" He turned to Blair. "I'll knock this runt down a few pegs and my guys will get some answers out of your mom. I get what I want and you get to be first in line for Director. Win, win."

Blair caught Aiden and Elodie as they stole a glance at each other. Blair's insides boiled. "You can do whatever you want with that one." She thrust her finger at Elodie. "She's the reason all of this has happened. But you won't harm my family."

"Blair! Enough!" Aiden charged forward. Rhett lashed out with the stock prod. Metal spikes jabbed Aiden's ribs, and he let out a strangled shout as he convulsed and collapsed.

Blair wobbled and gripped the edge of her desk as her brother's knees slammed against concrete.

Cath ran to Aiden's side and sank to the floor beside him. "This is *my* doing!" she shouted. "*I'm* the reason Aiden joined Eos."

And now Blair knew. It had been Cath, not Elodie. Cath had taken Denny away just as that monster had taken their real mother and father. The Key had never matched Cath for a reason. The Key knew she shouldn't have had children. She didn't know how to care for them. How to nurture them. She hadn't been the one who stayed up with Aiden all night as he sobbed for the parents who were never coming back. That had been Blair. She had always been there—would always be there. How had this happened? Cath had destroyed Aiden. Blair's *brother*. Her Denny. Her love and her life and her reason for being.

Aiden grunted as he struggled to his knees. "Mom, don't—"

Cath leaned into Aiden and kissed the top of his head before rising to her feet. "I'm the one you want, Blair. I'm Echo."

Blair felt as if someone had sucked all of the air out of the room. "*What?*" she wheezed as she pressed herself away from her desk.

Rhett clapped his hands on top of his head. "You've got to be fucking kidding me." He seemed to harden as his eyes bore into Blair. "Our most wanted person in Westfall is your fucking *mother?*"

How could she have missed this? Blair surged toward her imposter of a mother. "How?" She bit off the word so ferociously, spittle flecked Cath's cheeks.

Aiden coughed. "Mom, don't tell her anything."

"She is not your mother!" The words burned Blair's lips as she spewed them at Aiden like acid.

With a snarl, Rhett stomped forward. The prod's metal tines crackled and sparked as he stabbed the air in front of Cath and forced her up against the wall next to Elodie. He holstered his weapon and returned to Aiden. His fingers twitched over the shiny black rod as he slammed his boot against Aiden's chest and shoved him back against the wall.

The door hissed open, but Blair couldn't tear her attention away from Rhett looming over her injured brother. "You said you'd do all sorts of unspeakable things to them back at *your* warehouse. *This,*" she ground her pointed heel into the rug, "is mine. And I have bots that will cart you away and burn your body before it's even cold. I said not to touch my family."

Maxine glided ghostlike from the door to the corner of Blair's huge black desk. She didn't make a sound when she set down the gun.

Lava flowed within Blair's chest and heat crept up her neck. She squeezed her fists to keep from erupting. "Do not test me again, Major Owens."

Rhett's grip tightened on the prod as he shifted away from Aiden.

Blair kneeled in front of her battle-bruised brother. To her, he would never look older than he had that day in the clearing, his round face tipped up toward the moon. "Why won't you let me save you?" Tears burned her eyes. "I love you, Denny. And the only *true* love, love that can withstand anything, is that of family." Blair's gaze cut to Cath. "*Blood* family." Her chin quivered. "I love you, my sweet, sweet boy."

Aiden leaned back against the wall and rocked his head from side to side. "Spare me. Your one true love is your job. This office." He threw his cuffed hands in the air. "The Key. Not me or Cath or anyone else."

Blair pushed herself to her feet, shook back her tears, and smoothed out her black skirt. She would fix her brother later. He would see, they would all see, that everything she did, she did for him. But in order to cure Aiden of the poison these women had fed him, Blair needed to erase them from the picture.

"You started this," she snarled and stalked over to Cath. "You're the one who can end it. A recorded confession and answers to some questions will be a good place to start."

Cath studied Aiden and then Elodie, who had done a terrific job nearly blending into the wall. "You'll let them both go?"

Blair's gaze swept over the pistol on the corner of the desk and settled back on Cath. "I'll take you and let them go. I can fix the trouble they're in with the Council. Especially if I'm trading an Eos leader for two kissing teens." Blair crossed her arms over her chest. "As Director, I won't need any leverage. And the Key will appoint me immediately." She paused and hung a smile on her lips. "After all, this is what happens when citizens don't have effective leadership."

Cath's foot hung in the air for a moment before she committed to stepping forward.

Aiden pushed himself to his feet. "Mom! You can't. They'll kill you!"

Blair hiccupped back a sob. Aiden was choosing between them, and he wasn't choosing wisely.

Cath's eyes rested on Aiden as she clenched and unclenched her fists.

Blair swallowed her despair. "Holly, please record the events in the room." With Cath out of the way, she could fix all of this. She could fix Denny. "If you want to save your son, it's now or never, *Mother.*"

With her trademark poise and grace, Cath Scott walked forward to stand between her adoptive daughter and Major Owens. "My name is Cath Scott, although, to many, I am Echo." With her shoulders pulled back and her chin lifted skyward she continued in the even, slow lilt Blair had once found so comforting. "I've been a member of Eos since their inception. I regret nothing. I only wish I could have done more." Cath took a breath. Her eyes skimmed Blair before settling on Aiden. "I love you both deeply. You were the best decision I have ever made."

Cath surged forward at Rhett. She crashed into him. His arms windmilled as he fell into the corner of Blair's desk. His head hid the stone with a sickening crack as Cath struggled to her knees, spun, and grabbed the silver pistol.

Blair scrambled backward. She wasn't Cath's favorite, but Cath couldn't end her like this. Cath *wouldn't!* A sob flew from Blair's lips.

The gun glinted in the harsh light as Cath pressed the barrel under her own chin. "After the storm comes the dawn!" Cath cried, and pulled the trigger.

XLII

The gunshot was louder than Aiden expected. The kind of piercing sound that slaughtered all others. He felt it too. Like the sound itself had reached into his chest, grabbed his ribs, and rattled his bones like cage doors.

Aiden opened his eyes to blood and gore. Red so bright, so *alive*, that the streaks melting against the walls were like staring into the sun.

What had happened?

The smell of copper hit him as soon as he let himself inhale.

And then came the sound. The deep keening that flayed his skin and left him raw.

He had only heard it once before.

The night his parents died.

Aiden's fingertips dug into the carpet. His panting breaths blew around the dust bunnies Momma was always asking him to vacuum out from under his bed. Next time, he'd listen. Next time, he'd do anything Momma wanted as long as she and Daddy were okay.

Sobs tore through the closed door to his bedroom and seemed to scorch the air. "Momma! Daddy!"

It was his sister, screaming for their parents.

Tears burned Aiden's eyes and he clapped his hands over his mouth to keep his cries from escaping. Blair had told him to stay under the bed and stay quiet.

"Momma! Daddy!" Each of his sister's cries squeezed his heart.

The door to his room hissed open. Aiden pressed his hands against his lips, his fingernails digging into his soft cheeks.

"Denny?" Blair's voice was tiny, frail. She shuffled toward the bed. Her feet were covered in red, like she'd stepped in a bucket of paint and had forgotten to wash. She dropped to her hands and knees and peered under the bed.

Aiden reached out for his sister, but she didn't return the gesture. Instead, she pressed her cheek against the carpet and let out a quaking breath.

"Momma?" Aiden retracted his hand and wiped his cheeks. He couldn't stop crying. "Daddy?"

Blair swallowed. Her usual soft and loving expression had been replaced with something Aiden had never seen before. "Follow me, Denny, okay?" Silvery moonlight streamed in from the window, shining in the river of tears leaking from Blair's dark eyes. "And when we leave your room, look up, up, up." Her hand disappeared from view as she pointed toward the ceiling. "The moon is so bright you can see it through the roof."

Denny let out a shaky breath. "Nuh-uh."

Blair smiled and, for a split second, was his sister again. "Just try, okay? For me?"

Aiden crawled out from under the bed and followed his big sister's red footprints to the door.

Blair sucked in shaky breath, her trembling hand hovering over the door's keypad. "I'll always protect you, Denny." She typed in the code and the door hissed open. "Remember, look up, up, up."

"Aiden!" Someone had grabbed him, stood right in front of him, shaking him free of his memories. But shock clouded his senses. He was there, in the room with the red and the cries and the scent of burned flesh. But he was also gone, a specter, a placeholder for the man whose life this was. It wasn't Aiden's. It couldn't be.

Elodie filled his vision. Her hair stuck in untamed clumps against her crimson-splattered cheeks. Her scarlet-smeared lips moved as she spoke, but he could only hear the siren-like wails of his sister.

Elodie pressed something against his shackles and they popped loose. "Rhett will regain consciousness soon and the Key will be on their way."

Aiden's gaze swept around the room, pausing on the unconscious mound of Rhett Owens before settling on his sister and the petite woman next to her, frantically typing on her holopad. Blair rocked back and forth, her legs pressed against her chest, her face twisted by screams.

Elodie threw the handcuffs behind her. "They'll kill us. Your mother wouldn't want that."

Then he saw her, Cath, his mother, in a pool of unending red. "Momma . . ." The word spilled from his lips with a sob so deep and raw he felt inside out. Enough love, enough mothers, for two lifetimes. And he'd lost them both.

Tears carved clean paths down Elodie's blood-smeared cheeks.

He could save Elodie. Keep her safe, protected. Pour into her his everything. He wouldn't make the same mistakes again.

Something within him clicked, and the well of pain that streamed into his heart ceased overflowing. It ceased to fill at all. He scrubbed away the red and blocked out the cries and the stench and stored those sensations in the farthest corner of his mind. Being a protector didn't require sadness or grief. He stored those away too. Maybe he'd wrangle all of his emotions and stuff them into the dark as well. After all, hadn't his emotions gotten him here?

The room was a blur as Aiden followed Elodie toward the exit.

"Brother!" Blair wailed, bloody arms outstretched.

Aiden flicked his eyes to the floor and the heap of shattered pieces disguised as his sister. "You did this." His voice was even, firm.

The door opened in front of them and Elodie took Aiden's cold, trembling hand and pulled him from the wreckage of his broken family. Aiden didn't look back as the door hissed closed behind him.

XLIII

Cath's blood ran dark red against Blair's wall of windows, as if the sprinklers had rained rusty water. It was a good thing Blair had replaced her skin with the gloves Maxine had provided. She didn't have time to waste finding cleaning supplies. She had always been inventive, one of her best qualities, especially when she was under pressure. And look at how much pressure she was under now, bots buzzing around, a Key Corp soldier watching from her door. This was just another chance to shine.

"Just another chance to shine!" Blair bellowed as she balled up another clean corner of her plush throw rug and scrubbed at more rivulets of blood. She would return her office to its spick-and-span glory if it killed her.

"Blair?"

Blair's breathy pants fogged the section of window she'd just polished as she stilled and closed her eyes. Was that Cath's voice? Is that who was calling her? Had this all been a dream? Would Cath stand in front of her when Blair opened her eyes? Would she lean over Blair's bed, her fingers plucking the air that way they did while her halo of golden hair framed her kind and loving features?

"*Blair?*"

That was it. This had been a dream, a nightmare. It had to be. Blair would wake up and these false visions would fade into smoke and slip from her memory before she could even say what had happened. This wasn't real. She dropped the rug and pressed her hands against the glass. None of this was real.

"*Blair!*" Maxine slapped the window, and Blair's eyes flew open. "The bots will do that."

Blair went cold and hot all at once. This wasn't a dream, wasn't a nightmare. This was all too real. Goosebumps rose on her flesh, stopping when they reached her gloved forearms. "Cath . . ." she whimpered and turned to face her dutiful assistant.

Maxine shook her head. "She's gone, Blair." She said the words so matter-of-factly Blair had to lean against the window to steady herself. "And you need to snap out of it. There are Key Corp higher ups here—*investigators*. You don't want to embarrass yourself or appear weak, or—" she waved her hand in front of Blair's face. "Or frantic." Maxine tugged on the untucked end of her blouse. Pink spots stained the white silk.

Black fabric or not, Blair couldn't make herself look at her own outfit. "You cleaned off the blood."

Maxine's throat bobbed with a tight swallow. "I did what I had to do. That's something you taught me." A bot buzzed past the vague shape of Cath Scott on the floor.

Right now, Blair couldn't remember teaching anyone anything.

"So," Maxine said, with another pull at her blouse. "Snap out of it and do what needs to be done."

Maxine had said that twice now, *Snap out of it.* As if it was so easy. As if she'd ever had to *snap out of* anything in her privileged little blip of a life. Oh, Blair would *snap out of it* all right. She'd snapped out of worse than this.

"*This.*" The window squeaked as Blair dragged her gloved fingers down the glass. "Is *my* office. *Mine!*"

Maxine's eyelids fluttered as she steadied herself against Blair's unstable storm of emotions. "Yes, and, as I said, I don't want you to embarrass yourself."

Blair's cheeks puffed, ready to release another destabilizing blast, when a red blur caught the corner of her eye. Key Corp investigators. A swarm of them. All gathered outside the door around Major Rhett Owens. Blair stiffened and narrowed her eyes at Maxine. "Walk. Away." The words left her mouth as daggers. Maxine took a wobbly step back before she turned and walked past the Key Corp soldier standing in the doorway.

Blair brushed back her mane of soft curls, pausing when she reached a section crunchy with drying blood. It was everywhere. *Cath* was everywhere. Blair pressed the back of her hand against her mouth as she took in her office. Red chunks clung to the ceiling, the walls, rested in thick, gooey puddles on the floor. One of the soldiers had covered Cath's body with a sheet that radiated violet light. New tech. Blair dropped her hand and smoothed her fingers over her gloved forearms. The Key was always coming up with new tech.

To health. To life. To the future.

All three of those things had all been taken from Cath. They had all been taken by Eos. How had the Key not seen it coming? How had Blair not seen it coming? Eos had taken everything from her.

Blair surged forward and nearly tripped over the blood-smeared rug piled by her feet. "Rhett," she shouted over the hum of bots and men whose discussions were no doubt turning Cath's death into numbers. "Major Owens!" Blair repeated, stepping out of the office that had once given her such pride.

The red barrier of men parted and Rhett emerged, skittish and panting. His brows rocketed up his forehead and his gaze darted back and forth. Apparently, the Major wasn't used to violent, bloody ends.

Blair grimaced and motioned for him to follow her down the hallway. She couldn't stay near her office. She couldn't keep staring at the blood and the goo and Cath's lifeless body.

Rhett followed her. A dark purple lump protruded from just under his left eye, its swirl of color radiating like heatwaves. With each step away from the scene, he grew taller, more confident. By the time they reached the end of the hall, the frightened, shell-shocked soldier had faded. "Got some kind of fancy new nanite injection," he said. "Should be all cleared up by tomorrow." He winced as he grazed the swollen knot with his fingertips. "You've got a wicked desk in there." He nodded back down the hall toward the doorway and the onyx slab just beyond. "Doctor said that a few inches over and up," he tapped his temple, "and I'd be a goner."

Blair let out a bark of laughter. "My mother is dead." She bit the inside of her cheek. Cath wasn't her mother. Cath wasn't her mother!

Cath isn't my mother!

Red.

Rhett cleared his throat. "Yes, I am terribly sorry about what transpired. If I—"

"You're *sorry?*" Blair lifted onto the toes of her pointed stilettos. "I'll—I'll . . ."

I'll kill you!

Despite the fury burning hot within her veins, Blair couldn't say what she felt or follow it up with any action. She still needed Major Rhett Owens, the blockheaded lump of a man. Blair's teeth sounded like sandpaper as she gnashed them together. "Major Owens, where is Aiden?" Her voice shook, her hands shook, her legs shook.

Where is my brother?!

She dug her nails into her palms. It was fitting that the gloves protected her from the pain of her jagged nails and raw cuticles. Blair had always been protecting herself.

Rhett's good eye twitched. "I'll find him." Another twitch. "I'll find Elodie."

Tears bit at Blair's eyes. "People think living without them is hard." She tilted her chin toward the ceiling and blinked the tears back. "Living without them is the easy part. It's living *for them* that will rip you to shreds." Blair took a deep breath. In control of herself once again, she settled her gaze on Rhett. "You *will* find them, Major, and I'll be right there when you do." Blair sniffled and forced her grief and anger and panic into the luggage in which she stored the lies she told herself and the lies she told others. She'd unpack them later.

With studied ease and grace, Blair clasped her hands in front of her. "Thank you, Major Owens." She nodded, turned, and headed toward the restroom. The hairs on her arms rose and a sharp chill brushed her neck. The same kind of cold that welcomed blizzards and froze lakes.

As Blair took another step, she was sure she heard the distinct *crack* of fragile ice.

XLIV

Elodie had never run as fast as she'd run from the MediCenter. Somewhere along the way, as Westfall's downtown buildings blurred past, Aiden had yelled and told her to head toward the Warehouse District. Elodie hadn't needed the instruction. Even through the metallic tang of blood crusted against her lips and the burnt-earth scent of gunpowder seared into her nostrils, she still had her wits about her. She could still remember what Sparkman had told them.

I'll send them out to make one pass through this district at exactly twenty-three thirty.

Elodie and Aiden would be picked up soon. It was almost over. Her legs shook as she reached the Warehouse District and slowed down. They wanted to keep moving, keep the world at a blur so she didn't have time to think about Astrid and Cath, the guns and their lives being over. They'd died so easily, so quickly.

When they reached the Eos warehouse, Elodie slipped into the shadows next to Aiden and flattened herself against the concrete exterior. She tried her best to calm her ragged breathing and fill her burning lungs by inhaling smoothly, deeply.

"I used to think my life was boring," she said, her breath finally calming. "If only I could have seen into the future." Elodie couldn't help but smile. A cheerless, sardonic smile, but a smile nonetheless.

Aiden's boot scraped against the pavement. "Bet you wish you could have that life back."

Elodie chewed the inside of her cheek. "Not completely," she said and smoothed her collar between her fingers. "But somewhere in the middle, without the death."

Aiden continued to grind the sole of his boot against the ground. "Yeah, well, we can't go back now."

"What about your sister?" Elodie bit her lip. "Blair said that as long as Cath confessed, we could go free, and that she would sort everything out with the Council. We could pretend none of this ever happened."

"She only said those things to get what she wanted. She's always been that way." Aiden kicked a broken piece of concrete. It tumbled off the sidewalk and disappeared down the sewer grate.

"You're her brother. She loves you. And now you're the only family she has left."

Aiden wiped his nose on his sleeve. "Blair doesn't love me. She doesn't know how."

A nearby streetlight flickered before resuming its steady waterfall of light.

Elodie stood silently as Aiden continued to kick at the concrete beneath his boots. Clouds had hidden the stars, and all at once Elodie felt caged. "No one is supposed to die in VR." She felt the words leave her lips but wasn't sure why she'd said them.

Aiden stopped scuffing his boot against the sidewalk but remained quiet.

She brushed away the tears rolling down her cheeks. "Sparkman's team will pick us up and take us to a safehouse." She rested her head against the building and sighed. "It's almost over."

"We're not going to a safehouse," Aiden said as he stared at the flickering lamplight. "There's only one place where no one will look for us—where we can truly hide."

Bile burned the back of Elodie's throat. "Zone Seven." She'd known all along but hadn't wanted it to be real. She'd hoped something magical would happen and they'd all be rescued. But magic was only in stories, and all of those stories were banned.

Aiden twined his fingers together with hers. "New Dawn is out there. It has to be. We'll be safe, Elodie," he lifted her hand to his lips. They brushed against her skin as he spoke. "This time, I'll make sure of it."

An alert beamed bright white from her blood-spattered cuff, illuminating the mossy depths of Aiden's eyes.

"Shit!" He dropped her hand, yanked off his cuff, and threw it to the ground. "Take yours off. We have to destroy them." He stomped on his cuff. It flashed green then red then went dark. "We can't be traced. Not again."

Elodie scrambled to remove her cuff. It had been years since she'd taken it off. It was as much a part of her as the implant embedded behind her ear at birth. She followed Aiden's lead and drove her heel into the cuff until red light sputtered and it went dark. Elodie closed her opposite hand over wrist. Goosebumps rose against the soft skin once covered by the circle of plastic.

Aiden's fingertips grazed behind his ear. "Tech deleted your

VR profile, but we'll still have to get this." He tapped the spot where the implant was inserted.

Headlights bobbed along the street and Aiden craned his neck to get a better look.

Before she could question him, Aiden rushed toward the truck. With another surge of adrenaline, Elodie matched his stride. The unmarked black box truck seemed to grumble as it idled in the street between warehouses. Her breath stuck in her chest as she rounded the vehicle. A helmeted Key Corp soldier stood by the back of the truck, automatic weapon slung across the chest of his red uniform like a purse strap. He remained still and unfazed even as Elodie, blood smeared and frazzled, skidded to a stop. Her gaze flicked to Aiden, but he was stoic, unreadable. He had been since they'd left the MediCenter. Since Cath . . .

The soldier unlatched the door and pushed it open enough for them to climb through. "Sparkman said you'd need a way to Zone Seven." His nostrils flared under the visor covering his eyes.

Aiden nodded.

"My partner and I are making a run out there to drop off some gear and oxygen tanks." He motioned to the silver cannisters and stacks of black bins lining what they could see of the inside of the truck. "It'll be a week before we make another trip."

With another nod, Aiden gripped the side of the truck and hefted himself up into the cargo compartment.

The soldier checked something on his cuff before fixing his shielded gaze onto Elodie. "You in?"

Her hands were numb as she traced Aiden's steps and hoisted herself into the crowded back of the truck and onto the slim metal bench next to him.

The soldier followed her in and pulled a glowstick out of

his vest pocket before closing the door. It was pitch black for a moment, followed by the crunching snap of the glowstick and a cloud of white light.

The soldier held his gun against his chest as he struggled to fit his bulky gear between bins and boxes. He braced himself as the truck seemed to cough before it lumbered forward. "I have a couple packs for you," he said and dug through one of the bins. He pulled out two backpacks and dropped them in front of Elodie and Aiden before reaching back into the open box. "Some clothes too. By the looks of it, you need 'em." He set two pairs of neatly folded fatigues next to Elodie before he continued. "Sparkman got all of this together quick. I'm not sure each bag has everything you'll need, but one thing I do know is that you can't fit any type of shelter in there." His lips ticked with a frown. "You'll have to find New Dawn before you're out of food and water, or the elements," another frown, "or anything worse gets you."

Elodie twisted the bottom of her shirt around her finger. They were really going, and whether or not New Dawn existed no longer mattered. If they stayed in Westfall, they'd meet the same end as Astrid, as Cath.

Rhett now knew of Elodie's betrayal. There would be no more room for doubt when he found that she'd disappeared with Aiden instead of staying to seek forgiveness and nurse her fiancé back to health. Rhett wasn't a good man, but he was law abiding and determined. He'd hunt Elodie and Aiden down and make them pay. At least now, on their way toward the mystery of New Dawn, they had a chance. At least now they had hope.

Elodie stared down at her blood-spattered, grimy white tennis shoes. It was funny, the things she used to think were so import-ant—the things that most of Westfall's citizens thought were so important. Only a short while ago she never would have gone in public with a spot of dirt on her shoes. Her attention slid to Aiden's mud-caked boots. His lived-in messiness had been one of the things that had drawn her toward him. And look at her now . . .

Maybe this is payback, the universe punishing me for my sins.

Or maybe this is freedom. The war before the peace. The storm before the sweet breath of a newly cleansed day.

But what about Astrid? What about Cath? Their bodies painted the inside of Elodie's eyelids, haunting her with every blink.

Aiden cleared his throat and stuffed the fatigues into the backpack before he zipped it up and rested it between his feet. He offered Elodie a smile. It was meant to comfort her, but it didn't. The emptiness behind his eyes tainted his once bright, toothy grin. Now it was hollow. His lips performing an act he didn't feel.

She was losing him to the nightmare they'd just been through.

In the chemiluminescent glow of the back of the truck, time lost all meaning. Had it been minutes or hours since they'd left the warehouse district? Elodie closed her eyes and rested her head against the metal wall. Finally, the truck stopped. Elodie's breath hitched and her eyelids flew open. The Key Corp soldier pressed a gloved finger against his thin lips. They weren't in danger of Elodie speaking. She had nothing to say. The muffled voices of the guards outside the truck were nearly indistinguishable from the rumbling of the vehicle's engine. After a few sharp yeses from the driver, the truck jerked forward.

The soldier dropped his hand and steadied himself against the row of bins as he spoke. "We're crossing into Zone Seven. Almost at the drop-off point."

The ground became uneven, the ride bumpy as they bounced along the path into Zone Seven. Elodie gripped the edge of the steel bench. She desperately wanted a window. Even if their surroundings were horrible, it was better than letting her imagination run wild.

The acrid scent of charred earth crept into the truck. Aiden pulled a square of red cloth from his pack and covered his nose and mouth before tying it behind his head.

"Front pocket," he said, and pointed to her backpack.

Elodie lifted the bag onto her lap and unzipped the front. She pushed aside a flashlight and a few clear disks before finding her own handkerchief and knotting it behind her head. She rolled up her fatigues, stuffed them inside, clutched her pack against her chest and readied herself for what waited outside.

Aiden slid over, closing the distance between them. "We'll be okay. You know that, right?" He still smelled like pine, the trees after the rain, skateboarding dates, corn on the cob, kisses at the fair.

The truck stopped and the soldier again clutched his gun against his chest as he maneuvered around the boxes and back to the door. The door clattered as the soldier slid it up its track. He peered out into the dusty gray dawn and waited a moment before pounding his fist on the side of the truck and jumping out into the wilds of Zone Seven.

Ash floated around the guard like snow. His red uniform stood out from the muted grays and whites and blacks of the destroyed landscape like a tear in the skin of reality.

"All clear," he said, and motioned for them to follow.

Before Aiden had finished sliding the backpack over his shoulders, Elodie was at the edge of the truck.

This was her life and she was going to live it. That's the mistake she had made before—waiting. Waiting for life to happen *to* her.

Life had happened all right. Too much. Too fast. Never again. She'd be in control from now on.

She hooked her thumbs around her straps and looked over her shoulder at Aiden. "I know we'll be okay. I'll make sure of it." Without another thought, she leapt out of the truck. Ash plumed around her feet when they hit the ground.

Aiden followed, tightening the straps of his pack as he joined her.

The soldier climbed back into the cargo hold. "Good luck," he called as he cracked another glowstick and threw it into the depths of the truck. The door closed and the truck began its return journey, following the tire-worn path back to the only city Elodie had ever known.

Aiden shoved his hands into his pockets. "You okay?"

Elodie turned and faced the path not yet explored. She let out a hot breath against the handkerchief. "No," she answered honestly.

Aiden's backpack bobbed with a shrug. "Yeah, me either."

Elodie tightened the knot behind her head and tilted her chin toward the sky. Dirty white clouds pressed down above her. The same dingy pall as the ashen ground beneath her feet. She was trapped in a layer of the earth unfit for life.

The sky cracked overhead, and droplets speckled her ash-covered sleeves. Hope burned hot within Elodie's chest as the air thickened and the heavens thundered.

After the storm comes the dawn.

ACKNOWLEDGMENTS

Writing a book is hard. I'm grateful to have people in my life who make it just a bit easier.

To SA, one of the world's best editors. Sometimes I feel like we share a brain and sometimes I feel like I have so much left to learn from you that there couldn't possibly be enough hours left in my lifetime to do so. I cannot wait for our next adventure.

To my fabulous agent Steven Salpeter. Thank you for trusting me. This is only the beginning.

To the amazingly talented Deb Shapiro. Your wisdom and guidance have truly helped our team make this project successful.

To Josie Woodbridge, Courtney Vatis, Greg Boguslawski, and Blackstone Publishing. Thank you for helping me bring this book into the world.

To Holly Frederick and Maddie Tavis for your passion and expertise.

To Nathan and Mary, owners of The Stacks Coffeehouse.

Your business is my second home. Thank you for giving me space to craft my stories within its book-lined walls.

To Brooke, Emily, Pintip, and Rachel, whenever I falter, you are there to remind me of who I am and what I'm capable of. You bring out the best in me. I can't thank you enough for your friendship.

To Douglas and Gigi, I couldn't do any of this without you.